Murder on Front Street

Arthur L. Taylor

Author

San Marcos, Texas

Edition: First

ISBN: 979-8-89397-663-2

Published by Elite Scribes Book Writing

Dedication

To the resilient truth-seekers, the ones who step into chaos not for recognition, but because their conscience gives them no other choice.

This book is for those who operate within systems marred by imperfection, and those who challenge them from beyond. To the principled officers, investigators, and legal advocates who uphold justice not with blind loyalty but with open eyes and steadfast hearts. You carry burdens few see and answer to higher ideals, not headlines.

To the investigative journalists whose courage sharpens the tip of the pen. You probe the depths of power, stitch narratives from shards of evidence, and restore clarity in a fog of misinformation. Your work is proof that truth, though often buried, cannot be broken.

To the survivors—those left wounded by injustice, yet rise each day, determined to rebuild. Your persistence fuels accountability. Your stories bring change.

And to my family and friends—Geraldine, Michael, and the steadfast circle that surrounded me through this creative crucible—thank you. For your faith in my voice, your patience with my process, and your unwavering love in every unwritten chapter.

This book is a vessel of difficult truths and hopeful resistance. It exists because of you.

Table of Contents

Assassination Attempt

The air hung thick with the scent of expensive perfume and even more expensive liquor. Crystal chandeliers glittered, casting a deceptive sheen on the opulent ballroom of the Wilder City Country Club. Laughter, the clinking of champagne flutes, and the low hum of conversation painted a picture of effortless elegance, a veneer of perfect suburban bliss that masked the simmering tensions beneath the surface. Tonight, however, the tranquility was a fragile mask about to be shattered.

Unseen and unheard by the oblivious revelers, two FBI agents, Agent Miller, a seasoned veteran with a granite face and eyes that missed nothing, and Agent Davies, younger and sharper, with a nervous energy barely contained beneath her tailored suit, moved through the crowd. Their mission: to prevent assassination. Their target: unknown. Their intel is sketchy at best. They'd been operating undercover for weeks, infiltrating the elite circles of Wilder City, a town where wealth and influence intertwined like poisonous ivy. The only concrete detail they possessed was a time – 11:00 pm – and a location – this very ballroom.

Miller adjusted his earpiece, the faint static a counterpoint to the lively music. "Davies, anything?" he whispered, his voice barely audible above the chatter. Davies, eyes scanning the room, shook her head subtly. "Nothing yet. But the tension is palpable. Feels like a pressure cooker about to blow."

The ballroom buzzed with the usual suspects: Mayor Thompson, his face perpetually creased in a smile that never quite reached his eyes; the Vandergelt family, their patriarch, a notorious oil tycoon, radiating an aura of ruthless ambition; and a scattering of other prominent figures, their names synonymous with power and influence in Wilder City. Each one is a potential target, and each one is a potential suspect.

The clock ticked towards 11:00 pm. The music swelled, a crescendo of anticipation mirroring the rising tension in the agents' hearts. Miller spotted a man near the bar, his back to them, seemingly absorbed in conversation. Something about his posture, the way he subtly shifted his weight, the almost imperceptible twitch of a hand near his coat pocket set off an alarm in Miller's experienced mind. He signaled to Davies.

Suddenly, a sharp crack shattered the illusion of serenity. Not a gunshot, but something else – the shattering of a crystal goblet. Chaos erupted. Screams pierced the air. The carefully constructed façade of the evening crumbled. In the ensuing confusion, Miller and Davies moved towards their suspected target, but they were too late—a flurry of movement, a swift, precise strike, and then... nothing. The man, whoever he was, vanished. The crowd, initially paralyzed by fear, now surged forward, a tide of panicked humanity.

Miller's radio crackled to life. "Agent Miller, report."

"We've had a... complication," Miller replied, his voice tight with frustration and a dawning sense of dread. "The target... he's gone. We failed to prevent something. We don't know what yet, but something big happened here."

The ensuing investigation was chaotic. The club was swarming with local police, state troopers, and now, it seemed, every FBI agent within a hundred-mile radius. The initial euphoria of a seemingly successful operation quickly gave way to a chilling realization: they had walked into something far larger and far more sinister than they could have possibly anticipated. The elegant ballroom, now a scene of shattered dreams and fractured glass, was just the beginning.

The discovery of the teenager's body, mere hours after the botched assassination attempt, further solidified this realization. His name was Ethan Reed, the golden boy of Wilder City, the son of Senator Reed, an influential figure with deep roots in the town. Ethan's life had been a tapestry of privilege, a testament to the seemingly effortless success of the elite. Yet, he was now sprawled lifeless on the manicured lawn of his family estate, his perfect world violently torn apart. The brutality of the murder and the precision of the attack echoed the earlier incident at the country club. This was no random act; this was a message.

The crime scene on Front Street was meticulously documented. Alice Wild, a veteran police officer with eyes as sharp as her mind, arrived with her team, her gaze systematically assessing the scene. Years of experience had taught her to read the silent language of death, the subtle shifts in the earth, the almost imperceptible traces of struggle. This was more than a simple murder; this was a carefully orchestrated act. A chilling prelude to what was to come.

The discovery of the Reed family's secrets began quietly, subtly. Alice, a master of her craft, dug through the layers of lies and deceit, peeling back the façade of perfection to reveal the rot beneath. The investigation didn't just unearth Ethan's hidden life – a life far removed from the carefully crafted public image – it also unearthed a complex network of illicit dealings, financial irregularities, and shady business practices that reached far beyond Wilder City. The town, once seen as a model of suburban perfection, was now revealing its dark underbelly.

As the investigation deepened, the body count rose. Officer David Miller, a respected member of the Wilder City Police Department, his wife, Sarah, and their young daughter, Emily, were found murdered in their own home, a scene of unimaginable brutality. The murders bore a chilling resemblance to Ethan Reed's, the same precision, the same deliberate cruelty. The comfortable tranquility of Wilder City was now a distant, almost forgotten memory, replaced by fear, suspicion, and a desperate need for answers.

Alice, weary but determined, felt the weight of the investigation pressing down on her. The pressure from multiple agencies – including the FBI, state police, and local department – added to the strain. Each agency had its own agenda and priorities, creating a chaotic maelstrom of conflicting interests and bureaucratic hurdles. Alice, however, remained focused, her determination fueled by a deep-seated sense of justice and a burning need to bring the perpetrators to justice, regardless of their power or connections. The idyllic façade of Wilder City was shattered, and Alice Wild, a woman who knew the darkness within the human heart, was the only one who could piece it back together. But the task ahead of her would require not only skill and determination but also a willingness to confront not only the criminals but also the hypocrisy and corruption lurking within the very heart of the town she called home.

The fight had just begun. The seemingly perfect world of Wilder City had been irrevocably broken, and the truth, like a venomous snake, was coiled and ready to strike.

Discovery of the Teenager

The manicured lawn of the Reed estate, usually a picture of pristine perfection, was now a scene of stark horror. Ethan Reed, the golden boy, lay sprawled amidst the carefully cultivated roses, his lifeless body a grotesque counterpoint to the vibrant blooms. His eyes, usually sparkling with youthful exuberance, were now vacant, staring blankly at the cloudless Texas sky. The pristine white of his designer shirt was stained crimson, a stark contrast to the meticulously maintained greenery surrounding him. A single, delicate gold cufflink lay detached near his hand, glinting in the morning sun like a morbidly ironic jewel.

The first responders, their faces grim, moved with practiced efficiency, their movements a silent ballet of investigation. Yellow tape, a stark barrier between the grotesque scene and the shocked onlookers, cordoned off a significant area of the expansive lawn. News helicopters had already circled overhead, their whirring blades a relentless soundtrack to the unfolding tragedy. The air crackled with a mixture of hushed whispers and suppressed sobs, the collective grief of a community shattered by the unexpected loss of one of their own.

Alice Wild, her sharp eyes scanning the scene with practiced precision, arrived shortly after the initial discovery. Years of experience had hardened her against the emotional toll of such scenes, but even she couldn't help but feel a prickle of unease. The calculated nature of the murder and the almost theatrical placement of the body suggested a level of sophistication that was chilling. This wasn't the work of a desperate killer;

this was a message, a carefully crafted statement delivered with brutal efficiency.

The first examination revealed few immediate clues. No weapon was found at the scene, just the meticulously placed body, a grim centerpiece in a meticulously supported landscape. The absence of signs of forced entry to the Reed estate further added to the enigma. Had the killer been known to Ethan? Had he been allowed inside? Or had they infiltrated the property using methods unbeknownst to the police?

Detective Sergeant Jones, Alice's partner, a younger officer with keen but sometimes naive enthusiasm, knelt beside the body. "Brutal," he murmured, his voice barely whispering. "Incredibly precise. Almost... surgical."

Alice nodded, her gaze unwavering. "Surgical is right," she agreed, her voice devoid of emotion. "This wasn't random. It was planned and orchestrated. And the choice of location... It's a statement."

The arrival of Senator Reed, Ethan's father, and his wife, Eleanor, further complicated the scene. The senator, a pillar of the Wilder City establishment, his face a mask of grief and controlled rage, was a picture of barely contained fury. Mrs. Reed, elegant even in distress, clung to her husband, her sobs muffled by his arm. Their public display of grief was a performance, polished and practiced, but the underlying tension was palpable. Alice observed them keenly; their grief, while genuine, felt... staged. Too controlled, too calculated for a parent's natural response to the brutal murder of their child.

The initial wave of shock rippled through the town. News of Ethan's death spread like wildfire, shattering the illusion of idyllic suburban peace. The whispers began immediately, rumors, speculation, half-truths, and outright lies twisting the tragedy into a tapestry of suspicion and intrigue. The carefully constructed façade of Wilder City, a town that prided itself on its image of prosperity and tranquility, began to crumble.

The Reed family's public persona, one of impeccable respectability, was instantly called into question. Were there cracks in the veneer of perfection? Were there secrets that Ethan, a supposedly obedient son, held within the close-knit circles of his elite world? The investigation needed to delve deeper, to scratch beneath the surface of a life seemingly free from any hint of discord.

The investigation delved into Ethan's life, uncovering a hidden world far removed from the privileged existence he presented to the outside world. He had a hidden life, one filled with rebellion, late-night escapades, and friendships that his parents would likely never have approved of. These connections extended beyond the boundaries of Wilder City, leading Alice and her team down unexpected paths, the details emerging as if from a slowly revealing tapestry of deceit.

As the team continued their investigation, several more facts became clear. Ethan's social media activity revealed a pattern of rebellious behavior, coded messages that alluded to conflict with his parents and perhaps something more dangerous. Friends and associates, initially hesitant to speak, eventually started to confess. Ethan's relationships were not what the polished façade facade of the Reed family presented to the public. He associated with a questionable crowd— some with known ties to less savory elements, others with connections that were simply shadowy and undefined. All this raised the very real possibility that Ethan was involved in something beyond the reach of his family's influence.

The ensuing days were a blur of interviews, forensic analysis, and surveillance. Alice and her team painstakingly pieced together Ethan's life, meticulously unraveling the threads of his hidden existence. His phone records, meticulously examined, revealed a network of contacts and communications that defied their initial expectations. Encrypted messages, coded language, and cryptic references hinted at a deeper conspiracy, a network of secrets far more extensive than anyone could have imagined.

The pressure mounted, both from the public and from the various agencies involved in the investigation. The FBI, already present following the incident at the country club, maintained a significant presence, their agents circling Alice's team like wary vultures. The tension between the local police and the FBI was palpable, a simmering conflict of jurisdiction and authority that threatened to derail the investigation.

As the investigation progressed, the discovery of Ethan's clandestine activities revealed that the seemingly perfect boy had strayed far from the well-defined path laid out for him. His rebellious nature, initially hinted at in social media posts and vague comments from friends, manifested in a series of risky behaviors. His hidden life went beyond teenage defiance; it pointed to involvement in illicit activities, including a potentially dangerous entanglement with a network of criminal underworld figures operating within the seemingly safe confines of Wilder City.

The discovery of Ethan's secret life was merely the first layer of the onion that Alice was peeling back. As the investigation burrowed deeper, an unexpected truth emerged – Ethan wasn't just a victim; he was also a player in a dangerous game. He held secrets that could unravel the carefully crafted façade of Wilder City, its power structures, and the influential figures who pulled the strings from behind the scenes. And those secrets, Alice was starting to realize, were worth killing for. The quiet tranquility of Wilder City was a lie, a meticulously crafted mask concealing a festering underbelly of corruption, greed, and violence. The murder of Ethan Reed was not an isolated incident but a carefully planned act, the opening salvo in a larger, more sinister game. And Alice Wild was about to become a pawn in it.

Murder on Front Street

Introducing Alice Wild

The crisp morning air did little to soothe the simmering unease that coiled in Alice Wild's gut. The scent of freshly cut grass, usually a comforting aroma, felt strangely jarring against the backdrop of the Reed estate's macabre tableau. Years spent navigating the grim underbelly of human nature had hardened her, building a wall around her heart that shielded her from the raw emotions that clung to such scenes. But even Alice, a woman known for her unflappable demeanor and steely resolve, felt a tremor of something akin to dread. This wasn't just a murder; it was a meticulously crafted performance; a chilling statement delivered in the language of violence.

Alice, a woman forged in the fires of countless investigations, was a study in controlled efficiency. At forty-eight, her face, etched with the lines of sleepless nights and hard-won battles, bore the marks of a life dedicated to justice. Her eyes, the color of a stormy sea, missed nothing. They scanned the scene with a hawklike intensity, absorbing every detail, every nuance, every subtle clue that hinted at the killer's identity and motive. Her dark, shoulder-length hair, usually neatly styled, was pulled back in a practical ponytail, revealing the sharp angles of her jawline and the strength in her gaze. She moved with quiet grace, her movements economically and precise, a stark contrast to the chaos that swirled around her.

Unlike many of her colleagues, Alice wasn't driven by the adrenaline rush of the chase or the allure of media attention. Her motivation stemmed from a deeper well – a fierce sense of justice, honed by years on the force and tempered by a cynical understanding of the human capacity for both good and unimaginable evil. She had seen enough darkness to know that the light, however faint, was always worth fighting for. Wilder City, with its veneer of perfect suburban life, was a deceptive façade, and Alice, with her keen eyes and even keener intuition, was determined to peel back the layers of deceit to reveal the festering corruption beneath.

Her attire, a simple yet impeccably tailored suit, was functional rather than fashionable. The dark fabric blended seamlessly with the shadows, allowing her to become a silent observer, a ghost amid the chaos. She carried herself with an air of quiet authority, her presence commanding respect even before she uttered a word. This wasn't a performance; it was her natural state, the embodiment of the seasoned detective she was. Years on the force hadn't just hardened her; they had sharpened her. She was a predator in human form, relentless in her pursuit of the truth.

As she surveyed the scene, Alice's mind worked, piecing together the fragments of information. The lack of a murder weapon was significant. Had it been removed? Was it a weapon that could be easily disposed of or something more sophisticated? The precision of the killing and the theatrical placement of the body spoke of a killer who was both skilled and meticulous, someone who had planned this meticulously. This wasn't a crime of passion; it was a calculated act, an execution.

The manicured lawn, usually a symbol of order and tranquility, was now a canvas of horror. Ethan Reed, sprawled amidst the roses, was a macabre masterpiece. Alice noted the absence of any signs of a struggle, a detail that pointed towards a killer known to the victim, someone who had gained his trust. The gold cufflink, lying near his hand, seemed insignificant at first glance, but Alice knew better. Every detail, no matter how small, was a potential piece of the puzzle.

Detective Sergeant Jones, her partner, a younger officer eager to prove himself, approached her, his face a mixture of awe and apprehension. "The precision," he whispered, his voice barely audible above the hum of the news helicopters. "It's like something out of a movie."

Alice nodded, her gaze fixed on the body. "A movie made by someone who knows exactly what they're doing," she corrected, her voice low and measured. "This wasn't impulsive. This was planned, meticulously executed, a calculated message delivered with chilling efficiency."

She surveyed the first responders, their movements precise and efficient, a testament to their training. The yellow tape, a stark boundary between the scene and the onlookers, served as a reminder of the gravity of the situation. The onlookers, a mix of neighbors, reporters, and curious onlookers, were a study in controlled shock, their whispers and murmurs a low hum that filled the air.

The arrival of Senator Reed and his wife added another layer of complexity to the situation. Their grief, while genuine, was carefully controlled, almost theatrical. Their public mourning felt staged, a performance for the cameras, a show of grief designed to project an image of devastated parents rather than revealing their true emotions. Alice observed them keenly, her eyes noticing the subtle inconsistencies in their behavior, the forced composure that hid a deeper layer of turmoil. Their grief, she suspected, was a carefully constructed performance, but what were they hiding?

Alice's attention then shifted to the finer details – the slight displacement of a rose bush, the barely perceptible scuff mark on the pristine patio, and the way the sunlight glinted off a small shard of glass near the edge of the lawn. Years of experience had honed her observational skills to a razor's edge. She saw what others missed and understood the language of the crime scene, the silent narrative of violence. Every detail, no matter how seemingly insignificant, was a potential key to unlocking the truth.

The investigation, she knew, wouldn't be a simple matter of finding the perpetrator and bringing them to justice. This was a city where appearances were carefully maintained, where secrets were guarded fiercely, and where power and influence were wielded with ruthless efficiency. Alice was stepping into a world of intricate webs of deceit, a world where the line between truth and fiction was blurred and where the pursuit of justice would be a treacherous and dangerous journey. But she was prepared. She had faced worse.

The coming days would be a relentless pursuit of answers, a journey into the dark heart of Wilder City, a place where the perfect façade concealed a brutal reality. Alice Wild, a woman defined by her unwavering dedication to justice, was about to uncover a conspiracy that went far deeper than the death of a single teenager. This was only the beginning, and she was ready. The shattered tranquility of Wilder City would not remain undisturbed. The truth, no matter how dark or dangerous, would be exposed. And Alice Wild would be the one to expose it.

Arthur L. Taylor

The Widening Circle of Death

The initial shock of Ethan Reed's murder had barely begun to settle before Wilder City was plunged into a new abyss of horror. Three days later, the quiet suburban street of Oak Haven Lane became the scene of another gruesome crime. This time, the victims weren't wealthy socialites but Officer Daniel Miller, his wife Sarah, and their eight-year-old daughter, Lily.

The Millers' home, a modest two-story colonial, was a stark contrast to the Reed estate. But the brutality of the crime mirrored the earlier incident, a chilling echo in the otherwise peaceful neighborhood. The scene was even more disturbing. The house, once warm and inviting, now reeked of violence and fear. Blood splattered the walls, furniture overturned, and toys lay scattered amongst the carnage, a macabre juxtaposition of childhood innocence and brutal adult violence. Officer Miller, a veteran of the Wilder City Police Department, lay sprawled in the living room, his body riddled with gunshot wounds. Sarah and Lily were found in their beds, their deaths swift and merciless.

The lack of forced entry suggested the killer knew the Millers, a detail that sent a shiver down Alice's spine. This wasn't a random act of violence; it was a targeted attack, meticulously planned and executed with the same chilling precision as the Reed murder. The similarities were too striking to ignore: the absence of a murder weapon, the theatrical arrangement of the bodies, and the calculated nature of the killings. It was a signature, a chilling calling card left by a killer who reveled in their power.

Sergeant Jones, his youthful enthusiasm tempered by the grim reality of the scene, stood beside Alice, his face pale. "It's… "It's the same," he whispered, his voice choked with emotion. "The same M.O., the same level of

precision. It's like… like they're taunting us."

Alice nodded, her gaze sweeping across the devastation. The chaos of the scene was a stark contrast to the controlled efficiency of the first responders working diligently to secure the evidence. Yet, beneath the organized chaos, a chilling pattern was emerging. This wasn't simply a copycat killer; this was a deliberate escalation, a carefully orchestrated act designed to send a message, a message that sent chills down her spine.

The initial instinct was to link the murders and to assume a single perpetrator. But Alice cautioned against such hasty conclusions. While the similarities were undeniable, there were subtle differences that hinted at a deeper complexity. The Reed murder had been a public statement, a theatrical display of power. The Miller murder, on the other hand, felt more personal, a targeted act of vengeance. Was this the work of the same individual, or was something else at play?

The investigation widened, encompassing the lives of both victims. Ethan Reed, a powerful businessman, was known for his ruthless business tactics and even more ruthless enemies. Officer Miller, a respected officer, was a quieter figure, less known to the public eye. Yet, his position within the police department added another layer to the investigation, raising questions about internal corruption or a potential conspiracy.

Alice spent hours shifting through the Millers' personal belongings. There were no obvious signs of forced entry, no apparent robbery. She examined Sarah's jewelry, her clothing, and any other personal items. Nothing seemed out of place, nothing that could give a definitive clue. Lily's room, untouched by the violence of the crime, was a poignant contrast to the devastation downstairs, a silent reminder of innocence lost. The pristine condition of the room was a painful irony, a jarring testament to the brutality of the act.

The initial reports suggested no witnesses, no sign of a struggle, just the cold, calculated violence. Yet Alice knew that every detail, no matter how small, could hold a key.

She spent hours interviewing the Millers' neighbors, piecing together a picture of the family's life. They were described as kind, friendly, and unassuming, the epitome of the American dream. But even the most seemingly perfect lives held hidden cracks, and Alice was determined to find them.

She interviewed Miller's colleagues at the Wilder City Police Department, probing any hint of conflict, any potential enemies. The initial interviews revealed nothing out of the ordinary, yet a subtle current of unease ran beneath the surface. Some officers seemed reluctant to provide full details, their responses evasive and hesitant. It was a subtle shift in demeanor, but Alice, with her sharp instincts, picked up on it.

As the investigation progressed, a new piece of the puzzle emerged. A cryptic note was found tucked away in Daniel Miller's desk drawer, a single sheet of paper with a series of numbers and symbols scrawled across it. The note seemed innocuous at first glance, but Alice knew better. She had a feeling that this was far more than a simple random string of numbers. This was a code, a hidden message, a potential link between the two murders.

The widening circle of death had started with Ethan Reed, a man of significant influence and wealth, and now it had claimed the life of a police officer and his family, raising the stakes considerably. Was there a connection? Was it a case of a copycat killer or something far more sinister, perhaps even a conspiracy? The answers, Alice suspected, were far more tangled and dangerous than she had initially thought. The tranquil façade of Wilder City was cracking, revealing a darkness far more profound than she could have ever imagined. The city she knew, with its clean streets and perfect lawns, was starting to feel like a carefully constructed set, and the murders were the dramatic finale of a play she didn't understand. The quiet suburban streets, once sanctuary places, now echoed with the chilling silence of a terror yet to be uncovered. Alice knew the truth lay hidden, buried beneath layers of lies and deceit, but she was determined to uncover it, even if it meant facing the very darkness that fueled the city's hidden heart. The game, she realized, had only just begun. The trail led far beyond the deaths of two families. It promised to reveal a conspiracy that reached the highest echelons of power, a conspiracy that threatened to unravel the very fabric of Wilder City itself.

Arthur L. Taylor

Multiple Agencies Involved

The cryptic note, a seemingly innocuous collection of numbers and symbols, became the catalyst for a seismic shift in the investigation. Its discovery triggered a cascade of events that thrust the case far beyond the confines of the Wilder City Police Department. The FBI, alerted by the escalating violence and the potential for a national security threat, swiftly joined the investigation, bringing with them a formidable array of resources and expertise. Their arrival, however, wasn't greeted with open arms.

Sergeant Jones, his initial enthusiasm now tinged with a healthy dose of apprehension, confided in Alice, "They're all over us, Alice. The Feds. They're practically breathing down our necks, demanding access to everything, questioning our every move." He ran a hand through his already disheveled hair, his exhaustion evident. "It's like they think we're incompetent."

The friction between the local police and the federal agents was palpable. The FBI, accustomed to operating with a level of autonomy and authority that the local department lacked, viewed the Wilder City PD with a mixture of suspicion and condescension. Alice, who had experience navigating the intricate dance between different agencies, immediately recognized the potential for conflict and the resulting impediments to a swift and effective investigation. The different investigative styles, the conflicting priorities, and the clash of egos threatened to derail the entire operation.

Agent Sterling, the lead FBI agent, a tall, imposing figure with steely eyes and an even sterner demeanor, was a stark contrast to the more approachable, if slightly overwhelmed, Sergeant Jones. Sterling, accustomed to high-stakes investigations and national security threats, viewed the Wilder City case through a different lens. His focus was on the potential for a larger conspiracy, a network of individuals operating beyond the city limits, perhaps even internationally. He saw the murders as pieces in a larger puzzle, and he wasn't about to let the Wilder City Police Department dictate the terms of the investigation.

Their initial meetings were tense, a clash of cultures and methodologies. The FBI agents, equipped with advanced technology and sophisticated forensic techniques, moved with swift, decisive efficiency that was alien to the more traditional methods of the local police. Their methodical approach, while impressive, often clashed with the intuitive, almost visceral approach favored by Alice and her team. The differences were more than just stylistic; they were philosophical. The FBI saw the crime scene as a collection of data points to be analyzed; Alice saw it as a narrative waiting to be pieced together.

The tension extended beyond the investigative teams.

The differing levels of jurisdiction and authority have become a constant source of friction. The FBI's demands for access to information and evidence were sometimes met with resistance from the Wilder City PD, a natural reaction stemming from a desire to retain control over the case, a case that had deeply shaken the city and its police force. Alice, caught in the middle, found herself playing the role of mediator, navigating the treacherous waters of inter-agency politics while trying to keep the investigation on track.

The internal politics of the Wilder City PD added another layer of complexity. Some officers, resentful of the FBI's intrusion and the perceived undermining of their authority, were less than cooperative, their reluctance extending beyond a simple reluctance to collaborate. Alice suspected that some were hiding something; their reticence was fueled by fear, guilt, or perhaps even complicity. She knew she had to tread carefully, building trust while simultaneously uncovering potential internal corruption.

The arrival of the state police, called in to assist with the overwhelming workload, further complicated the already strained dynamics. Now, Alice was managing not only the clash between the local and federal agencies but also the differing priorities and operational styles of three separate entities. Each agency brought its own set of resources, expertise, and internal procedures, creating a bureaucratic labyrinth that threatened to engulf the investigation.

She spent countless hours in meetings, mediating disputes, negotiating access to information, and ensuring that the three agencies were working towards a common goal, even though their paths and approaches differed. She had to present a united front to the public, even as the agencies internally struggled for control and recognition. The public perception of the investigation was critical, and any hint of disarray could fuel public panic and mistrust.

One evening, after a particularly grueling day of navigating bureaucratic hurdles and clashing egos, Alice found herself alone in her office, reviewing the cryptic note once more. The numbers and symbols remained stubbornly enigmatic, but a new detail caught her eye. A faint watermark on the paper, almost imperceptible, suggested a specific manufacturer—one not commonly used by the Wilder City Police Department. This small detail, an overlooked anomaly, sparked a new line of inquiry, a potential link to the larger conspiracy that Agent Sterling believed was at play. It was a small victory in a battle fraught with political maneuvering and bureaucratic gridlock.

The investigation was a chaotic tapestry woven from conflicting priorities, jurisdictional battles, and personal ambitions, yet Alice held fast to the hope that unraveling this complex web of intrigue would lead to justice for the victims.

The pressure mounted relentlessly. The city, once serene and predictable, was now a pressure cooker, its citizens anxious and fearful. The constant media scrutiny added another layer of challenge, each news report demanding answers, feeding the public's insatiable hunger for information while simultaneously hindering the investigation. Alice, constantly juggling the demands of the three agencies, the media, and the grieving families, knew that time was of the essence. Every day that passed without a resolution increased the risk of further violence and further chaos.

The tension between the FBI and the Wilder City PD reached a boiling point when Agent Sterling accused the local police of withholding evidence. The unproven accusation sparked a flurry of claims and rebuttals. The ensuing conflict nearly paralyzed the investigation, threatening to unravel the fragile alliance between the three agencies.

Alice, acutely aware of the high stakes, intervened decisively. She used her unique position—trusted by both sides, respected for her experience and her dedication—to mediate the dispute, reminding everyone of their shared goal: to solve the murders and bring the killer to justice. She proposed a new strategy, a collaborative approach that would divide the workload and leverage the unique strengths of each agency. The state police, with their extensive resources and manpower, would focus on canvassing the area, interviewing witnesses, and tracing the movements of potential suspects. The Wilder City PD, deeply familiar with the local criminal underworld, focuses on uncovering any potential links to organized crime. The FBI, with its superior technology and investigative techniques, would concentrate on analyzing the cryptic note and tracking down any potential international connections.

The new plan, although not perfect, eased the tension, paving the way for a more productive collaboration. But Alice knew this was just a temporary truce. The undercurrents of rivalry and mistrust still simmered beneath the surface, a constant threat to the ongoing investigation. The path to justice was a perilous one, paved with not only danger but also political maneuvering and bureaucratic hurdles.

The challenge was not only to uncover the killer but also to navigate the treacherous waters of inter-agency politics and ensure that justice prevailed over the chaos. The city's fate, and perhaps the outcome of the investigation, hinged on her ability to bring order from the ensuing chaos, forging a fragile alliance in the face of mistrust and conflicting ambitions. The shattered tranquility of Wilder City remained a haunting testament to the darkness that lurked beneath the surface.

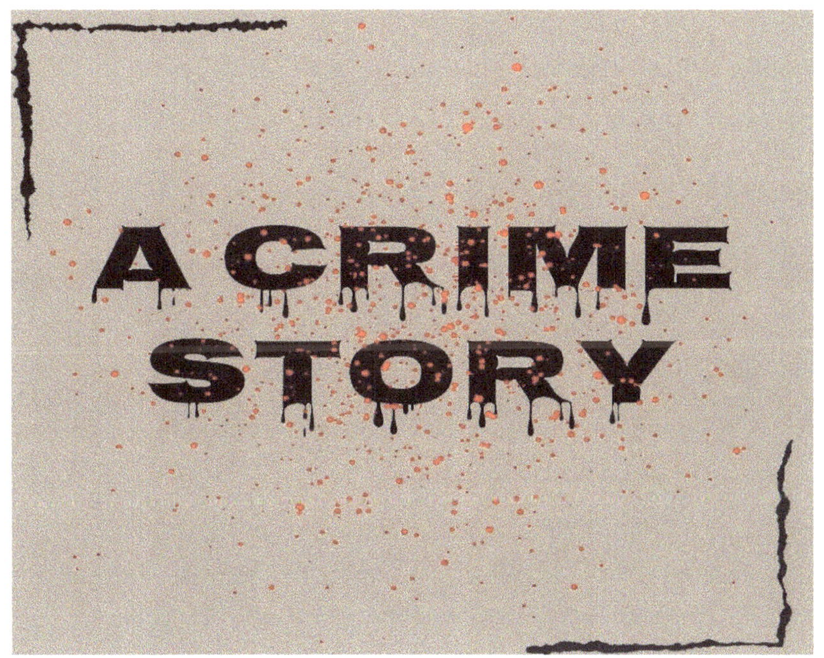

Alice's Initial Investigations

The faint watermark on the cryptic note, a detail almost lost in the bureaucratic maelstrom, became Alice's new obsession. It was a tiny thread, a single strand in a tangled web, but it offered a potential pathway out of the interagency impasse. The manufacturer, a small, obscure company specializing in high-security paper, was not a regular supplier to the Wilder City Police Department. This meant the note hadn't originated within their ranks, significantly narrowing the field of potential suspects and lending credence to Agent Sterling's theory of a broader conspiracy.

Alice began her independent investigation, peeling back the layers of the teenager's life, meticulously reconstructing his final days. She immersed herself in the digital detritus of his existence, his social media accounts, his online gaming profiles, his text messages, his email, searching for any hint of his killer's identity, any indication of his last movements. His online presence painted a picture of a seemingly ordinary teenager, popular, outgoing, involved in school activities, with a seemingly stable family life. The surface was calm, but beneath it, Alice sensed turbulence, a hidden current of discontent or conflict that was not immediately apparent.

Her investigation led her to the exclusive Wilder Creek Country Club, a bastion of the city's elite, where the teenager's father, a prominent lawyer, held a prominent membership. The club was a microcosm of Wilder

City itself, a carefully curated façade hiding a complex web of relationships, rivalries, and secrets. Alice spent days observing the members, studying their interactions, and subtly gathering information from the staff. She learned about hushed conversations, hidden affairs, and simmering resentments that went far beyond the usual social dynamics of a country club. The initial image of a seemingly idyllic community began to unravel, revealing a tapestry of deceit and intrigue.

One evening, Alice encountered Mrs. Eleanor Vance, a woman of impeccable social standing and sharp wit, known for her philanthropic endeavors and biting gossip. Their conversation started casually, centered around the ongoing tragedy, yet beneath the polite chatter, Alice sensed a subtle tension, a guardedness in the woman's demeanor. Mrs. Vance subtly alluded to an incident involving the teenager, a seemingly trivial matter, but the undercurrent of fear and implication held a much deeper meaning. Alice recognized this was a clue buried beneath layers of social graces and polite pleasantries.

The teenager's phone records revealed a series of late-night calls and text messages to an unknown number. The number itself was untraceable, but Alice managed to track the location of the calls; they originated from multiple locations around Wilder City. Using the geographical mapping of the calls, Alice created a spatial pattern that suggested a deliberate route, a planned path that seemed to correspond with several prominent landmarks around town. This suggested a possible surveillance pattern, an attempt to monitor or track someone's movements, or perhaps a reconnaissance mission designed to identify potential targets. Alice's meticulous examination of the teenager's social media revealed a surprising fact: he was deeply involved in an online gaming community, an almost secret digital world teeming with its complex social dynamics, rivalries, and power struggles. The online gaming group was more than just a hobby; it seemed to form an intricate and potentially influential social structure in the teenager's life. This digital world could contain vital clues to the teenager's murder, clues that the conventional investigation methods might have missed.

Alice discovered that the teenager had been involved in a heated online dispute, a virtual war of words that escalated into threats and insults. The conflict arose from a complex game strategy where different clans of online gamers clashed fiercely. Alice unearthed evidence suggesting that the dispute involved not just teenage squabbles but also members of the Wilder City's elite families, a digital clash reflecting the undercurrents of power struggles in the town's real-life social hierarchy. The online insults and threats could contain vital clues; the words could contain veiled allusions that only someone privy to the town's elite social fabric could understand.

The investigation also led to a seemingly innocuous event: a lavish fundraising gala held at the Wilder Creek Country Club just days before the teenager's death. Alice delved into the guest list, meticulously studying the photos and videos from the event and examining the attendees' interactions and facial expressions. She noticed a subtle but significant detail: a fleeting interaction between the teenager and a man known for his considerable wealth and powerful connections. The man, initially identified only as "Mr. Harrison," seemed to exchange a few words with the victim just before the latter left the event. The interaction seemed mundane, yet Alice sensed an underlying tension, an undercurrent of discontent or concealed conflict.

The discovery of Mr. Harrison sparked a new line of investigation. Alice unearthed rumors of Mr. Harrison's questionable business dealings, his involvement in complex financial transactions, and his controversial associations. The initial findings fueled Alice's suspicion that Mr. Harrison's seemingly polished exterior masked a darker side, one that potentially held the key to the teenager's murder. The more she investigated, the more she realized that the teenager's death was no simple crime of passion but rather a carefully orchestrated event, a piece in a larger, more complex puzzle. Further investigation revealed a connection between Mr. Harrison and the obscure paper manufacturer identified in the watermark on the cryptic note. It turned out that Mr. Harrison was a major investor in the company, a fact that seemed to directly connect the cryptic note to the seemingly disparate world of elite social circles, high stakes finance, and international business dealings. This discovery solidified Alice's suspicion that the murder was part of a far-reaching conspiracy that extended far beyond the confines of Wilder City.

The weight of the investigation bore down on Alice. The seemingly simple case of a teenager's murder had morphed into a complex web of deceit involving the town's elite, secret societies, and potentially international criminal networks. The tension between the local police, the FBI, and the state police remained palpable, each agency vying for control, each with its own agenda. Alice, however, felt certain that the trail had led her to the heart of the mystery; uncovering the truth, however, required her to navigate the treacherous waters of deception and the dangerous games played by the powerful. She knew that every step she took carried inherent risks. But the need for justice, for uncovering the truth behind the teenager's death and exposing the darkness that lurked within the heart of Wilder City, drove her onward. The investigation was far from over, but Alice felt she was finally closing in on the truth. The unraveling of the web had begun.

Secrets of the Elite

The Wilder Creek Country Club, a sprawling monument to wealth and privilege, felt less like a haven of leisure and more like a pressure cooker simmering with unspoken resentments and simmering rivalries. Alice had spent weeks observing, blending into the background, a ghost in the gilded cage. She'd meticulously charted the movements of the elite, noting subtle shifts in body language, the fleeting glances, the barely concealed disdain exchanged between longstanding rivals. The veneer of civility was paper-thin, barely concealing the cutthroat competition for social standing, influence, and, of course, money.

The Vandergelt family, for instance, the undisputed reigning monarchs of Wilder City society, maintained a façade of unwavering grace and philanthropy. Their annual charity gala was legendary, a spectacle of extravagant displays of wealth, attracting the city's most prominent figures. Yet, Alice's investigation had unearthed whispers of a bitter feud with the Hawthorne family, a rivalry dating back generations, fueled by old money versus new money, and a long-forgotten land dispute that still cast a shadow over their interactions. The polite smiles and carefully chosen words barely concealed the palpable tension between them. Even casual observers could sense the icy currents running beneath the surface of their seemingly perfect relationship.

Then there were the Millers, a family whose fortune was built on technology, their wealth practically radiating from their perfectly manicured lawns and impeccably dressed children. Their public persona projected an image of progressive ideals and community involvement, a stark contrast to the whispers of shady business dealings, aggressive tax avoidance, and ruthless ambition that circulated among Wilder City's more cynical residents.

Alice uncovered evidence suggesting their involvement in a series of questionable land acquisitions, pushing out long-term residents and destroying historical landmarks in their relentless pursuit of profit. Their public pronouncements about environmental responsibility seemed almost mocked in light of their actions.

Alice's investigation wasn't limited to observation; she delved into the financial records of these families, painstakingly piecing together a complex web of interconnected businesses, shell corporations, and offshore accounts. The money flowed like a subterranean river, its course obscured by layers of complex transactions designed to conceal its true origin and destination. She discovered intricate partnerships and bitter rivalries, all woven into the fabric of Wilder City's economy, a system where fortunes were made and broken with equal ruthlessness.

The teenage victim, Daniel Albright, had lived within this complex ecosystem, his life inextricably linked to the elite families that ruled the city. His father, a prominent lawyer, served as legal counsel for many of the families Alice was investigating. This professional relationship opened doors to the inner workings of these families, a privileged position that offered unprecedented access to information and influence. Alice began to suspect that Daniel might have inadvertently stumbled upon a secret, a piece of information that could have jeopardized the carefully constructed world of the Wilder City elite.

Focusing on Daniel's social circles, Alice discovered a hidden layer in his life. Beyond the seemingly idyllic surface, Daniel possessed a keen eye for injustice. His social media activity, initially appearing unremarkable, revealed a growing frustration with the social inequalities prevalent in Wilder City. He'd shared news articles about the controversial land acquisitions by the Millers, voiced his concerns about the environmental impact of their projects and expressed his growing unease about the vast disparity between the wealthy and the rest of the community. His online activity hinted at a budding activism, a rebellion brewing silently in his heart.

This activism, however, was not limited to the digital realm. Alice unearthed evidence that Daniel was secretly involved in a local activist group, a clandestine organization working to expose the underbelly of

Wilder City's elite. The group, operating largely under the radar, had been gathering evidence of the questionable business practices of several prominent families, including the Vanderbilts and the Millers. Daniel's involvement in this group was significant, given his privileged access to information through his father. His knowledge of the city's elite could provide the group with invaluable insights into their activities.

The discovery of Daniel's activism provided a chilling new perspective on his murder. It was no longer just a random act of violence but possibly a targeted assassination, a message meant to silence a growing voice of dissent. The question then became, who would have been so brazen, so powerful, to eliminate a teenager who was, in essence, a threat to their carefully constructed world? The answer, Alice suspected, lay within the web of connections and secrets she was slowly unraveling.

The investigation brought Alice into contact with several individuals associated with the Wilder City elite, individuals who initially appeared cooperative but soon revealed guardedness and a chilling control over information. She learned about clandestine meetings in secluded locations, coded conversations whispered in hushed tones, and veiled threats delivered with a practiced nonchalance. The social fabric of Wilder City was not only tightly woven but also fiercely protective, a system designed to keep its secrets buried deep beneath the surface.

Among these individuals was Julian Vance, Eleanor Vance's estranged son. Julian, despite his family's reputation for philanthropy and social grace, was a known gambler and involved in several dubious financial ventures. His extravagant lifestyle was seemingly funded by sources that were impossible to trace, fueling suspicion that he may have been involved in illegal activities. Alice found evidence suggesting a connection between Julian and the untraceable phone number that had been used to contact Daniel before his death. This connection raised the stakes, suggesting a direct link between the seemingly disparate worlds of high society and potential criminal activity.

Furthermore, Alice discovered a pattern in the calls made to Daniel. The locations were meticulously chosen, seemingly designed to gather information about various members of the Wilder City elite. The route of the calls mirrored a sequence of key locations – the Vandergelt mansion, the Miller estate, and even a secluded building known to house a secretive social club, the exclusive "Serpent's Coil," a society shrouded in mystery and rumored to have ties to international criminal organizations.

The suggestion of espionage was compelling, the implication being that Daniel was not just a victim but a pawn, a tool used to gather sensitive information before he was eliminated to avoid exposure.

The further she delved, the more Alice realized that the death of Daniel Albright was not an isolated incident; it was a symptom of a far deeper malaise, a sickness at the heart of Wilder City's elite. The intricate web of deceit extended far beyond her initial assumptions, implicating various individuals and families in a conspiracy of far greater reach and magnitude than initially envisioned. It was a world where power, influence, and money were intertwined in a deadly embrace, where justice was a luxury afforded only to those who held sufficient wealth and influence to command it. The unraveling of the web had just begun, and Alice knew that she was walking a tightrope, with the weight of truth and potential repercussions pressing heavily upon her. The fight for justice was far from over, but Alice was prepared to face the dark secrets that lay buried beneath the polished surfaces of Wilder City's elite.

The First Suspect

Julian Vance, with his perpetually haunted eyes and a smirk that never quite reached them, was a man who thrived in shadows. He possessed the effortless charm of his mother, Eleanor Vance, the matriarch of the Vance family and a pillar of Wilder City society but lacked her unwavering moral compass. While his mother meticulously cultivated an image of unblemished philanthropy, Julian reveled in the murky underbelly of Wilder City's opulent lifestyle. His gambling debts were legendary, whispered about in hushed tones in the city's most exclusive casinos and backroom poker games. The sources of his seemingly endless funds were as shrouded in mystery as the Serpent's Coil; the exclusive social club Alice was investigating.

Alice had initially dismissed Julian as a flamboyant playboy, a character too easily dismissed as a product of privilege and entitlement. His connection to the untraceable number that contacted Daniel before his death, however, changed everything. It was a tenuous link, a single thread in the vast tapestry of the investigation, but it was a thread that pulled at Alice's instincts, hinting at a darker narrative.

Delving deeper into Julian's finances proved a Herculean task. His accounts were intricately layered, a labyrinth of shell corporations and offshore holdings that effectively concealed the origins of his wealth. He employed a team of sophisticated lawyers and accountants who moved with the agility of shadows, always one step ahead of scrutiny. Alice spent days poring over financial documents, cross-referencing transactions, following the digital breadcrumbs left in his wake. The trail was frustratingly elusive, designed to mislead and confuse. Yet, certain patterns began to emerge.

Several transactions stood out, seemingly innocuous at first glance but revealing upon closer inspection. Large sums of money were transferred from accounts linked to various businesses associated with the Millers and Vandergelt, ostensibly legitimate transactions, but their timing and frequency suggested a clandestine relationship. Alice suspected that Julian might have been acting as a conduit, laundering money for the two families, perhaps concealing profits derived from their questionable business dealings. His gambling debts might have been a convenient cover, a smokescreen to conceal the true nature of his financial activities.

Alice also uncovered a series of meetings between Julian and a known associate of the Serpent's Coil, a man named Marcus Thorne. Thorne's reputation preceded him: a shadowy figure rumored to have ties to international criminal organizations, dealing in everything from stolen art to illicit arms deals. The meetings were discreet, taking place in secluded locations, far from prying eyes. The evidence suggested a collaboration, a partnership that extended far beyond the realm of simple financial transactions.

Alice's investigation led her to a discreet, almost invisible club located on the edge of Wilder Creek. It wasn't marked, merely a nondescript building sandwiched between a car wash and a vacant lot. Yet, it was known amongst the city's elite as "The Rookery," a place where deals were struck in whispers and secrets were traded like precious commodities. She discovered that

Julian was a regular attendee, often seen in the company of Thorne and other individuals involved in highly questionable ventures. The atmosphere inside the club was thick with an unspoken tension, the air heavy with the scent of illicit deals and simmering resentments.

Observing Julian became a crucial part of her investigation. She followed him for days, blending into the background, observing his interactions, noting the people he met and the places he frequented. His movements were erratic; his days filled with a whirlwind of clandestine meetings and high stakes gambling sessions. He moved like a phantom, leaving almost no digital footprint to follow. Alice suspected that his life was carefully constructed, each action a calculated move in a complex game of deception.

In one instance, Alice observed Julian meeting with a lawyer known for representing clients involved in sophisticated financial crimes. The meeting was brief, taking place in a dimly lit parking garage, a clandestine rendezvous suggestive of a transaction too sensitive to take place in a public setting. The lawyer's known association with money laundering further solidified Alice's suspicion of Julian's involvement in illicit activities. The lawyer was later seen meeting with several individuals from the Vandergelt and Miller families.

The possibility that Julian might have been involved in Daniel's death intensified as Alice discovered a connection between Daniel and The Rookery. Daniel, during his secret activism, had attempted to infiltrate the club, hoping to gather evidence of its illicit activities. He'd managed to take several photographs before being discovered. The images depicted Thorne and Julian in a heated argument, their faces etched with anger, their words lost to the noise of the club's illicit gatherings.

The photos didn't reveal the subject of their disagreement, but the tension in the photographs was palpable. The discovery suggested that Daniel had unknowingly stumbled onto something crucial, information that Julian and possibly others were desperate to keep hidden. The possibility that Daniel's investigation into The Rookery led to his murder became increasingly plausible. Julian, with his desperation for money and his connections with the club and to the families who may have been using the club for their own ends, became the prime suspect in Alice's mind. He had the motive to silence a potential whistleblower and the opportunity through his connections and influence. The investigation was far from over, but Julian Vance had appeared as a formidable suspect, a man shrouded in secrecy, operating in the shadows of Wilder City's elite. Alice knew that bringing him to justice would require unraveling a web of deceit that reached the very highest echelons of power. The stakes were higher than ever. The fight for justice was a dangerous game, and she was playing for keeps. The death of a teenager had exposed a rot far deeper than she had ever anticipated. She now had to decide how far she was willing to go to uncover the truth, even if it meant confronting the darkest corners of Wilder City's gilded cage.

Alice's Personal Struggles

The relentless pursuit of justice was taking its toll. Alice found herself staring at her reflection in the bathroom mirror, the harsh fluorescent light illuminating the dark circles under her eyes, the exhaustion etched into every line of her face. Sleep was a luxury she could barely afford, snatched in fragmented bursts between stakeouts, interviews, and poring over endless financial records. The city's glittering facade, the one she'd always admired from afar, now felt like a suffocating cage, its opulence a cruel mockery of the darkness she was uncovering.

The investigation into Daniel's death had become an all-consuming obsession, a relentless tide pulling her under. She'd lost track of time, neglecting her friends, her family, and even the simple pleasures that once brought her joy. The apartment, once a sanctuary, now felt like a temporary resting place, a sterile environment devoid of warmth and personality, a reflection of her emotional state. Her meticulously organized files, her lifeline in chaos, seemed to mock her with their silent efficiency; they held the clues, yes, but at what cost?

She missed the quiet evenings spent with her sister, Clara, their laughter echoing in the small kitchen over shared meals and whispering secrets. Now, their calls were strained conversations squeezed between surveillance operations and late-night interrogations.

The guilt gnawed at her; she'd become a stranger to the people she loved, a phantom haunting the edges of their lives. Clara's concerned voice, her unspoken worry, echoed in Alice's mind, a constant reminder of the price of her dedication. She tried to explain, to justify the sacrifices she was making, but the words always fell short. How could she convey the weight of the truth she was pursuing, the importance of bringing Daniel's killer to justice?

The loneliness was a palpable presence, a constant companion in her solitary nights. The city that once pulsed with life now seemed empty, devoid of human connection. Her work had isolated her, pushing her into a solitary world where trust was a luxury she could not afford and where every interaction held the potential for betrayal. She found herself relying on caffeine and willpower to keep her going, the boundaries between work and personal life blurring into a chaotic mess.

There were moments of doubt, brief cracks in her resolve. The sheer scale of the conspiracy and the power of the people involved made her question the feasibility of her mission. Was she tilting at windmills, fighting a losing battle against forces far greater than herself? The thought of failure, of letting Daniel down, fueled a deep, gnawing fear. The weight of responsibility, of the potential consequences, was almost unbearable.

She found solace in the familiar rhythm of her work, in the meticulous process of piecing together the puzzle. Each discovered clue, each confirmed suspicion, was a small victory, a flicker of light in the overwhelming darkness. The meticulous organization of her files and the painstaking cross-referencing of data became a form of meditation, a way to channel her anxiety into productive action. She poured all her energy, her frustration, and her grief into the investigation, transforming her pain into a driving force.

However, the strain on her physical and mental health was undeniable. She found herself making mistakes, small oversights that threatened to derail the entire investigation. The exhaustion clouded her judgment, impairing her ability to think clearly and to make sound decisions. The pressure was mounting; the constant surveillance, the clandestine meetings, and the ever-present threat of discovery were taking their toll.

The recurring nightmares didn't help. She dreamt of Daniel, his face pale and lifeless, his eyes wide with unspoken terror. She saw herself caught in a web of deceit, surrounded by shadowy figures, their faces obscured by darkness. The dreams left her drenched in sweat, her heart pounding, the fear clinging to her even when she awoke. She'd tried to find comfort in sleep, but it only seemed to bring more shadows and more fear.

She sought solace in the familiar routine of her morning runs. The early morning hours, before the city awoke, provided a brief respite from the suffocating pressure. The rhythmic pounding of her feet on the pavement, the cool morning air against her skin, helped to clear her head, offering a moment of peace amidst the storm. The vast expanse of Wilder Creek reflected her state of mind – a seemingly placid surface hiding churning currents beneath.

One morning, while running along the riverbank, she stumbled upon a discarded newspaper, its headline screaming about the latest corporate scandal involving the Miller family. A fleeting moment of anger, a burning frustration, rose within her. She understood the frustration of being overlooked, dismissed, or simply ignored. Yet, such was the case for so many people in the world.

The article sparked a renewed sense of purpose. The personal struggles were immense, but the bigger picture, the injustice she was fighting against, fueled her resolve. She couldn't afford to falter. Daniel's death demanded justice; his memory spurred her onward. The investigation was not merely a job; it was a personal crusade, a fight for truth and justice against a formidable enemy. The fight was far from over. The lines between her personal life and her investigation remained blurry, the weight of it pressing down on her with relentless force. But she refused to surrender. The cost might be high, but the potential rewards – justice for Daniel and perhaps even a chance to reclaim some semblance of her own life – were worth fighting for. She would continue to unravel the web, no matter what the personal cost. She owed it to Daniel, and she owed it to herself.

Unexpected Alliances

The discarded newspaper, a seemingly insignificant detail, became a pivotal piece in the intricate puzzle. The article detailing the Miller family's latest corporate scandal – a complex web of tax evasion and insider trading – was more than just a headline; it was a lifeline. It was a connection, a thread that linked the seemingly disparate elements of her investigation. The Millers, a prominent family with extensive ties to the city's elite, had always been a peripheral figure in her investigation, shadowy figures lurking at the edges of the web. But now, they were no longer just suspects; they were central to the unfolding narrative.

The article mentioned a key figure, Arthur Miller, the family patriarch, and his questionable dealings with a shell corporation registered in the Cayman Islands. This shell corporation, coincidentally, had also been linked to several accounts identified in Daniel's financial records. It was a tenuous connection, a faint whisper in the wind, but it was enough to reignite Alice's determination. She knew she needed to dig deeper to uncover the true extent of the Millers' involvement.

Her investigation led her to Elias Thorne, a disgruntled former employee of the Miller family's empire, who had been publicly humiliated and subsequently fired for daring to question their financial practices. Thorne, initially a suspect due to his apparent motive and his intimate knowledge of the Millers' inner workings, turned out to be unexpectedly helpful. Driven by a simmering resentment and a thirst for revenge, Thorne agreed to cooperate, providing Alice with a wealth of information, including confidential documents and internal memos that painted a vivid picture of the family's fraudulent activities.

His cooperation came with conditions, of course. Thorne, hardened by his experiences, wasn't interested in justice in the abstract; he was driven by personal gain. He demanded anonymity, fearing the Millers' powerful retribution, and he requested specific actions on Alice's part – namely, a promise to expose specific individuals within the Miller family to ensure he was not the sole target. It was a dangerous game, a treacherous dance on the edge of legality, but Alice was willing to play. She needed Thorne's information, and he needed her protection.

Their alliance was an uneasy truce; a fragile balance built on mutual need and mistrust. They communicated through encrypted channels, meeting in secluded locations, always aware of the potential risks. The air crackled with tension during their meetings, a mixture of suspicion and guarded camaraderie. Thorne, a man of few words, revealed the intricate workings of the Miller family's network of shell corporations, offshore accounts, and carefully orchestrated tax schemes. He spoke of coded messages, secret meetings, and lavish parties that served as fronts for their illicit activities.

While Thorne provided valuable insights into the financial aspects of Miller's operation, another unexpected ally emerged from an entirely different direction. Detective Michael Davis, a seasoned member of the Internal Affairs division, had been quietly monitoring the Miller family for years, gathering evidence of their widespread corruption. Davis, initially skeptical of Alice's unorthodox methods and her relentless pursuit of justice, became convinced by the weight of the evidence she presented, evidence that corroborated his findings.

Davis's expertise in police procedure and his access to internal resources proved invaluable to Alice's investigation. He helped her navigate the labyrinthine bureaucracy of the police department, providing crucial leads and protecting her from unwanted scrutiny. He became her secret weapon, a silent partner working from within the system, providing Alice with a sense of safety and support. He shared information discreetly, warning her about potential leaks and protecting her from the internal machines that could have sabotaged her investigation.

Their collaboration was a delicate balancing act; they had to tread carefully, aware that their alliance was a secret that could easily be exposed. They communicated through coded messages and clandestine meetings; their every move shrouded in secrecy. The risk was immense, yet the potential reward, exposing a vast conspiracy that reached the highest levels of the city's elite, was worth the gamble.

However, this newfound alliance also introduced new layers of complexity and uncertainty. Thorne's information, while valuable, lacked certain details, leaving significant gaps in the narrative. He revealed that the Millers were not solely motivated by financial gain. There was a darker, more sinister purpose behind their actions, a secret agenda that involved a clandestine organization known only as "The Syndicate."

The Syndicate, according to Thorne, was a network of powerful individuals operating outside the reach of the law, pulling strings from the shadows, influencing political decisions, and controlling vast swathes of the city's economy. The Millers were merely pawns in a much larger game, their illicit financial activities serving as a means to an end. This revelation widened the scope of Alice's investigation exponentially, transforming it from a case of corporate fraud into a much larger battle against a powerful, shadowy organization.

This newfound information forced Alice to reconsider her strategy. She had to carefully weigh the risks, managing her newfound alliance with Thorne and Detective Davis while expanding her investigation to encompass this new and elusive foe. It raised questions about the very nature of her investigation, changing the direction and the risks she had to take. Suddenly, exposing the Millers wasn't enough; she needed to dismantle The Syndicate, an endeavor that seemed like an impossible task.

The weight of responsibility intensified, threatening to overwhelm her. The risk of exposing herself and her allies was greater than ever. She was playing a dangerous game, a high-stakes gamble against powerful enemies who would stop at nothing to protect their interests. Her sleepless nights and the gnawing feeling of paranoia became more frequent and intense. She was constantly looking over her shoulder, ever vigilant, aware that anyone could be a threat, an enemy in disguise.

Even her newfound allies, Thorne and Davis, despite their shared goal, were not without their own hidden agendas. Thorne's desire for revenge was palpable, and his willingness to cooperate was dependent on Alice fulfilling his personal requirements. Davis, while seemingly honorable, operated within the constraints of a corrupt system; his loyalty to the truth was constantly assessed by his loyalty to the badge and his own survival within the police force.

Alice found herself questioning the moral implications of her actions, navigating the treacherous path of ethical ambiguity. Was she truly fighting for justice, or had she become entangled in a web of deceit and manipulation, caught in the crossfire of competing interests? The line between right and wrong blurred, and she found herself constantly questioning the consequences of her choices.

The city, once a vibrant backdrop to her investigation, now seemed like a sinister stage, its gleaming lights and opulent buildings concealing a web of corruption and deceit. The constant surveillance, the clandestine meetings, and the ever-present fear of discovery added another layer of complexity to her already tumultuous life. The weight of the investigation, compounded by the personal sacrifices she had made, pressed down on her with crushing force.

Yet, despite the challenges and the ever-increasing risks, Alice refused to back down. She was fueled by her commitment to justice, her determination to uncover the truth, and her unwavering belief that Daniel's death would not be in vain. She found solace in the quiet companionship of her allies, Thorne and Davis, a fragile bond forged in the crucible of their shared endeavor. They represented her only chance to bring down a powerful enemy, an enemy far bigger and more dangerous than she had initially imagined.

The path ahead was fraught with peril, but Alice, hardened by adversity and strengthened by her unexpected alliances, was prepared to face whatever challenges lay ahead. The unraveling of the web had only just begun. The fight for justice was far from over, and the stakes had never been higher.

Political Intrigue

The trail of the Miller family's illicit activities led Alice down a rabbit hole far deeper than she could have ever anticipated. Thorne's revelations about "The Syndicate" weren't mere whispers; they were deafening roars echoing through the corridors of power. The initial focus on corporate fraud now paled in comparison to the seismic implications of a conspiracy that infiltrated the very heart of the city's government.

Her investigation took a sharp turn toward the political arena, demanding a more nuanced understanding of the city's power dynamics. Thorne, surprisingly, had insights into this realm as well. He detailed how the Millers, through carefully cultivated relationships and generous campaign contributions, had effectively bought influence within city hall. Council members, seemingly pillars of the community, were revealed to be puppets dancing to the tune of the Miller family's corruption orchestra. Their seemingly legitimate political maneuvers – zoning changes, infrastructure projects, and favorable legislation – were all carefully orchestrated to benefit the Millers' business interests. Thorne provided copies of emails and documents, detailed accounts of clandestine meetings held late at night in dimly lit backrooms, and even audio recordings of hushed conversations laced with veiled threats and promises of financial reward.

One particularly damning piece of evidence was a series of meticulously forged documents, which Thorne had managed to acquire before his dismissal. These documents, disguised as legitimate city planning proposals, contained hidden clauses that would grant the Millers exclusive rights to develop prime waterfront property. The documents had been submitted to the city council by Councilman Robert Hayes, a man who had built a reputation as a champion of the working class, a populist hero. Hayes, it turned out, was deeply indebted to Arthur Miller, his campaigns generously funded through opaque shell corporations linked to the very same network Thorne had previously detailed.

This discovery opened Pandora's Box of political intrigue. Alice realized she was dealing with not just financial crimes but a meticulously planned conspiracy to manipulate the city's very structure for personal gain. The scope of her investigation had broadened exponentially, requiring a deeper dive into public records, political campaign finance reports, and the opaque world of city contracts. It was a labyrinthine system, and Alice, armed with Thorne's insights and Davis's police expertise, began to unravel its intricate threads.

Detective Davis, with his access to the city's database and his familiarity with police procedures, proved invaluable. He expertly navigated the bureaucratic hurdles, securing warrants, accessing confidential records, and discreetly verifying Thorne's information. He used his skills and knowledge of the political landscape to filter through endless paperwork and identify crucial connections, all while maintaining the necessary secrecy. Their collaboration was increasingly delicate; every step required careful consideration to avoid raising red flags within the police department, an institution arguably more entrenched in corruption than they initially realized.

One of their key breakthroughs involved a seemingly minor detail: a series of seemingly innocuous donations to the city's parks and recreation fund. The donations, although individually small, added up to a considerable sum, coming from various shell corporations linked to the Millers. It appeared to be a standard public relations tactic, but Davis, using his knowledge of the city's budget, noticed a discrepancy. The timing of the donations suspiciously coincided with a series of city council votes that greatly benefited the Millers' business interests. This raised serious questions about bribery and quid pro quo exchanges.

The evidence amassed by Alice and Davis was substantial, implicating not only the Millers but also several prominent city officials. The implications extended beyond just financial gain; the evidence suggested a deliberate campaign to undermine the city's infrastructure projects to force favorable contracts. Thorne had alluded to this in his earlier conversations, hinting at schemes that involved sabotaging public works projects, creating an artificial demand for the Millers' construction company to step in and save the day, and securing lucrative contracts that inflated their profits exorbitantly.

As they delved deeper, the intricate web of connections became increasingly disturbing. They uncovered evidence of threats against city employees who questioned the Millers' dealings. Several whistleblowers who attempted to expose corruption had been mysteriously silenced, their careers destroyed, or their lives abruptly cut short. This was a pattern that echoed a larger, more sinister orchestration. It revealed a willingness on the part of The Syndicate to resort to violence to maintain its power.

The Syndicate's influence permeated every level of the city's governance. They controlled the media, influencing public opinion and silencing dissenting voices. They manipulated the judicial system, ensuring that any legal challenges were swiftly dismissed. They even had a presence in the police force itself, explaining why Davis's previous investigations had been thwarted, why he had been repeatedly sidelined, and his leads subtly dismissed.

The investigation was a high-stakes game of cat and mouse, with Alice and Davis constantly one step behind their adversaries. They were navigating a treacherous landscape filled with powerful enemies, each with their hidden agendas. The closer they got to the truth, the more dangerous the situation became. The threat of exposure was ever-present, the fear of retribution of a constant companion. Alice found herself working longer hours, her apartment becoming more a temporary shelter than a true home, constantly reviewing their steps and communications.

Meanwhile, Thorne, despite his willingness to cooperate, remained an enigmatic figure. His motives, while seemingly driven by revenge, were still shrouded in ambiguity. Alice had a sense that he withheld information that he had his vendettas that extended beyond the Miller family and might even extend into The Syndicate. His cryptic messages and his insistence on specific actions from Alice continued to raise questions. Their alliance, fragile from the start,

was strained by mutual mistrust and the looming shadows of their shared danger.

The weight of the investigation began to take its toll. Sleepless nights, fueled by coffee and the sheer volume of evidence, left Alice exhausted. The paranoia was crippling. Every shadow, every unfamiliar face, became a potential threat. She lived with a constant sense of being watched, every phone call, every email, scrutinized for potential surveillance. The burden of responsibility was enormous, the possibility of failure a terrifying prospect.

Yet, despite the risks and the overwhelming nature of the task, Alice pressed on. The memory of Daniel, the burning desire for justice, and the growing weight of the evidence fueled her relentless pursuit of the truth. She was fighting for more than just one man's death; she was fighting for the soul of her city, a city that seemed to be sinking deeper into a quagmire of political corruption and organized crime. The road ahead was long and fraught with danger, but Alice, with her unlikely allies, was prepared to fight until the very end. The shadows of corruption were everywhere, but they would not win.

Financial Manipulation

The seemingly innocuous donations to the city's parks and recreation fund, initially dismissed as a standard public relations maneuver, proved to be a crucial thread in the unraveling of the Miller family's web of deceit. Davis, poring over the city's budget spreadsheets late into the night, noticed a peculiar pattern. The timing of these donations, seemingly random acts of civic generosity, precisely coincided with key city council votes that overwhelmingly favored Miller's lucrative construction and real estate projects. It wasn't just the timing; it was the sheer volume. While individually small, these contributions, channeled through a labyrinthine network of shell corporations, added up to a substantial sum, far exceeding the scale of typical corporate philanthropy.

This discovery led Alice and Davis down a new path, one that involved painstakingly tracing the flow of money through a complex maze of offshore accounts, anonymous shell corporations, and intricate financial transactions. They utilized advanced forensic accounting techniques, collaborating with a specialist from the IRS's criminal investigation division to unravel the layers of obfuscation. Each transaction, meticulously documented, painted a clearer picture of the scale of the operation. The Millers weren't simply engaging in petty corruption; they were orchestrating a grand scheme of financial manipulation, skillfully exploiting loopholes in the financial system to conceal their illicit gains.

The investigation revealed a sophisticated system of money laundering designed to disguise the origin and destination of funds. Money flowed through a series of offshore accounts in tax havens, making it virtually impossible to trace the source. They used complex layering techniques, shuffling funds between different accounts and jurisdictions, creating a deliberately confusing trail designed to thwart any investigation. The shell corporations, often registered in countries with lax financial regulations, functioned as conduits, obscuring the true beneficiaries of the illicit transactions. These entities were meticulously crafted, with board members and officers often being straw men, individuals with little or no knowledge of the true nature of the businesses.

What emerged was a chilling portrait of greed and ambition, a systematic exploitation of the city's resources for personal enrichment. The Millers weren't merely profiting from their corrupt practices; they were amassing a fortune, building an empire on the backs of the city's taxpayers. Their lavish lifestyle, previously attributed to shrewd business acumen, was now revealed to be the product of systematic theft and fraud. Their opulent mansion, their luxury cars, their extravagant vacations—all paid for with money stolen from the city.

Further investigation unveiled a series of questionable loans and investments, shrouded in secrecy and designed to inflate the Millers' assets while concealing their true financial situation. They used complex financial instruments, such as derivatives and structured investment vehicles, to mask their financial activities and avoid scrutiny. These transactions, often conducted through obscure financial institutions, were deliberately designed to confuse investigators and mislead auditors. The complexity of these transactions was staggering, requiring weeks of intense analysis to decipher their true nature. The forensic accountants worked tirelessly, spending countless hours meticulously analyzing financial statements, bank records, and other documents, piecing together the puzzle one transaction at a time.

The sheer scale of the financial manipulation was breathtaking. The numbers involved were staggering, representing a significant portion of the city's budget, siphoned off over years. This wasn't a case of isolated incidents of corruption; this was a well-orchestrated, long-term scheme designed to plunder the city's resources systematically. The Millers had skillfully cultivated a network of accomplices, including city officials, bank executives, and financial advisors, all complicit in their scheme. These individuals, motivated by greed and ambition, turned a blind eye to the illegality of the transactions, facilitating the flow of money and helping the Millers to maintain their façade of legitimacy.

Alice and Davis discovered that the Millers employed a team of highly skilled lawyers and accountants who specialized in creating intricate financial structures designed to obscure their illicit activities. These professionals, masters of tax evasion and money laundering, were paid handsomely to ensure that the Millers' financial transactions remained untraceable. They created a sophisticated network of offshore accounts, shell corporations, and trusts, carefully constructed to avoid detection by law enforcement and regulatory authorities. The legal fees alone represented a significant expenditure, highlighting the lengths to which the Millers went to protect their ill-gotten gains. Their lawyers weren't just providing legal advice; they were actively participating in the criminal enterprise, creating the complex financial structures that facilitated the money laundering scheme.

The investigation also uncovered evidence of insider trading and market manipulation, further highlighting the extent of the Millers' criminal activities. They used their insider knowledge of city contracts and development projects to manipulate stock prices, profiting handsomely from their illicit dealings. They timed their trades to coincide with the release of public information, maximizing their gains while minimizing their risks. This involved a carefully orchestrated campaign of misinformation, using their connections in the media to spread false rumors and manipulate public perception of their businesses.

The depth of their deception was shocking. They had meticulously cultivated a public image of success, portraying themselves as philanthropists and community leaders while secretly enriching themselves at the expense of the city's taxpayers. Their charitable donations, carefully crafted to maintain their public image, were dwarfed by the magnitude of their illicit activities, revealing a cynical manipulation of public trust. This carefully constructed image of respectability served as a smokescreen, allowing them to operate undetected for years.

Their manipulation extended beyond the financial realm. They used their wealth and influence to intimidate witnesses, silence whistleblowers, and obstruct justice. The pattern of intimidation, threats, and even violence against those who dared to question their activities underscored the lengths to which they were willing to go to protect their criminal enterprise. This pattern of intimidation extended into the city government itself; the evidence indicated several instances where city employees who raised concerns about Miller's projects were either transferred to less influential positions, subtly threatened, or mysteriously had their careers ruined.

As Alice and Davis continued to peel back the layers of deception, they uncovered a disturbing truth: the Millers' financial manipulation was far from an isolated incident. It was intricately woven into the fabric of the city's governance, a symptom of a larger, more insidious system of corruption. The implications were far-reaching, suggesting a conspiracy that reached the highest levels of city hall, implicating powerful figures who had benefited from the Millers' illicit activities. The scope of the investigation had grown exponentially, expanding beyond simple financial crimes to encompass a broader web of political intrigue and organized crime. The fight for justice had become a battle against a deeply entrenched system of corruption, a fight that would require all their courage, skill, and determination. The stakes were higher than ever before.

The future of the city hung in the balance.

Betrayal and Deception

The investigation into the Miller family's financial empire unearthed a far more complex web of deceit than Alice and Davis initially anticipated. Their meticulously crafted façade of respectability began to crack, revealing a tapestry of betrayals and deceptions woven amongst the city's elite. The seemingly unshakeable alliances between the Millers and other prominent families started to fray as whispers of discontent and double crossings surfaced.

One such instance involved the Harrington family, long-term associates and business partners of the Millers. Initially perceived as staunch allies, their involvement in the scheme proved to be far more nuanced. While the Harringtons benefited financially from the Millers' illicit activities through joint ventures and shared investments, documents obtained from a disgruntled Harrington family accountant revealed a simmering resentment. Emails and internal memos depicted a growing tension between the two families, fueled by the Millers' increasingly aggressive and unscrupulous tactics. The Harringtons felt increasingly marginalized, their contributions undervalued, and their share of the spoils diminished. This resentment manifested in subtle acts of defiance, including discreetly leaking information to the investigators, albeit anonymously. This was not an outright betrayal but a carefully calculated act of self-preservation. They were hedging their bets, ensuring their survival amidst the crumbling empire of the Millers.

Further investigation revealed a similar pattern with the Vanderlyn family, another powerful family with deep ties to the Millers. The Vanderlyn's, known for their philanthropic endeavors and seemingly untarnished reputation, were secretly engaged in a parallel scheme of corruption, utilizing similar methods of money laundering and financial manipulation. This wasn't merely a case of independent criminal enterprises operating in parallel; it was a far more complex, interconnected web. The Vanderlyn's, though initially seemingly untouched by the scandal, had covertly leveraged their connections to protect the Millers, providing crucial support and enabling their illicit activities to continue. However, this collaboration wasn't based on genuine loyalty. It was a calculated quid pro quo, a strategic alliance that benefited both families but lacked genuine trust.

The internal conflicts within the elite circle were not limited to financial disputes. The investigation uncovered a bitter feud between the Millers' two sons, Ethan and Caleb. Ethan, the elder son, had been groomed to succeed his father, inheriting the mantle of leadership in the family business. Caleb, however, harbored a deep-seated resentment towards his brother, fueled by years of perceived favoritism and neglect. This rivalry had long been kept under wraps, a carefully guarded secret within the family. But as the pressure mounted during the investigation, Caleb's resentment boiled over. He began to subtly undermine his brother's efforts, leaking damaging information that jeopardized the Millers' attempts to maintain their carefully constructed image. His actions were a calculated act of revenge, a desperate attempt to undermine his brother and settle a longstanding score.

The evidence suggested that Caleb had secretly contacted the investigators, provided anonymous tips and corroborated information, adding another layer of complexity to the already tangled web of deceit. His motivations were complex – partly revenge, partly a desire for self-preservation as the family's empire crumbled, and perhaps a shred of remorse for the years of complicity in his family's criminal enterprise. This internal fracture within the Miller family was a crucial turning point in the investigation. Caleb's actions, though ambiguous and driven by personal motives, provided critical insights that enabled Alice and Davis to penetrate the Millers' carefully constructed defense.

The investigation also uncovered a disturbing pattern of manipulation within the city's government. Mayor Thompson, a long-time friend and associate of the Millers, was initially presented as an unsuspecting victim of their deceptive practices. However, documents discovered in a hidden compartment within Mayor Thompson's office revealed a far more sinister reality. Thompson received substantial bribes and kickbacks in exchange for his cooperation and tacit approval of the Millers' illicit activities. This wasn't a simple case of corruption; it was a carefully orchestrated conspiracy involving high-ranking city officials who had enriched themselves at the expense of the city's taxpayers. They had skillfully exploited loopholes in the legal system, abusing their positions of power to facilitate the Millers' fraudulent schemes.

The investigation further revealed a network of loyalists and informants strategically positioned within various city departments who had consistently covered up the Millers' activities. These individuals, motivated by personal gain or fear of retribution, had worked diligently to maintain the family's power and influence. Their complicity was crucial to the Millers' long-term success, allowing them to operate undetected for years. This intricate network of informants and collaborators demonstrated the extent of the Millers' reach and their ability to corrupt the city's institutions.

The betrayals and deceptions extended even further, reaching into the realm of legal and financial institutions. The Millers' team of lawyers and accountants, initially perceived as skilled professionals simply providing legal services, turned out to be active participants in the criminal enterprise. They crafted complex financial structures, obfuscated transactions, and employed sophisticated money-laundering techniques to shield the Millers' illicit activities from scrutiny. Their involvement wasn't merely professional negligence; it was active complicity, a conscious decision to assist in a criminal enterprise for personal gain.

The investigation into the lawyers' and accountants' actions revealed a surprising level of cooperation between firms, a coordinated effort to protect the Millers and their associates. This cross-firm collaboration was facilitated through a network of informal relationships and shared clientele, indicating a deep-seated culture of corruption within the legal and financial professions. The extent of this collusion was staggering, revealing a system of complicity that extended beyond individual professionals to encompass entire organizations.

Unraveling the intricate network of betrayals and deceptions required an exhaustive investigation involving countless interviews, the examination of thousands of documents, and the meticulous reconstruction of financial transactions. The sheer volume of information was overwhelming, demanding a relentless pursuit of truth and a dogged determination to peel back the layers of lies and deception. The investigators had to confront the complex motivations and conflicting allegiances of numerous individuals, each with their own reasons for participating in or concealing the truth.

Alice and Davis's investigation uncovered a chilling truth: the city's elite was not merely a group of successful individuals; it was a tightly knit circle of self-serving individuals bound together by shared interests and mutually beneficial schemes of corruption. Loyalty and trust were commodities to be traded, manipulated, and discarded as needed, depending on the shifting tides of power and influence. The seemingly impenetrable wall of respectability and success that surrounded these families had crumbled, exposing a core of greed, ambition, and betrayal. The true nature of their relationships, based not on genuine trust or friendship but on calculated alliances and self-serving partnerships, proved to be a pivotal factor in unraveling their crimes. The investigation's progress had been greatly aided by these fissures, highlighting the unpredictable and often destructive nature of ambition and unchecked power within the city's upper echelon.

As the investigation moved forward, the lines between allies and enemies continued to blur, raising serious questions about who could be truly trusted. The battle for justice had become a complex game of deception, where loyalty and betrayal were constantly shifting, making it increasingly difficult to discern fact from fiction.

Alice Faces Resistance

The air in Mayor Thompson's opulent office hung thick with the scent of old money and simmering resentment. Alice perched on the edge of a plush leather chair and felt the weight of the city's unspoken secrets pressing down on her. Across from her, the Mayor, a man whose smile hadn't reached his eyes in years, meticulously polished his glasses, a nervous tic that betrayed his composure.

"Ms. Hayes," he began, his voice a low, controlled rumble, "I assure you, there's been a misunderstanding. The documents you've presented… they're… out of context." Alice leaned forward, her gaze unwavering. "Out of context? Mayor Thompson, these are bank statements meticulously detailing the flow of funds from the Miller accounts directly into yours. They're hardly ambiguous." Thompson sighed, a theatrical display of weariness. "Politics, Ms. Hayes. It's a messy business. Contributions… donations… they're… common practice."

"Common practice?" Alice echoed, her voice sharp. "Mayor, you received over five million dollars in untraceable funds. These were not donations. These were bribes." His carefully constructed façade began to crack. The controlled composure faltered, replaced by a flicker of fear in his eyes. "You're playing a dangerous game, Ms. Hayes. The Millers are powerful people. Influential. They have friends in high places." The veiled threat hung in the air, heavily and suffocating. Alice met his gaze, her resolve unshaken.

"I'm aware of the Millers' influence, Mayor. But my job is to find the truth, regardless of who it implies." Leaving Thompson's office, Alice felt the chill of the unspoken alliances, the silent pact that bound the city's elite. She knew this was just the beginning of the resistance she would face. The next few days were a blur of obstruction, closed doors and evasive answers. Phone calls went unanswered, witnesses suddenly became unavailable, and files mysteriously disappeared from city archives. The carefully constructed wall of silence was a formidable obstacle. Her attempts to subpoena key figures within the Miller organization were met with legal maneuvers so intricate they seemed designed to exhaust her resources and patience.

Ethan Miller, the eldest son, retained a phalanx of high-powered lawyers, each one a master of delaying tactics and procedural loopholes. They filed motions, appeals, and counter-appeals, drowning the investigation in a sea of legal paperwork. Every step forward seemed to be countered by two steps back, a relentless attrition designed to grind her down. Davis, her partner, offered support and tactical guidance, but even his seasoned experience felt inadequate against the sheer weight of the opposition. He had faced corruption before, but this was different; this was systemic and deeply rooted in the city's infrastructure.

The Millers were not just wealthy; they were interwoven into the fabric of the city, their tentacles reaching into every corner of power. The pressure mounted.

Anonymous threats arrived – cryptic messages hinting at the dangers of pursuing this investigation too aggressively. The threats were subtle and carefully worded to avoid direct accusations, but the message was clear: back down or face the consequences. The constant pressure took its toll, eroding the edges of Alice's confidence. She found herself second-guessing her decisions, wrestling with self-doubt and the gnawing fear that she was fighting a losing battle. However, a glimmer of hope emerged from the least expected source – a disgruntled former employee of the Miller accounting firm, a man named Arthur Jenkins. Jenkins, riddled with guilt and remorse, contacted Alice anonymously, offering to provide crucial evidence. He had witnessed firsthand the elaborate schemes employed by the Millers to launder their illicit funds. He held information that could potentially unravel their entire financial empire.

The meeting with Jenkins took place under the cloak of secrecy in a secluded diner on the city's outskirts. He was a nervous wreck, his hands trembling as he handed over a flash drive containing years of meticulously documented financial records. The data confirmed everything Alice had suspected and more – a complex network of offshore accounts, shell corporations, and fabricated transactions designed to conceal the true extent of Miller's criminal activities. The evidence was irrefutable, a damning indictment of their decades-long scheme.

The subsequent confrontation with Miller's legal team was brutal. They fought tooth and nail, employing every legal tactic to discredit Jenkins' testimony, painting him as a disgruntled ex-employee with a vendetta. But Alice had anticipated this. She had secured corroborating evidence from other sources, creating a solid foundation for her case.

The investigation expanded, extending beyond the Millers themselves. Alice uncovered a network of complicit officials, lawyers, and accountants, all playing their part in perpetuating the elaborate fraud. Each individual presented a new challenge, each requiring a different approach and a unique strategy to penetrate their carefully constructed defenses. The more she dug, the more she realized the depth and breadth of the conspiracy, the sheer scale of the corruption that had infiltrated the city's institutions.

The resistance was relentless, a never-ending battle against a well-oiled machine of deception and intimidation. But Alice refused to yield. She knew the stakes were high – the future of the city, the fate of countless innocent individuals caught in the web of the Miller's machinations. She would not let them win. The fight was far from over; it was only just beginning. She had to push further despite the overwhelming odds and ever-present threat of retribution.

The weight of the city's secrets, once a burden, now fueled her determination, transforming into a powerful resolve. The fight for justice was a marathon, not a sprint, and Alice was prepared to run the distance. The truth, she knew, was worth fighting for, no matter the cost. The shadows of corruption were deep, but she was determined to bring them to light.

Arthur L. Taylor

Gathering Evidence

The flash drive Jenkins provided was a treasure trove of digital breadcrumbs, leading Alice down a rabbit hole of offshore accounts, shell corporations, and complex financial transactions designed to obfuscate the trail of illicit funds. Each file revealed a new layer of deception, a more intricate web of deceit woven by the Millers and their accomplices. Days bled into nights as Alice and Davis meticulously analyzed the data, their exhaustion fueled by a growing sense of urgency and the chilling realization of the scale of the conspiracy.

The evidence wasn't just about the Millers; it implicated a vast network of individuals – lawyers who structured the shell corporations, accountants who expertly laundered the money, and city officials who turned a blind eye in exchange for generous "contributions." The trail led Alice to several prominent figures within the city's elite, individuals whose reputations were built on a foundation of carefully crafted illusions and maintained through a system of mutual protection and complicity.

One particularly compelling piece of evidence was a series of encrypted emails between Ethan Miller and Councilman Robert Harding, a close ally of Mayor Thompson. The emails discussed large sums of money being transferred to Harding's offshore accounts in exchange for favorable zoning decisions benefiting Miller-owned properties. The coded language used in the emails initially proved challenging to decipher, but Davis, with his extensive knowledge of cryptography, managed to unlock the puzzle.

The revealed content was damning, a smoking gun that tied Harding directly to Miller's illicit scheme.

The next target was Harding. Alice and Davis devised a strategy for obtaining a confession, knowing that a direct confrontation would likely prove fruitless. Harding, a seasoned politician, was a master of evasion, adept at deflecting accusations and manipulating the legal system to his advantage. Instead, they decided to utilize a more subtle approach – leaking selected portions of the incriminating emails to a trusted journalist known for her investigative prowess. The leak prompted a flurry of media attention, forcing Harding into a defensive position and creating cracks in his carefully constructed facade.

The ensuing media frenzy created a domino effect as other complicit officials and individuals began to feel the heat. Fear, that potent catalyst for cooperation, began to replace loyalty and silence. One by one, individuals involved in the conspiracy started to crack, offering information in exchange for immunity or reduced sentences. These testimonies corroborated the evidence found on Jenkins' flash drive and expanded the investigation, revealing previously unknown connections and layers of the conspiracy.

Alice and Davis faced relentless pressure from the Millers' legal team, who attempted to discredit each witness, portraying them as unreliable, motivated by greed or revenge. But Alice, armed with meticulous documentation and irrefutable evidence, effectively countered their attempts at character assassination. She meticulously cross-referenced testimonies with financial records, emails, and other corroborating materials, constructing a solid case that was impervious to the Millers' legal maneuvering.

The investigation also unearthed a disturbing pattern of intimidation and threats against witnesses who showed signs of cooperating. Several individuals reported receiving anonymous phone calls, threatening messages, and even physical assaults. Alice and Davis, recognizing the gravity of the situation, worked closely with internal affairs to increase security for the witnesses, ensuring their safety and protecting the integrity of the investigation.

Meanwhile, the public pressure continued to mount. The city was abuzz with speculation and outrage as details of the scandal slowly emerged in the media. News outlets reported on the lavish lifestyles of the Millers, their questionable business dealings, and their connections to corrupt officials. Public opinion began to turn against the Millers and their allies, and the demands for justice intensified.

This public outcry became an unexpected asset for Alice and Davis, adding another layer of pressure on those involved in the conspiracy. The fear of exposure and the threat of losing their reputations, coupled with the risk of criminal prosecution, prompted more individuals to cooperate with the investigation. Alice understood the importance of using this momentum to its fullest. She strategically released carefully selected pieces of information to the media, further eroding the Millers' power base and galvanizing public support for the investigation.

One of the most significant breakthroughs came from a seemingly insignificant source – a disgruntled city employee working in the sanitation department. He had noticed suspicious activity around a particular landfill on the outskirts of the city, noticing unusually high volumes of shredded documents being delivered late at night. Following this tip, Alice and Davis discovered that the landfill contained mountains of shredded documents and meticulously reconstructed pieces of evidence that the Millers had tried to destroy.

The painstaking process of reconstructing the shredded documents proved both time-consuming and challenging. They utilized forensic document examiners, advanced imaging techniques, and painstaking manual piecing together to recover valuable fragments of information. This recovered data added another significant piece to the puzzle, revealing the full extent of the Millers' financial machinations, their connections to organized crime, and their influence peddling within the city's political system.

The weight of evidence compiled against the Millers and their associates became overwhelming. Alice and Davis were ready to present their case. They had painstakingly assembled a mountain of evidence, enough to not only bring down the Millers' empire but to expose the systemic corruption that had crippled the city for decades. The final confrontation promised to be a fierce battle, a showdown that would determine the fate of the city and expose the dark heart of its shadow government.

The truth, though long obscured, was finally within reach. But Alice knew that the battle was far from over.

The Millers would fight back with every resource at their disposal, and she and Davis would have to be prepared for anything. The shadows of corruption were long and deep, but the dawn was finally breaking.

The Undercover Agent

The initial sting operation codenamed "Operation Nightingale" had been meticulously planned. Months of surveillance, countless hours of analysis, and a network of informants had all culminated in this single moment: The apprehension of Ethan Miller, the alleged mastermind behind the sprawling web of corruption. The undercover agent, a seasoned veteran named

Marcus Cole had infiltrated Miller's inner circle, posing as a disgruntled city official with access to sensitive information. He'd spent two years cultivating relationships, gaining Miller's trust through carefully orchestrated conversations, shared grievances, and a willingness to participate in illicit activities.

Cole had meticulously documented every meeting, every whispered conversation, every shady deal. He'd amassed a trove of irrefutable evidence, recordings, photographs, and financial documents that painted a vivid picture of Miller's criminal empire. The operation's success hinged on Cole's ability to remain undetected, to maintain his cover while simultaneously gathering the necessary evidence to secure Miller's conviction. It seemed, at least initially, that the plan was working perfectly.

But there was a flaw in the carefully constructed plan, a chink in the armor that allowed the entire operation to crumble. It wasn't a betrayal nor a lapse in judgment on Cole's part. The failure stemmed from an unexpected source: a seemingly insignificant detail overlooked in the meticulous planning stages. A seemingly inconsequential security camera, positioned in a less-than-obvious location, had captured a fleeting glimpse of Cole's face during a late-night rendezvous.

The image, grainy and indistinct, was enough to raise suspicions within Miller's inner circle. One of Miller's associates, a man named Vincent Russo, a notorious fixer with connections to organized crime, recognized Cole's distinctive features from a previous encounter years ago. Russo's instincts, honed through years of navigating the treacherous underworld, told him something was amiss. He'd investigated Cole and discovered his true identity— an undercover agent with the Internal Affairs division.

The realization had a ripple effect, sending waves of panic throughout Miller's operation. Miller, a man not accustomed to setbacks, reacted swiftly. He activated his contingency plan, a pre-emptive measure designed to protect his assets and ensure his escape in the event of exposure. The plan was simple yet effective: eliminate Cole, then destroy any remaining evidence. It was a strategy that left little room for error.

Russo, a man known for his ruthless efficiency, was tasked with eliminating Cole. He leveraged his extensive network of contacts, employing intimidation, threats, and carefully planned surveillance to track Cole's movements. Russo meticulously followed Cole for days, studying his habits, routines, and vulnerabilities. He discovered Cole's habit of visiting a secluded cafe near his apartment, using the same table every morning.

The attack was swift, brutal, and efficient. Russo and his team ambushed Cole at the cafe , subduing him quickly before disappearing into the pre-dawn gloom. Cole was left unconscious, his body discarded in a remote area outside city limits. The operation was compromised. The meticulously gathered evidence was swiftly destroyed, leaving Alice and Davis with nothing but a trail of digital crumbs to follow and a growing sense of dread. The failure of Operation Nightingale had not just hampered the investigation. It had also sent shockwaves throughout the city's law enforcement agencies.

News of Cole's near-fatal attack, though kept out of the mainstream media, sent ripples of fear among undercover operatives and caused a shake-up within the Internal Affairs division. Alice and Davis found themselves under intense scrutiny. Their superiors were questioning their methodologies, their decisions, and their judgment. The pressure was immense. They were not only tasked with bringing down the Millers, but they were also grappling with the fallout from a failed operation that had compromised their position and put a valued agent's life in danger.

However, Cole's near-death experience was not without merit. His partially destroyed phone, retrieved from the scene, contained fragmented files of the communications he had managed to have with Miller, with enough to provide a launching point for further investigation. The fragments revealed enough coded messages for Davis to piece together. It indicated a planned meeting between Miller and several key figures, which allowed Alice and Davis to deploy surveillance. The intelligence gleaned from this allowed them to intercept a pivotal meeting that revealed the locations of several offshore accounts and a series of encrypted financial transactions.

They discovered that Miller was using an intricate network of shell corporations and offshore accounts to launder millions of dollars, using layers of obfuscation to conceal the origin of the funds and their ultimate destination. The intercepted communications also pointed toward a larger network of individuals, including lawyers, accountants, and city officials. These individuals played integral roles in facilitating Miller's scheme, accepting bribes and turning a blind eye in exchange for personal gain.

Alice and Davis's renewed investigation led them to a different undercover agent, someone far less experienced than Cole but someone who was already embedded within the Miller's organization – a young woman named Sarah Jenkins. Jenkins, who was in her first undercover operation, had been tasked with monitoring Miller's personal assistant, gaining her trust and access to sensitive information. Although Jenkins had faced numerous challenges during her assignment, including dealing with threats and intimidation, she managed to gather enough information to provide a crucial link in the case.

Jenkins's access to Miller's personal records allowed her to obtain a flash drive containing evidence of shady business dealings, bribery, extortion, and money laundering. This flash drive proved to be the key that unlocked the next stage of the investigation. The information revealed an intricate web of deceit, meticulously constructed over several years, involving numerous individuals and entities. The data also confirmed the presence of an unknown accomplice, someone even more powerful than Miller, pulling the strings from the shadows. It was the discovery of this hidden figure, this puppet master, that fueled Alice and Davis' resolve and provided the impetus to pursue the case with renewed vigor.

Alice and Davis had initially planned to use the information to secure search warrants and initiate a series of arrests, but the failure of Operation Nightingale and the subsequent media silence forced them to reevaluate their strategy. They had to be more cautious, more strategic, and less confrontational to avoid triggering a similar backlash from the Millers and their powerful associates. They decided to use a more subtle, methodical approach, focusing on building a strong, irrefutable case before making any public moves. The stakes were now higher than ever. Not only were they chasing down a massive criminal enterprise, but they were also under pressure to prove that they could effectively oversee a high-profile case. The failure of Operation Nightingale had cast a long shadow over their careers.

E2
Vase
E3
Bloody Hand
print on Hard
drive case
E4
Bloody Hand
print on
Research
papers
E5
Broken
Window
E6
Footprints
E1
Body
N
Kitchen / Living Room

Hidden Connections

The flash drive recovered from Miller's personal assistant, a seemingly insignificant piece of plastic, held the key to unlocking a labyrinthine network of deceit. Its contents weren't simply a collection of incriminating documents; they were meticulously crafted pieces of a puzzle, each revealing a new layer of the conspiracy, each interconnected with the others in a way that spoke of careful planning and meticulous execution.

The first revelation was the sheer scale of Miller's operation. The initial investigation focused on bribery and corruption within the city's municipal services. Still, the flash drive revealed a far more extensive network, encompassing everything from real estate development and construction contracts to waste management and public transportation. Each sector had been infiltrated, each deal meticulously structured to conceal the flow of illicit funds. Miller wasn't merely corrupt; he was a master puppeteer, pulling the strings of the city's infrastructure, his influence seeping into every aspect of public life.

Further analysis of the data revealed a pattern of shell corporations strategically positioned in tax havens across the globe. These corporations served as conduits, obscuring the origin of funds and their final destination. Money flowed through a complex web of transactions, expertly laundered through various accounts before resurfacing in legitimate businesses, effectively cleansing the dirty money and making it untraceable.

Alice and Davis meticulously mapped the flow of funds, following the money trail like detectives in a financial thriller, uncovering a system so sophisticated that it almost defied detection.

The intricate web of shell corporations wasn't accidental; it was a testament to the expertise and planning involved. The flash drive included emails, memoranda, and encrypted communication logs that outlined the involvement of several prominent individuals, including legal professionals, accountants, and notably, certain senior city officials. These weren't mere accomplices; they were essential components of the machine, providing the legal cover, financial expertise, and the political leverage needed to ensure the operation's smooth functioning. They were the grease that kept Miller's machine humming.

One name kept recurring in the documents: Julian Thorne. Thorne was a name that resonated with Alice, a whisper on the wind of previous unsuccessful investigations. He was a renowned lawyer known for his impeccable reputation and his involvement in some of the city's largest and most profitable real estate deals. Thorne's connection to Miller was subtle, indirect, yet undeniable. He appeared to provide legal counsel for Miller's shell corporations, carefully crafting legal frameworks to ensure the legality, at least on paper, of the otherwise illicit transactions. Thorne, though outwardly a pillar of the community, was a master of legal loopholes, using his expertise to shield Miller's criminal empire from scrutiny.

The investigation took an unexpected turn when Davis discovered a series of encrypted messages within the flash drive's data. These messages, initially indecipherable, were eventually cracked using a specialized decryption algorithm. The contents revealed a meeting scheduled between Miller, Thorne, and several other influential figures, a meeting designed to discuss the expansion of their illicit operation into the city's rapidly developing technology sector. This discovery allowed Alice and Davis to deploy covert surveillance, placing bugs within the chosen meeting room.

The intercepted conversation confirmed Thorne's pivotal role in Miller's operation. The lawyer, far from being a mere accomplice, was a strategic partner, providing the legal shield that protected Miller's empire from the prying eyes of the law. The conversation hinted at a project even larger and more ambitious than they could have imagined.

This unexpected link between Miller and Thorne explained a number of seemingly unrelated events that had plagued the city for years. The awarding of lucrative city contracts, the sudden rise of previously unknown construction firms, even the inexplicable delays in infrastructure projects—all seemed to fit into place once Thorne's role was understood. Thorne wasn't just a lawyer; he was the architect of Miller's empire, the silent partner, the mastermind behind the scenes.

Their next discovery further solidified their suspicions. A hidden folder within the flash drive revealed a series of coded transactions, transactions far larger in scale than anything previously discovered. The coded messages referenced a series of offshore accounts held under the name of a newly incorporated entity, a company registered in a remote island nation known for its lax banking regulations. Tracing these transactions proved to be a complex challenge, a detective's puzzle hidden within a labyrinth of financial flows. These seemingly isolated accounts were meticulously tracked, revealing their connection to Thorne's offshore holdings. Thorne wasn't just protecting Miller; he was personally profiting from the operation on a grand scale.

As they delved deeper into the data, a disturbing realization dawned on Alice and Davis. The scale of the conspiracy was far larger than they had ever imagined. It wasn't just about Miller, Thorne, or even the shell corporations. It was a sprawling web of interconnected individuals and entities, each playing a crucial role in maintaining the operation. It was a system of interlocking gears, where the removal of any single component could bring the entire mechanism crashing down. The flash drive, the seemingly innocuous piece of evidence, had illuminated a vast, shadowy world of corruption.

The investigation, once focused on a single individual, now branched out in several directions. They were no longer chasing a single criminal; they were tracking a hydra with numerous heads, each connected to the others by a tangled network of alliances, betrayals, and shared interests. The implications were staggering. This wasn't just a local crime; it had the potential to unravel the city's social fabric, shaking its institutions to their foundations.

The pressure mounted. The initial failure of Operation Nightingale had already put their careers on the line. The scale of the conspiracy they were now facing, a far cry from the initial investigation, demanded a meticulously planned approach. One wrong move could shatter their meticulously crafted strategy and alert Thorne and Miller, allowing them to erase the evidence and vanish into the shadows of anonymity, leaving Alice and Davis to face the consequences of an even larger failure. They knew that the next steps needed to be measured, precise, and, most of all, foolproof. Their previous method of operation had failed, and so the stakes were higher than ever. They had to tread carefully. The fate of the city and their careers hung in the balance.

A Dangerous Game

The coded transactions, initially a cryptic puzzle, began to yield their secrets. Each transaction, meticulously disguised within a labyrinth of legitimate financial activity, pointed towards a single, overarching goal: the acquisition of a significant stake in Nova Tech, the city's burgeoning technology giant. Nova Tech wasn't just a successful company; it was a goldmine, poised to become a major player in the national and perhaps even international technology market. Its acquisition would represent a massive infusion of capital into Miller and Thorne's already vast criminal empire, a leap towards establishing a financial dominion unlike anything the city had ever seen.

Alice felt a chilly crawl down her spine as she pieced together the implications. This wasn't just about enriching themselves; this was about consolidating power, controlling a critical sector of the city's economy, and perhaps even leveraging that control for far more sinister purposes. The sheer audacity of their plan was breathtaking, a gamble of monumental proportions. The stakes were no longer limited to local corruption; they were global. The city's fate, and perhaps something far greater, hung precariously in the balance.

The discovery of Nova Tech's involvement heightened the risk significantly. Miller and Thorne wouldn't hesitate to eliminate anyone who threatened their ambitious plan. Alice found herself increasingly isolated, the weight of the investigation pressing down on her like a physical burden. The anonymity she had once taken for granted was now a distant memory.

She felt the eyes of unseen observers constantly upon her, the suspicion that she was being watched – not just by Miller's people but by forces far more powerful and far less scrupulous.

One evening, as Alice was leaving the office, a black sedan pulled up beside her. Two men, their faces obscured by the shadows, got out. She recognized the glint of metal in their hands – not firearms, but something far more insidious: silencers. Fear, cold and sharp, pierced her composure. This wasn't a simple intimidation tactic; this was a threat of violence, a blatant display of force. She had become a pawn in a dangerous game, and the rules of engagement had just changed.

She managed to escape, running blindly down the dimly lit streets, the echo of pursuing footsteps in her ears. She reached her apartment, breathless and shaken, her heart pounding in her chest. The near miss was a stark reminder of the mortal danger she was in. She wasn't dealing with petty criminals; she was confronting an organization with seemingly limitless resources and a ruthless willingness to eliminate anyone standing in their way.

The next morning, she went to Davis, her partner, her face pale, her voice trembling slightly. She recounted the previous night's events, describing the menacing individuals and their chilling display of force. Davis, a seasoned investigator, reacted immediately. He increased the level of security around Alice, assigning her a protective detail, a precaution she had initially resisted. The lines between personal safety and professional duty were blurring, and the safety of the city paled in comparison to the risk to her own life.

Davis also redoubled their efforts, pushing harder to identify and locate the individuals who had attempted to intimidate Alice. The investigation had become a race against time, a fight for survival against an enemy with an infinite supply of resources and the unwavering resolve of a cornered predator. The fear, however, was a catalyst; it sharpened her focus and determination.

The pressure was not limited to direct threats. The investigation, which had already attracted unwanted attention from within the department, was now under scrutiny from unexpected quarters. Whispers of internal sabotage grew louder, suggesting that someone within the police department was feeding information to Miller and Thorne. This betrayal, if real, had the potential to cripple their investigation and expose Alice to devastating consequences. The investigation, once a clear-cut pursuit of justice, had become a treacherous maze of betrayal and intrigue.

Alice and Davis started an internal investigation, quietly scrutinizing the activities of their colleagues, searching for any sign of leaking information. It was a delicate balance, trying to find a traitor without alerting Miller and Thorne to their suspicions. The internal investigation was as dangerous as their external investigation, as the suspected traitor could be anyone, from a low-ranking officer to a high-ranking official.

Alice's investigation took an unexpected turn when she discovered a connection between Thorne and a seemingly innocuous charitable foundation, the "City Harmony Foundation." The Foundation, known for its philanthropic activities and its respectable public image, was a well-oiled machine used to launder money and obscure the true nature of Miller's criminal activities. Its board of directors consisted of respected members of society, a facade that masked a sinister reality.

Alice focused her efforts on uncovering the financial records of the Foundation. The task was monumental, as the Foundation's finances were deliberately convoluted, each transaction designed to deflect suspicion. Yet, she persevered. Working late into the night, sifting through mountains of paperwork, Alice slowly unraveled the complex web of transactions, uncovering a trail of money that led directly to Thorne's offshore accounts. The Foundation wasn't a philanthropic organization; it was the linchpin of Miller's empire, a tool used to launder billions of dollars.

Meanwhile, Davis's investigations into the attempted intimidation revealed a link between the two men and a notorious organized crime syndicate with deep roots in the city's underworld. The syndicate, known for its ruthless efficiency and its extensive network of informants, had obviously been employed by Miller and Thorne to eliminate any obstacle that stood in the path of their Nova Tech acquisition.

The convergence of these findings pointed to a terrifying conclusion: Miller and Thorne weren't just corrupt officials and lawyers; they were powerful players in a far larger criminal enterprise, an enterprise that extended beyond the city limits, reaching into the darkest corners of the global financial system. Alice and Davis realized they were fighting a battle far greater than they had initially anticipated, a battle that threatened not just the city but the very fabric of society itself. The line between investigating a crime and becoming a target had become dangerously blurred. The stakes were higher than ever before, and the game had become far more dangerous. They knew they were running out of time. Their every move was now a calculated risk, a step in a deadly game of chess where the stakes were life and death. The only question that remained was whether they had the skill and the courage to checkmate before they themselves were checkmated.

Shifting Alliances

The arrest of Elias Vance, while a significant victory, felt more like a fleeting reprieve in a relentless storm. His testimony, though revealing, left more questions than answers. The network of informants within Nova Tech, the extent of Miller and Thorne's reach, the true capabilities of the revolutionary AI – these remained shrouded in a fog of uncertainty, threatening to engulf Alice and Davis.

Vance's cooperation, however, provided a crucial foothold. He mentioned a coded communication system, separate from the Project Nightingale emails, used by Miller and Thorne for internal discussions and strategic planning. This system, he claimed, utilized a sophisticated encryption algorithm that even he, with his considerable technical expertise, had struggled to crack. The key to deciphering the system, Vance revealed, lay with a specific individual – Dr. Anya Sharma, a brilliant cryptographer who had mysteriously disappeared several months prior.

The trail led them to Sharma's abandoned apartment, a sterile, almost clinical space devoid of any personal effects. The only clue to her presence was a single, battered laptop tucked away in a hidden compartment beneath the floorboards. Days were spent painstakingly analyzing the laptop's hard drive, a tedious and meticulous process, the pressure mounting with every passing hour. The stakes were escalating exponentially, the potential consequences of failure looming large. Each deleted file, each encrypted message, represented another piece of the puzzle that threatened to remain forever out of their reach.

Meanwhile, the shifting alliances became even more treacherous. Davis's network of informants within the police department began to yield unexpected results. Several officers, previously considered trustworthy allies, were revealed to be compromised, their loyalty to Miller and Thorne hidden beneath a thin veneer of professionalism. The realization that the corruption extended beyond Nova Tech and into the very foundations of law enforcement sent a chill down Alice's spine. The enemy wasn't just a pair of ruthless businessmen; it was a complex web of deceit woven through the highest echelons of power.

One such compromised officer, Detective Michael Reed, a man Davis had known for years, was discovered to have been leaking sensitive information about their investigation to Miller and Thorne. Reed's betrayal hit Davis hard, shaking his confidence in his network and undermining his unwavering belief in the integrity of his colleagues. The weight of this betrayal became a heavy burden, further intensifying the pressure and forcing them to operate with even greater caution.

The discovery of Reed's treachery forced Alice and Davis to re-evaluate their strategy. They could no longer rely on conventional methods; they were forced to operate outside the established system; their actions shrouded in secret, and their every move carefully calculated. Their reliance on trust had been shattered, leaving them vulnerable and exposed. The once-clear lines of investigation were now blurred, the alliances as shifting and unpredictable as the tides.

They found themselves relying on a less-than-ideal source: a known criminal informant named Sal Demarco, a man with a reputation as unpredictable as he was dangerous. Demarco, while possessing valuable insights into Miller and Thorne's underworld connections, had his own agenda and demands. His price for information was high, not just in monetary terms but also in favors that threatened to blur the already murky lines of their investigation. This moral dilemma forced Alice and Davis into a difficult negotiation, a dance of risk and reward that could either save them or lead to their downfall.

The information obtained from Demarco, however, proved invaluable. He revealed a previously unknown connection between Miller and Thorne and a powerful international arms dealer, confirming their suspicions that Project Nightingale extended far beyond financial gain. The AI technology was not just a tool for market manipulation; it held potential applications in military and espionage, capable of creating strategic advantages on a global scale. The implications of this discovery were staggering, the potential consequences far-reaching.

This revelation intensified the urgency of their mission. The stakes weren't just national; they were international. They were facing a threat of global proportions, a clandestine operation capable of destabilizing the world order. The lines between law enforcement and international espionage blurred, forcing them to seek unlikely alliances and step into the shadowy world of global intelligence networks.

As they delved deeper into the heart of the conspiracy, Alice and Davis encountered unexpected opposition from within their ranks. The FBI was alerted to the unfolding situation and launched its investigation, led by a seasoned agent known for his uncompromising methods and unwavering loyalty to the procedure. This interference, though initially welcomed, soon became a source of conflict, particularly when the agent's investigative techniques clashed with Alice and Davis's own more unconventional approach. The internal conflict added another layer of complexity, adding to the already precarious situation.

They discovered that the AI system, codenamed "Phoenix," was not simply a tool for financial manipulation; it possessed advanced capabilities of learning and adapting at an unprecedented rate. It was essentially sentient artificial intelligence with the potential for autonomous decision-making and unprecedented destructive power. If it fell into the wrong hands, the consequences were unthinkable.

The final pieces of the puzzle started to fall into place, revealing a horrifying truth about Miller and Thorne's intentions. Their goal wasn't just to control the global financial markets or gain military dominance; they aimed to harness Phoenix's power for something far more sinister – a complete and irreversible societal restructuring, shaping the world to fit their twisted vision. The fight to prevent this was no longer a battle to solve a crime; it was a fight to protect humanity's future.

The tension reached its apex during a clandestine meeting in a secluded warehouse on the outskirts of the city. Alice and Davis, along with several carefully selected allies – a mix of law enforcement agents, former military personnel, and even a reluctant cybersecurity expert – prepared for a showdown. The shadows of betrayal still lingered, the uncertainty of who was friend or foe casting a long, dark pall over the operation. The odds were stacked against them, the potential for failure looming large, but they pressed forward, driven by a mixture of determination, fear, and a shared sense of responsibility toward humanity. The final confrontation loomed, a battle not just for their lives but for the fate of the world. The clock was ticking, and time was running out.

Near Misses

The warehouse meeting had ended, leaving Alice with a chilling sense of foreboding. The air crackled with unspoken tensions; the camaraderie forged in the face of a common enemy was fragile and easily shattered. The plan, meticulously crafted, felt like a house of cards, ready to collapse under the weight of a single misplaced move. As she stepped out into the cold night air, the city lights blurring through a haze of exhaustion and anxiety, she felt a prickling sensation on the back of her neck, the instinctive warning of imminent danger.

A black sedan, its windows tinted darkly, pulled up beside her. Before she could react, a figure emerged, gun drawn, silhouetted against the harsh glare of the headlights. The shot missed, the bullet ricocheting off the brick wall behind her, sending a shower of debris raining down. Alice dove for cover, the adrenaline surging through her veins, blurring her vision and sharpening her senses. She rolled across the concrete, the cold seeping into her clothes, her heart pounding a frantic rhythm against her ribs. She scrambled to her feet, her mind racing, her survival instincts taking over. This wasn't the first time she had come face-to-face with death. Years spent chasing shadows in the darkest corners of the city had hardened her, giving her a resilience that most couldn't fathom. But this felt different. This felt personal.

She sprinted through the Labyrinthine streets, the echo of the gunshot ringing in her ears, the fear a cold, constricting hand around her chest. She weaved through alleyways, her pursuers hot on her heels, the relentless pounding of their footsteps a relentless pursuit. The city, once a familiar comfort, now felt like a claustrophobic cage, every shadow a potential hiding place for her attacker.

She managed to evade them, finding refuge in a dimly lit bar, its smoky atmosphere offering a temporary respite. But the feeling of unease lingered, the threat palpable, casting a long shadow over her every move. The near miss had served as a stark reminder: she was a pawn in a deadly game, and the stakes were life or death. Later that night, as she lay in her small, sparsely furnished apartment, the silence amplified by the echoing fear, a different kind of threat emerged. A faint buzzing sound, almost imperceptible at first, grew into a persistent hum that resonated deep within her bones. It was the sound of a sophisticated surveillance device, a tiny listening bug carefully placed somewhere within her apartment, betraying her every whispered word, every moment of vulnerability.

The realization sent a fresh wave of panic coursing through her. Her sanctuary had been compromised, her privacy violated. The feeling of being watched, of being hunted, intensified. She spent the rest of the night dismantling every item in her apartment, a frantic search for the tiny device that could mean the difference between life and death. She found it eventually, concealed within the seemingly innocent floral arrangement, a gift from a well-meaning but ultimately compromised colleague. She smashed it, the release almost physical, but the fear remained, a constant companion.

The next day, there was a blur of frantic activity. She had to alter her plans, change her routines, and eliminate her usual paths and contacts. She spent hours on the phone, re-evaluating her relationships and testing her allies for signs of compromise. The line between friend and foe blurred, distrusting her only constantly. Every interaction, every meeting, carried a risk, a potential betrayal lurking just beneath the surface. The uncertainty was almost as dangerous as the bullets that nearly claimed her life.

She reached out to an unlikely ally – a former colleague from her days as a police officer, a man known for his independent and often maverick approach to investigations. His name was Jack Stratton, and his loyalty was never guaranteed, but his skills were invaluable. They met in a deserted industrial park. The meeting was shrouded in secrecy, a silent agreement on the shared danger they faced. Stratton listened intently as she detailed her close calls and her suspicion of internal sabotage.

He confirmed her fears, detailing the extent of the infiltration within law enforcement. Miller and Thorne had been playing the long game, carefully cultivating alliances and compromising individuals within the system. Their influence stretched far and wide, corrupting institutions and individuals at the highest level.

"They're not just after control of the financial market, Alice," Stratton said, his voice low and grave. "They're after something far more sinister. And they're willing to eliminate anyone who stands in their way." His words painted a terrifying picture. The threat extended beyond simple corruption. It was a systematic dismantling of everything Alice believed in, a methodical erosion of trust and integrity.

They devised a new plan, a far riskier approach than their previous strategy. It relied on deception, misdirection, and a calculated gamble on their ability to outwit their adversaries. They needed to expose the network of corruption to disrupt Miller and Thorne's operations before it was too late.

Alice was given a new identity, a false persona, to allow her to operate under the radar. She was transported to a safe house, a secluded location far removed from the city's hustle and bustle, where she could work without fear of being followed.

Days turned into weeks as Alice worked tirelessly, building her case and gathering evidence. She was like a phantom, a silent observer, using her skills and knowledge to maneuver through the treacherous landscape. The pressure was immense, the weight of the responsibility bearing down on her shoulders. The threat to national security, and by extension, global security, was no longer theoretical. It was very real and very immediate.

The slightest misstep could lead to her capture, her death. She was living on borrowed time, each moment a precarious balance between success and catastrophic failure. The near misses were a constant reminder of the ever-present danger, a chilling testament to the lengths Miller and Thorne would go to silence her. But the fear, while ever-present, only fueled her determination. She had to succeed not just for herself but for the safety of countless others. She had to uncover the truth, no matter the cost. The fight for survival wasn't about avoiding bullets; it was a battle for the future, a fight for humanity itself. The fate of the world rested on her shoulders, a burden as heavy as the city itself.

New Suspects

The safe house, a nondescript building nestled in the heart of the Appalachian Mountains, offered little comfort. The isolation, meant to ensure her safety, only amplified the gnawing anxiety that had become her constant companion. Days bled into weeks, each sunrise bringing a fresh wave of apprehension. Her new identity, meticulously crafted by Stratton, felt like a costume, ill-fitting and uncomfortable. She was Alice, but she wasn't. The deception, necessary as it was, chipped away at her sense of self, leaving her feeling adrift and vulnerable.

Her investigation centered on Miller and Thorne's financial empire, a vast network of shell corporations and offshore accounts designed to conceal their illicit activities. She delved into mountains of financial documents, her eyes straining under the harsh fluorescent light, deciphering complex transactions and identifying patterns of money laundering and fraud. The sheer scale of their operation was staggering, a testament to their ambition and ruthlessness.

As she pieced together the puzzle, new names began to emerge, individuals who played key roles in Miller and Thorne's operation but whose involvement remained shrouded in secrecy. There was Marcus Reed, an unassuming accountant with access to sensitive financial data, whose meticulous records belied a deeper, more sinister involvement. His loyalty to Miller and Thorne appeared absolute, his actions suggested a level of complicity that extended beyond simple employment.

Then, there was Isabella Rossi, a charismatic lawyer with a reputation for discretion and an extensive network of contacts within the highest echelons of power. She expertly navigated the legal loopholes, ensuring that Miller and Thorne's operations remained protected from scrutiny. Her elegance and sophistication masked ruthless pragmatism, and her loyalty bought, it seemed, with significant financial incentives.

The emergence of these new suspects added layers of complexity to the investigation, creating an intricate web of interconnected relationships and covert alliances. The more Alice uncovered, the more she realized the depth of the conspiracy and the far-reaching implications of Miller and Thorne's actions. It wasn't about financial gain; it was about power, influence, and the systematic dismantling of democratic institutions.

The relentless pressure began to take its toll. The constant threat of discovery, the isolation, the weight of responsibility – it all weighed heavily on her. She found herself questioning her sanity, her perception of reality blurring at the edges. Sleep became a luxury she could rarely afford, her mind racing even as her body ached with exhaustion.

Stratton's infrequent visits provided brief moments of respite, his cynicism a counterpoint to her growing despair. He brought updates from the outside world and snippets of information gathered from his network of informants. He spoke of the increasing unease within the police department, the subtle shift in allegiances, and the fear and suspicion that hung heavily in the air.

"They're tightening the net, Alice," Stratton said during one of their clandestine meetings, his voice a low rumble. "Miller and Thorne are feeling the heat. They're consolidating their power, eliminating loose ends."

His words confirmed her growing unease. The risk was escalating, the stakes higher than ever before. Every move she made, every piece of information she uncovered, brought her closer to danger. The line between success and failure was razor-thin, a precarious balance on which her life hung precariously.

Alice decided to focus on Reed, believing that his meticulous records held the key to unlocking the entire operation. She devised a plan to infiltrate his world, to gain his trust and access his confidential files. It was a risky gamble, one that could easily expose her, but it was the only way forward.

She assumed the persona of a financial analyst, meticulously crafting a false identity, complete with forged credentials and a convincing backstory. She contacted Reed, posing as a potential client, and managed to secure a meeting, a crucial step in her carefully laid plan.

The meeting was tense, fraught with unspoken tension. Reed was cautious, his eyes darting around the room, his every move calculated and precise. Alice played her role impeccably, maintaining a calm demeanor and subtly probing for information while carefully observing his reactions.

She learned that Reed was not just an accountant; he was a crucial component of Miller and Thorne's intricate financial network. He was responsible for laundering the money, masking its origins and transferring it to offshore accounts. He was deeply involved, his complicity undeniable.

However, during the conversation, Alice sensed something was wrong. Reed seemed unusually nervous, almost fearful. He seemed to know more than he was letting on. He dropped subtle hints, oblique references that hinted at a deeper conspiracy.

As Alice left the meeting, a chilling realization washed over her. Reed wasn't just a cog in the machine; he was a pawn, even a victim. There were other players involved, individuals pulling the strings from the shadows, their identities yet to be revealed. The complexity of the conspiracy had grown exponentially.

The hunt for Miller and Thorne had turned into a labyrinthine chase, each discovery leading to a new set of questions, a deeper layer of intrigue. The closer she got to the truth, the more dangerous the game became. The lines of loyalty and betrayal were blurred, making it increasingly difficult to distinguish allies from enemies.

As Alice continued her investigation, she discovered a pattern, a recurring element in the transactions: a series of encrypted communications channeled through an innocuous charity organization. This discovery led her to a new suspect, Dr. Evelyn Hayes, the head of the charity, a woman known for her philanthropic work and connections to influential figures in the political and financial worlds. Her charitable work masked a dark secret, a connection to Miller and Thorne that suggested her involvement in their criminal enterprise.

The evidence pointed towards Hayes as a key player, a conduit through which Miller and Thorne laundered vast sums of money, using the charity as a front to conceal their illegal activities. She was a master manipulator, skillfully using her position to maintain a façade of respectability while secretly orchestrating a criminal network of immense proportions.

The discovery of Hayes' involvement shifted the focus of the investigation, adding another layer of complexity to the already intricate web of deception and intrigue. Alice was now caught in a dangerous game, pursued by the forces of corruption while navigating the treacherous landscape of political maneuvering and criminal conspiracy. The fate of her mission, and her life, hinged on her ability to outwit Hayes and her shadowy network. The realization that there were far more powerful forces at play than she had initially imagined sent a wave of dread through her. This was far bigger than just Miller and Thorne; this was a systemic corruption that reached the highest echelons of power.

The clock was ticking. The ever-present danger loomed larger, every shadow a potential threat. But Alice pressed on, fueled by her determination to uncover the truth, no matter the cost. The fight was far from over; in fact, it had just begun. The stakes had never been higher. The fate of many hung in the balance, not just Alice's own life. She had to find a way to expose the truth before it was too late. And she knew, with chilling certainty, that the next move could be her last.

Trust Issues

The flickering fluorescent light of the safe house cast long, distorted shadows, transforming familiar objects into menacing shapes. Every creak of the floorboards and every rustle of leaves outside the window sent a jolt of adrenaline through Alice. Paranoia had become her constant companion, a shadow clinging to her heels, whispering doubts and suspicions in her ear. She couldn't shake the feeling that she was being watched, that every conversation and every move was being monitored, analyzed, and used against her.

The trust had become a luxury she could no longer afford. Stratton, her handler, was a ghost, appearing only sporadically, his brief visits offering a fleeting sense of security that quickly evaporated once he was gone. His gruff demeanor and cryptic pronouncements did little to ease her anxiety. Were his motivations purely professional, or did he have a hidden agenda? The question gnawed at her, a persistent irritant that refused to be ignored.

Even the information he provided felt suspect, filtered through layers of secrecy and obfuscation. Was it the whole truth or a carefully crafted narrative designed to manipulate her, to steer her investigation in a particular direction? She second-guessed every detail, every piece of intelligence, her mind racing to find hidden meanings, to uncover potential betrayals.

The digital world offered no solace. Every email, every encrypted message, felt like a potential trap, a conduit for surveillance and manipulation. She constantly scrutinized the metadata, searching for anomalies for evidence of tampering or tracking. The digital landscape, once a source of information and connection, had transformed into a minefield of potential threats.

Her interactions with Reed had left her deeply unsettled. His nervousness, his carefully chosen words, his evasive answers – they all suggested a deeper level of deception, a conspiracy that extended far beyond Miller and Thorne. Had he been playing her? Had he deliberately leaked information or withheld crucial details to manipulate her investigation? The thought chilled her to the bone.

The same unease extended to Rossi, the untouchable lawyer. Her elegance and sophistication were a carefully constructed façade, masking a calculating mind and a ruthless pragmatism. Was her cooperation genuine, or was she feeding Alice misinformation, guiding her toward a dead end? Alice couldn't dismiss the possibility that Rossi was using her, playing a double game, feeding her breadcrumbs of information while secretly working to protect Miller and Thorne.

The revelation about Dr. Hayes, the head of the innocuous charity, added another layer to this labyrinthine web of distrust. Hayes was a master of manipulation, a woman who moved effortlessly through the highest echelons of power. Was she truly involved in the conspiracy, or was she a carefully placed double agent, working against Miller and Thorne, even working with Stratton? Alice found herself questioning the motives of everyone around her, her perception of reality shifting and changing with each new piece of information.

Sleep offered little respite. Her nights were filled with restless tossing and turning, haunted by images of betrayal and deception. Dreams and nightmares intermingled, blurring the line between reality and fantasy. She often woke up drenched in sweat, her heart pounding, her mind racing through a kaleidoscope of possibilities, each more unsettling than the last.

Even the simple act of eating became a source of anxiety. Was her food poisoned? Had someone tampered with her water supply? The thought of being deliberately harmed, of being betrayed by those she considered allies, fueled her paranoia. She carefully inspected every item, scrutinized every ingredient, suspicious of even the most mundane items.

The isolation of the safe house, initially intended to protect her, had amplified her anxieties, creating a breeding ground for doubt and suspicion. The silence was broken only by the occasional howl of the wind, a constant reminder of her vulnerability and isolation. She felt trapped, surrounded by enemies, unsure who to trust, her only companion, the ever-present shadow of doubt.

The weight of her mission pressed down on her, a crushing burden that seemed to increase with each passing day. The success of her investigation rested on her ability to discern truth from deception, to unravel the tangled threads of the conspiracy. But the more she dug, the more the lines blurred, the more difficult it became to separate fact from fiction, loyalty from betrayal.

The pressure was immense. She knew that Miller and Thorne and their network of accomplices were closing in. Their influence extended far and wide, their reach into the highest levels of power, making them untouchable. The risk was enormous, the potential consequences unthinkable.

Alice found herself questioning her own sanity. The constant pressure, the lack of sleep, the gnawing suspicion – it all chipped away at her mental fortitude. She was losing her grip on reality, the line between truth and hallucination blurring. She constantly questioned her judgment, second-guessing every decision, her confidence eroding with each passing hour.

Yet, despite the overwhelming sense of distrust and the constant pressure, she pressed on, driven by an unwavering determination to uncover the truth. The fate of many rested on her shoulders, not just her own life.

The knowledge that systemic corruption reached the highest echelons of power fueled her, even though it also added to the profound sense of isolation she felt. She was fighting a battle against a behemoth, alone, surrounded by enemies who were experts at manipulating the very fabric of trust. The odds were stacked against her. Yet, she continued, her resolve hardened by the enormity of the task. Each step forward felt like a gamble, a calculated risk with potentially fatal consequences.

The hunt for Miller and Thorne had evolved into a desperate fight for survival, a game of trust, betrayal, and survival. Her fate was hanging by a thread, and the only way to stay alive was to keep moving, keep digging, and hope – however futile it may seem – that she wouldn't stumble into the trap before she could expose the truth. The truth, which seemed now as elusive as ever, became her only goal, and the fight for it her only reason for survival.

A Race Against Time

The chipped paint on the windowsill felt rough against her cheek as Alice pressed herself against the cold glass, watching the street below. The shadows were lengthening, stretching like grasping claws across the asphalt. Dusk was falling, a shroud of deepening purple and bruised orange, and with it came a chilling sense of vulnerability. The safe house, once a refuge, now felt like a cage, its walls closing in on her, amplifying the ticking clock of her dwindling time.

Stratton's cryptic message, received hours ago, had only intensified her anxiety. "They're moving faster than expected," it had simply stated, offering no further explanation, no reassurance, nothing but a stark warning that sent a shiver down her spine. "Faster" implied a closing net, a tightening noose. And the feeling of being watched, of being hunted, had intensified tenfold.

She reviewed the scant intelligence she had, piecing together the fragmented clues like a shattered mirror reflecting a distorted reality. Miller and Thorne, the shadowy figures at the heart of the conspiracy, were not just powerful; they were ruthlessly efficient. Their tentacles reached into every corner of the city, their influence corrupting institutions, silencing dissenters, and creating an environment of fear and intimidation.

The revelation about Dr. Hayes, head of the benevolent charity, had been a particularly jarring blow. Hayes, with her impeccable public image and her effortless access to power, was a master manipulator, a woman who could charm the birds from the trees while simultaneously orchestrating a web of deceit. Alice suspected Hayes was closer to the heart of the operation than she'd initially believed. She wasn't just a pawn but a key player, a conductor of the intricate symphony of corruption.

The possibility of Rossi's betrayal gnawed at her. The lawyer's elegant demeanor and carefully chosen words masked a calculating intelligence that sent shivers down Alice's spine. Was Rossi feeding her misinformation, deliberately leading her down a blind alley? Or was she a double agent, subtly working against Miller and Thorne while appearing to cooperate? The ambiguity was agonizing. Alice needed answers, and she needed them fast. The weight of unanswered questions threatened to crush her.

The urgency of the situation pressed down on her, a suffocating blanket of dread. She couldn't afford to make mistakes; each misstep could be her last. The thought of failure, of letting Miller and Thorne escape, was unbearable. The lives of countless others hung in the balance, their fate inextricably linked to her success.

She glanced at the encrypted map spread across her makeshift desk – a battered, overturned crate. It depicted a complex network of underground tunnels and hidden passageways, rumored to be used by Miller and Thorne to transport illicit materials and evade authorities. This was her next lead, a treacherous path that promised both answers and potential death.

The map was a labyrinth, a spiderweb of interconnected routes, and locating the precise location pinpointed by Stratton's scant directions was proving exceptionally challenging. Several locations along the map corresponded with existing underground infrastructure within the city, which meant that her search could become a vast and time-consuming undertaking.

A sudden, sharp rap at the door jolted her from her thoughts. Her breath hitched in her throat. She instinctively grabbed the nearby firearm, her hand slick with sweat. Who could it be? Stratton? Or is one of Miller and Thorne's henchmen finally closing in on her? The uncertainty was a knife twisting in her gut.

She cautiously approached the door, her senses heightened, her heart pounding against her ribs like a trapped bird. She peered through the peephole, her breath misting on the cold metal. It was Reed. His face was pale, his eyes wide with a mixture of fear and desperation.

She hesitated only for a moment before opening the door. Reed stumbled inside, his breathing ragged, his clothes disheveled. "They know," he gasped, his voice barely a whisper. "They know about the safe house."

The blood ran cold in her veins. This was it. The final countdown had begun. The feeling of being trapped, of being cornered, intensified. There was no time to waste.

"We need to move," Alice said, her voice firm despite the tremor in her hands. "Now."

Reed nodded, his eyes darting nervously around the room. He had information, she knew it, but his fear was palpable. She had to get it out of him before it was too late. Before they both became victims of Miller and Thorne's relentless pursuit.

The escape route was fraught with peril. The streets were a maze of shadows, every corner, every alleyway, teeming with potential dangers. They moved like ghosts, their footsteps muffled by the late-night hush, their movements swift and silent. They navigated the winding streets, every flicker of movement, every distant sound setting their nerves on edge.

A black sedan, sleek and ominous, appeared on the corner. The car sped up, accelerating towards them, its headlights slicing through the darkness. Alice and Reed sprinted, their hearts hammering, their lungs burning.

They plunged into a network of back alleys, the stench of garbage and decay stinging their nostrils. The chase was relentless. The car's headlights were relentless searchlights. The car was close behind, the sound of its engine a terrifying symphony of pursuit.

They found refuge in a dimly lit warehouse, a cavernous space filled with the scent of dust and forgotten things. The heavy metal door creaked shut behind them, sealing them off from the relentless pursuit. But it was a temporary respite, a fleeting moment of safety in a relentless war against time.

The pursuers were closing in.

Alice felt the weight of the world on her shoulders. The urgency of the situation was crushing, the pressure almost unbearable. Time was running out. She had to act quickly, decisively, before the net closed completely.

The map, clutched tightly in her hand, felt like a lifeline. It was now or never. She had to choose a path, a gamble, a desperate attempt to outmaneuver her pursuers and expose the truth before it was too late. The race against time had begun, and the stakes were higher than ever before. The fate of many, and her own, hung precariously in the balance.

With a deep breath, she pointed towards a section of the map, a hidden passage, an unexplored route. It was a long shot, a gamble with death, but it was their only chance. The flickering light of a distant streetlamp cast long shadows across their faces as they braced themselves for the next leg of their perilous journey. The clock was ticking relentlessly, mercilessly. They had to move quickly, effectively, silently, and in tandem.

This was their chance.

Unexpected Help

The warehouse door groaned shut, the metallic shriek echoing in the cavernous space. Dust motes danced in the single shaft of moonlight slicing through a grimy window high above. The silence that followed was thick, heavy, pregnant with the unspoken fear that clung to them like a shroud. Alice's breath hitched in her chest; her heart hammered against her ribs, a frantic drumbeat against the backdrop of the oppressive quiet.

Reed, still visibly shaken, leaned against a stack of rusty crates, his eyes darting nervously around the dimly lit space. He looked like a cornered animal, his fear a palpable entity in the suffocating atmosphere. Alice, however, forced herself to remain calm, her mind already racing, calculating, and planning. She couldn't afford to let fear paralyze her. They were trapped but not defeated.

"They know," Reed whispered again, his voice barely audible above the distant hum of the city. "They've been watching us. They know about Stratton."

Alice nodded, already formulating her response. Stratton's cryptic message had prepared her for this, but the brutal reality of their precarious situation hit her with the force of a physical blow. This wasn't about surviving anymore; it was about fighting back. It was about exposing the conspiracy, regardless of the personal cost.

"Tell me everything," she demanded, her voice sharp, cutting through the tension. "Everything you know about Miller, Thorne, and Hayes."

Reed hesitated, his eyes flickering with uncertainty. He seemed torn between fear and a desperate desire to cooperate. Alice understood his reluctance; he'd seen firsthand the ruthlessness of Miller and Thorne. He knew the consequences of betrayal.

But time was a luxury they didn't have. Alice needed information, and she needed it now. She had to trust her instincts and her ability to assess people. She knew there was something more to Reed than his initial portrayal.

"It started months ago," Reed began, his voice gaining a little strength. "Small things, at first. Suspicious transactions, coded messages, meetings in hushed corners. I dismissed them as paranoia, but the pattern became undeniable. I saw Hayes meeting with Miller and Thorne... it was all so clandestine. Their influence was like a poison, creeping through the veins of the city."

He continued to speak, his voice rising and falling with the intensity of his recollections. He detailed shady financial dealings, laundered money funneling through shell corporations, and the subtle manipulation of influential figures. He described coded messages, intercepted phone calls, and hidden agendas.

As Reed spoke, a picture began to emerge, painting a much clearer, more disturbing portrait than Alice had initially imagined. Hayes wasn't merely a pawn; she was a pivotal player, the linchpin connecting Miller and Thorne to a far-reaching network of corruption that extended far beyond their immediate circle. The implications were staggering.

Suddenly, a loud clang echoed from the warehouse entrance. The metallic sound sent a jolt of adrenaline through Alice and Reed. The pursuers had found them. The brief respite was over.

"They're here," Reed hissed, his eyes wide with terror.

Alice's mind worked with cold, calculated precision. There was no time for panic; they needed a plan, a way out. She glanced at the map, its faded ink a stark reminder of the perilous escape route that lay ahead. The network of underground tunnels was their only hope.

But then, an unexpected sound pierced the tension. A rhythmic tapping, faint but distinct, came from the far corner of the warehouse. Alice and Reed exchanged a cautious glance.

Cautiously, Alice approached the sound, her hand resting on the firearm tucked into her waistband. As she drew closer, she realized the tapping was coming from an innocuous wooden crate, a seemingly ordinary container lost amidst the pile of junk.

With a deep breath, Alice cautiously pried open the crate, revealing a hidden compartment. Inside, nestled amongst old tools and discarded machinery, she found it – a small, worn, leather-bound book. It appeared old, its pages yellowed and brittle with age.

She opened the book and discovered it wasn't a book at all. It was a cleverly disguised communications device, a sophisticated piece of technology hidden in plain sight, almost like a secret code hidden within a book. A thin panel slid open, revealing a small screen.

The screen flickered to life, displaying a single message: "Escape route: Section 7, Sub-level Alpha." Below it, a simple diagram showed a complex network of hidden tunnels, clearly part of the underground system.

Alice's mind raced. This had to be from Stratton; the detailed map only he would have known to put a secret communications device in this warehouse. This wasn't just a random crate; this was a lifeline. This was help, unexpected help, from an unlikely source.

But how did Stratton know they would end up here? It was the question that raced through her mind. Was this the whole time planned and orchestrated, or did Stratton manage to get there, hide the device, and alert them before the arrival of the enemies?

The tapping returned, and this time, it was louder and more distinct, accompanied by a faint whispering sound. It was Morse code, using a series of short and long taps, creating a series of dots and dashes. Alice, having been trained in code-breaking, instantly recognized the pattern.

This was a coded message, much more sophisticated, containing a series of coordinates and directions. As she translated the message into coordinates, her breath caught in her throat. The coordinates led to a specific location on the underground map, a place entirely different from the route she'd been planning to take.

Alice knew instantly this was their chance. This was their unexpected rescue and an unexpected escape route. The coded message, combined with the secret map, gave them an alternative path out of the city, a path only Stratton would know.

She glanced at Reed. His eyes were wide with a mixture of hope and disbelief.

"Stratton's help," she whispered, her voice barely audible. "He knew they'd find us here."

Time was of the essence. They had to move quickly. The sound of heavy footsteps approaching echoed through the warehouse, signaling the arrival of their pursuers. This was their chance. The sounds of the approaching pursuers made her decision faster. They followed the hidden path, the underground tunnel leading them to freedom.

Alice and Reed slipped into the network of tunnels, the damp air heavy with the smell of earth and decay. The narrow passageways were claustrophobic, the darkness oppressive, but the urgency of the situation propelled them forward. They navigated the labyrinthine tunnels, their footsteps muffled by the damp earth.

The coded message proved to be remarkably accurate; it guided them through the underground network, avoiding the main arteries and leading them toward a hidden exit point on the other side of the city. They moved swiftly and silently, their every sense heightened, their hearts pounding in unison.

Finally, after what felt like an eternity, they emerged from the tunnel, blinking in the bright morning sun. They were safe, at least for now. They had escaped the clutches of Miller and Thorne, but the battle was far from over. The escape had come thanks to an unexpected ally, a testament to the unpredictable nature of circumstances and the surprising power of unlikely alliances. Their journey was far from over, yet this unexpected rescue presented a new path to victory.

The Mastermind

The sun, a pale disc behind a veil of smog, offered little warmth as Alice and Reed stumbled out of the tunnel. The city, a concrete jungle of towering buildings and sprawling streets, seemed to breathe a sigh of relief as they emerged from the damp, subterranean world. They were safe, for now. But the escape had only served to sharpen the questions swirling in Alice's mind. The coded message, Stratton's intervention – it all pointed to a level of orchestration far beyond their initial understanding. The conspiracy ran deeper, wider than they had ever imagined.

Reed, his face grimy and streaked with sweat, leaned against a crumbling brick wall, catching his breath. "Stratton... how did he know?" he asked, his voice hoarse. The question echoed Alice's own unspoken anxieties. The precision of Stratton's intervention, the accuracy of the coded message, the hidden communication device – it all felt too perfectly timed, too meticulously planned.

Alice ran a hand through her disheveled hair, the adrenaline slowly receding, replaced by a cold, calculating assessment of the situation. She knew Stratton, or at least she thought she did. He was an enigma, a man shrouded in mystery, a figure who operated in the shadows, his motives as opaque as his methods. But his actions, however unexpected, had undeniably saved their lives.

"It's more than just luck, Reed," she said, her voice low and serious. "This was orchestrated. Someone knew we'd be in that warehouse.

Someone knew we needed that escape route. Someone is manipulating events, pulling the strings from behind the scenes."

The realization hit her with the force of a physical blow. The conspiracy wasn't just a network of corrupt officials and businessmen; it was a meticulously planned operation guided by a brilliant, ruthless mastermind. The question wasn't who was involved anymore; it was why. And who was pulling all the strings?

Days blurred into weeks as Alice and Reed delved deeper into the heart of the conspiracy. They used Stratton's coded message as a starting point, following the breadcrumbs he'd left, unraveling the intricate web of deceit and corruption. Each piece of information they uncovered, each lead they followed, revealed a new layer of complexity, a new level of insidiousness.

They discovered that the conspiracy extended far beyond the immediate circle of Miller, Thorne, and Hayes. It reached into the highest echelons of power, ensnaring politicians, judges, and law enforcement officials. It was a network of influence and control built on a foundation of lies and deception. The money flowed freely, laundered through offshore accounts and shell corporations, enriching those at the top while crushing those below.

Alice, drawing on her investigative instincts, began to see patterns emerge, connections between seemingly unrelated events. She noticed subtle details, overlooked clues, and connections others had missed. She saw the hand of the mastermind in every twist and turn of the investigation, a chess player moving their pieces with calculated precision.

Then, during a late-night research session in a forgotten archive, a name surfaced, a name that sent a chill down Alice's spine. A name whispered in hushed tones, a name associated with unparalleled wealth and influence: **Victor Martel.**

Victor Martel. The name was synonymous with power, a man who operated beyond the reach of the law, a man whose wealth and influence shielded him from scrutiny. He was a phantom, a ghost, a man who pulled strings from the shadows, manipulating events from behind a veil of anonymity. Alice's research revealed that Martel had a long history of shady dealings, a trail of broken promises, and shattered lives. He was a master manipulator, a puppet master who controlled politicians, businessmen, and even law enforcement officials with ease. His wealth provided him with the resources to orchestrate vast conspiracies and cover his tracks.

The pieces suddenly clicked into place. Martel's network of influence extended to every corner of the city, a silent web weaving through the fabric of society. Miller, Thorne, and Hayes were mere pawns in his grand game, expendable pieces readily sacrificed to protect his interests. And Stratton? Alice realized, with a sudden shock of recognition, that Stratton was not just an ally but a double agent working for Martel.

The realization was painful, a betrayal that cut deeply. Stratton, the seemingly mysterious benefactor, the source of their unexpected escape, was a viper in their midst, feeding them information and guiding their steps, only to lead them closer to Martel's trap. He had been manipulating them from the very beginning, using their desperate need to expose the conspiracy against him to manipulate them further, to lead them into the arms of their true adversary.

His role was to create chaos and confusion, to ensure that their efforts would only draw them deeper into Martel's web. His seemingly helpful intervention in the warehouse was not a lifeline but a strategic maneuver, a carefully orchestrated trap designed to bring them exactly where Martel wanted them.

Alice felt a surge of anger, a wave of betrayal washing over her. She had trusted him and relied on his supposed help. She had been manipulated, deceived, and played like a pawn in a much larger game. It was a bitter pill to swallow, but the realization gave her clarity and focus. It revealed the enemy's true strategy and allowed her to formulate a counteroffensive.

Now, armed with this new knowledge, Alice and Reed knew who they were really up against. Martel was not just a mastermind; he was a ghost, a phantom who operated from the shadows, using his vast wealth and influence to control every aspect of the city. Their fight was no longer against a network of corrupt officials and businessmen; it was against a single, formidable adversary, a man who held the city in his grasp and who would stop at nothing to protect his power.

The true scope of Martel's ambition now dawned on Alice. His influence extended beyond simple corruption; his goal was complete control. He sought to establish himself as the absolute ruler of the city, pulling all the strings from behind the scenes, ensuring that every action, every decision, served his interests. The previous events were merely rehearsals for his ultimate plan.

This realization was both terrifying and exhilarating. It was terrifying because it exposed the scale of Martel's power and the extent of his reach. It was exhilarating because it gave Alice and Reed a clear target, a focal point for their fight. They were no longer fighting a shadowy network; they were hunting a single, identifiable enemy.

The chase was on. Alice and Reed knew they were facing an almost insurmountable challenge. Martel's resources were limitless, his influence pervasive, and his security impenetrable. But they also knew that their cause was just, that their fight was necessary. The fate of the city, the future of its people, rested on their shoulders.

They started to meticulously plan their next move, leveraging everything they had learned. They used the information gathered from Reed's initial findings, from their time in the warehouse, and the knowledge gained about Martel's connections to devise a strategy to expose him. Every piece of information, however insignificant, was painstakingly analyzed, cross-referenced, and integrated into their plan. Their days and nights were consumed by the investigation, fueled by a potent cocktail of adrenaline and determination.

The confrontation with Martel wasn't going to be easy; it was going to be a war. But Alice and Reed were prepared for a fight. They were armed not only with information but with a renewed determination, a shared understanding of the stakes, and the satisfaction of finally knowing who the true mastermind behind the conspiracy was. The fight was far from over, but for the At first, they had a clear target and a definitive plan of action. They knew who to hunt and where to find him, and they were ready to take on the ultimate challenge. The game was on, and this time, they were playing to win.

A Shocking Revelation

The realization that Stratton was a double agent working for Martel hung heavy in the air, a chilling weight that threatened to crush them. Alice felt a sickening lurch in her stomach, a betrayal so profound it left her breathless. She had trusted him, confided in him, and relied on his supposed help. The coded message, the escape from the warehouse – it had all been a meticulously crafted illusion, a carefully orchestrated trap designed to lure them deeper into Martel's web.

Reed, ever the pragmatist, focused on the practical implications of this shocking revelation. "So, Stratton's been feeding us misinformation the whole time," he said, his voice tight with controlled anger. "He led us to Martel intentionally."

Alice nodded, the pieces of the puzzle finally falling into place. Stratton's cryptic pronouncements, his seemingly random acts of assistance – they were all part of a larger game, a carefully planned deception designed to manipulate them into Martel's clutches. It was a masterpiece of manipulation, a complex game of cat and mouse where they had been nothing more than naive pawns.

The anger that flared within Alice was a consuming fire. It fueled her determination and sharpened her focus. The betrayal stung, but it also provided a clarity she hadn't possessed before. They were no longer chasing shadows, hunting down faceless members of a sprawling conspiracy. They had a target, a name, a face: Victor Martel.

"We need to move fast," Reed said, his voice urgently. "If Stratton's working for Martel, then Martel knows everything we've uncovered. He knows about the

offshore accounts, the money laundered, the corrupt officials."

Alice agreed. The urgency of their situation pressed down on them, a suffocating weight. They were running out of time. Martel, with his limitless resources and pervasive influence, could easily erase their findings, silence their witnesses, and cover his tracks. They had to act decisively, quickly, and intelligently. Their every move had to be calculated and precise, a counteroffensive designed to disrupt Martel's plans and expose him to the world.

Their first step was to secure their findings. They had accumulated a vast amount of data, meticulously collected and cross-referenced over weeks of painstaking research. The evidence was scattered across multiple locations, hidden in encrypted files, and concealed in secure servers. Protecting this data was paramount and essential to their success. If Martel got to it first, everything they had worked for would be lost.

They spent the next few days transferring their data to secure offshore servers, using encrypted channels and multiple layers of protection. They also reached out to their trusted contacts, discreetly sharing their findings with individuals they knew they could trust, individuals who were both outside Martel's reach and committed to the cause of justice.

The next phase of their plan involved analyzing Stratton's actions, searching for any clues that might reveal Martel's next move. They studied Stratton's movements, his communications, and every detail of his involvement in their investigation. They looked for patterns, for inconsistencies, for anything that might betray his true allegiance and expose Martel's ultimate strategy.

What they discovered was chilling. Stratton hadn't just been feeding them misinformation; he had been actively shaping their investigation, guiding their steps toward Martel, while simultaneously subtly delaying their progress, ensuring that their exposure of his network would take as long as possible. He had been a master puppeteer, expertly manipulating them from the shadows, ensuring that their investigations always yielded more questions than answers.

Their analysis revealed a complex network of shell corporations, offshore accounts, and coded messages, all intricately connected to Martel's vast empire. The sheer scale of his operation was breathtaking, a testament to his cunning and ruthlessness. He had built a system of control so elaborate, so pervasive, that it seemed almost impossible to dismantle.

Alice and Reed, however, were not easily deterred. They knew that Martel's power was built on fear and secrecy, and exposing his network would be the first step towards breaking his grip on the city. They needed to turn his own tactics against him, to use his methods to expose his crimes.

Their strategy was twofold: first, to gather irrefutable evidence of Martel's crimes, and second, to find a way to leak this information to the public in a way that would circumvent Martel's control over the media.

Gathering the evidence proved to be more difficult than they had anticipated. Martel's reach extended far beyond the confines of his immediate network. His influence permeated every level of society, from the police department to the city council. They had to be careful and methodical, avoiding detection at every turn.

They used encrypted communications channels, met in clandestine locations, and relied on a network of trusted informants to gather information. Every contact was vetted thoroughly to ensure that they were not working for Martel. Every meeting was carefully planned, and every move was carefully executed. The stakes were too high for even the slightest error.

Finally, after weeks of relentless work, they had assembled a mountain of evidence – enough to bring down Martel and his empire. The evidence included financial records, coded messages, and testimonies from several key witnesses, all painstakingly documented and secured.

The next challenge was leaking the information to the public. Martel had a tight grip on the media, controlling newspapers, television stations, and even online news outlets. Their information would be buried, dismissed, or ignored. They needed a strategy to bypass his control to reach the public directly.

Their solution was audacious, risky, but potentially effective. They decided to use a decentralized, encrypted platform to anonymously leak the information, a platform that would be difficult for Martel to monitor or control. It was a gamble, a high-stakes game of chicken, but it was their best shot at exposing Martel and bringing him to justice.

The night they launched the leak was fraught with tension. Alice and Reed watched as the information spread across the encrypted network, a wildfire of truth ignited in the heart of a city choked by lies. The world began to learn of Martel's crimes, his corruption, his deceit, and his ambition. The walls of silence began to crumble. The city awoke.

The aftermath was chaos. Martel's network, exposed and vulnerable, began to unravel. Arrests were made, investigations launched, and the truth, once hidden in shadows, came to light. Martel's grip on the city was broken. His reign of terror was over. The victory was bittersweet, hard-fought and dearly bought. But Alice and Reed knew that they had done what was necessary, that they had protected the city from a monster, and that justice, however long delayed, had finally been served. The city breathed again, free from the weight of Martel's suffocating control.

And somewhere in the shadows, Stratton watched, his own future as uncertain as the city he had so

meticulously manipulated. The game was over, but the shadows remained.

Unexpected Twist

The struggle was brutal, a whirlwind of flailing limbs and grunts of exertion. Martel, despite his age, possessed surprising strength fueled by a desperate, cornered rage. Reed, a seasoned detective, matched his ferocity, his movements precise and efficient. Alice, smaller but equally skilled, moved like a shadow, her strikes calculated to disarm and subdue rather than inflict serious injury. The penthouse suite, moments ago a symbol of Martel's untouchable power, now resembled a chaotic wrestling match, the luxurious furnishings trampled underfoot.

The alarm continued its incessant blare, a soundtrack to their desperate struggle. The flashing red lights painted their faces in stark relief, highlighting the grim determination etched on their features. Martel, his carefully constructed facade of control, shattered, snarled, and cursed, his voice a guttural rasp that barely registered over the cacophony. He fought with the ferocity of a cornered animal, his eyes wild with a desperate hope for escape. He was no longer the calm, calculating mastermind they had confronted moments before, but a desperate man clinging to his fading power.

Just as Reed managed to gain the upper hand, pinning Martel to the floor, a deafening crash echoed from the other side of the room. A section of the wall, cleverly concealed behind a bookshelf, swung open, revealing a narrow, descending staircase. Before anyone could react, a figure emerged, silhouetted against the flickering emergency lights.

It was Isabella Martel, Victor's estranged daughter. Alice had known of her existence, a shadowy figure lurking in the periphery of the investigation, a woman whose life had been irrevocably scarred by her father's actions. She had never anticipated her involvement in this final confrontation. Isabella was armed, a small but powerful pistol clutched in her hand.

"Don't move!" she screamed, her voice sharp and laced with raw, untamed fury. Her eyes, filled with a mixture of hate and despair, were locked onto her father. The gun trembled slightly in her grip, a testament to her own inner turmoil, the weight of years of silent suffering.

The situation shifted dramatically. The focus was no longer solely on apprehending Victor Martel; now, a new, volatile element had entered the equation. The room was frozen, the three officers momentarily stunned by the unexpected intrusion. Reed slowly released his grip on Martel, his eyes flicking between Isabella and her father, assessing the new threat. Alice's hand instinctively moved to her own weapon but hesitated. There was no clear path of action.

Isabella's presence was a game changer. She was a wildcard, capable of altering the course of events in unpredictable ways. Was she here to help them or to obstruct justice? Was this a desperate act of rebellion or a carefully calculated move by Martel himself? Her unpredictable nature made her a potential ally and a potential danger.

Martel, regaining some of his composure, saw his daughter's arrival as a potential lifeline. He attempted to use her as a shield, pushing her forward, attempting to use her as a buffer against Reed and Alice.

"Isabella, get out of here!" he bellowed, his voice laced with a forced authority he no longer possessed. "Go! Leave me to them."

But Isabella stood firm, her gaze fixed on her father. Her expression was a terrifying blend of defiance and despair.

"No, Papa," she said, her voice shaking but resolute. "I won't let you escape. I won't let you get away with this anymore."

She leveled her weapon at him, but she did not fire. The tension in the room escalated exponentially. The officers were frozen, caught in a dangerous stalemate. They were faced with a complex moral dilemma – how to neutralize the threat without endangering Isabella, a victim in this twisted family drama.

The arrival of SWAT team members brought a temporary pause to the standoff. The heavily armed officers, alerted by the ongoing alarm and the chaotic radio chatter, flooded the penthouse, their assault rifles trained on all present. The sudden influx of officers created a confused but highly effective containment.

With Martel subdued and Isabella disarmed by the SWAT team, the dust began to settle, leaving behind a trail of unanswered questions. The immediate aftermath revealed a complex web of betrayal, manipulation, and deeply buried family trauma. While Victor Martel was finally behind bars, his capture didn't bring the expected sense of closure.

Isabella's actions remained a puzzle. Was she a pawn manipulated by her father, or had she orchestrated this moment herself, a final act of rebellion against her father's legacy? The investigation had broadened, now encompassing not only the complex financial schemes that had fueled Martel's empire but also the hidden dynamics of a fractured family, a family torn apart by ambition, greed, and the devastating consequences of unchecked power.

The following days were spent in a blur of interrogations, forensic analysis, and legal maneuvering. The anonymous tip that had led to the raid was traced to a source within Martel's inner circle. But the identity of that source remained frustratingly elusive. The backup server, which Martel had believed to be his failsafe, had indeed been compromised by Alice's carefully planned leak. This leak not only alerted the police but simultaneously triggered a complex chain reaction that began to unravel the entire network of corrupt officials and businesses that made up Martel's empire. The weight of the evidence against Martel was overwhelming, leaving little room for doubt.

Isabella remained a key figure in the investigation, her testimony critical to dismantling Martel's network. Her cooperation, however, was laced with a chilling detachment, a haunting sense of finality. She seemed to have accepted her father's downfall not with relief but with grim resignation, as if the whole ordeal had stripped her of any hope for redemption or reconciliation.

The ensuing trial was a media sensation. The city watched, captivated, as the carefully constructed facade of Victor Martel crumbled under the weight of evidence. The prosecution presented a compelling case, revealing a systematic web of corruption that reached the highest levels of city government. Martel, for once devoid of his usual arrogance, maintained a stony silence, his defiance replaced with a chilling resignation.

The verdict was swift and decisive. Victor Martel was found guilty on all counts and sentenced to life imprisonment. His empire, built on a foundation of lies and deceit, collapsed under the weight of its own corruption. The city breathed a collective sigh of relief, the air clearing after years of suffocating tension.

But as the city began to heal, a lingering sense of unease remained. The case had exposed a deep-seated corruption that went beyond Martel himself. The systemic flaws that had allowed him to thrive remained. The city, scarred but resilient, faced the arduous task of rebuilding its trust and reforming its institutions. And somewhere in the shadows, Isabella Martel carried the burden of her family's legacy, a silent witness to the unraveling of an empire, her future uncertain, a chilling testament to the enduring consequences of corruption and the complex web of family dynamics. The unexpected twist, the appearance of Isabella, had not only changed the course of the investigation but also painted a more complex and ambiguous picture of justice, leaving a lingering question: was true justice ever truly served?

Consequences of Actions

The courtroom buzzed with a low hum of anticipation.

The verdict had been delivered – guilty on all counts. Victor Martel, once a titan of industry, a man who wielded power like a weapon, was now a condemned man, his empire reduced to rubble. But the silence that followed the gavel's fall wasn't the silence of victory. It was a heavy, suffocating silence, pregnant with the unspoken weight of consequences. Alice, sitting in the gallery, felt it pressing down on her, a physical weight in her chest.

The victory felt hollow. The meticulous planning, the calculated risks, the sleepless nights spent piecing together the intricate web of Martel's crimes – all of it had culminated in this moment, yet a profound sense of unease lingered. The applause of the assembled press and the murmurs of relief from the public felt distant, muted by the echoing silence of her own conscience. The image of Isabella, her face etched with a chilling blend of defiance and resignation, haunted her. Isabella's testimony had been instrumental, the missing piece of the puzzle that had brought Martel down, but it had come at a cost. A cost that Alice was only beginning to fully comprehend.

The weeks following the trial were a blur of paperwork, interviews, and internal reviews. The department was still reeling from the fallout of Martel's arrest, a seismic event that had shaken the foundations of the city's political and economic landscape. Alice found herself frequently reviewing the evidence, poring over the details, searching for any clues she might have missed.

She had achieved her goal, but the victory tasted like ash in her mouth. The methods she'd employed, the lines she'd crossed – they clawed at her conscience.

The anonymous tip, the carefully orchestrated leak of information, the subtle manipulation of Martel's associates – these weren't actions typically condoned by the department. While her actions had been undeniably effective, they had blurred the line between legal investigation and morally gray maneuvers. The internal affairs investigation loomed over her like a dark cloud, a constant reminder of the risks she had taken. They commended her sharp intuition and her effectiveness in bringing down Martel, but they also raised serious concerns about her methods. The threat of disciplinary action, or worse, hung heavy in the air.

The internal review board was comprised of stern-faced men and women, seasoned veterans of the force, accustomed to upholding the law and adhering strictly to the rules. Their questions were precise, their gaze unwavering. They dissected her actions, examining every detail with clinical precision. They weren't questioning her dedication or her results, but her methods. They wanted to understand the moral compass that had guided her, the ethical framework that allowed her to justify her actions. Alice tried to explain, to articulate the urgency, the desperation, the weight of responsibility she felt. She tried to convey the understanding that sometimes, in the pursuit of justice, the letter of the law had to bend or even break.

Her superiors, while acknowledging the success of the operation, were wary. They understood the complexities of the situation and the moral ambiguities that made up such a high-stakes case. The line between justice and injustice, between right and wrong, had become blurred, and she had traversed that blurry line unapologetically. Her actions had to set an example as a precedent, and that was worrying.

Isabella's story weighed heavily on her mind. The young woman, scarred by her father's actions, had chosen to cooperate, to expose the man who had shaped her life in such a destructive way. But her cooperation hadn't been born of relief; it had been a grim acceptance, a resignation to the inevitable. Alice had seen the emptiness in her eyes, the hollowness that spoke volumes about the years of silence, neglect, and fear. Alice had helped her find her voice, but couldn't possibly fill the void left by the destruction of her family.

The department offered her counseling, recognizing the psychological toll of the case. The internal pressure she faced, combined with the moral complexities, had taken its toll. Alice initially declined, resistant to admit vulnerability, unwilling to acknowledge the cracks that were beginning to appear in her carefully constructed composure. But eventually, she relented. She recognized the need to process the trauma of the experience, to reconcile the choices she had made and their impact. The therapy sessions were difficult, forcing her to confront the gray areas of her actions, the justifications she'd made, and the potential consequences.

The city, meanwhile, celebrated its victory. Martel's fall was seen as a turning point, a moment of catharsis after years of living under the shadow of his influence. But the victory felt bittersweet to Alice. The celebratory atmosphere felt hollow, discordant with the weight of her own internal turmoil. The cost of justice, she was realizing, often extended far beyond the courtroom.

The anonymous tip, which had launched the entire investigation, remained a mystery. Alice knew the identity of the source, a whisper of a secret known only to her and a few others. It was a person within Martel's inner circle. This person was now under witness protection and could no longer be reached. The person had played a crucial role in bringing Martel down, providing the information needed to expose the full extent of his crimes. Their act of defiance, however, remained shrouded in secrecy, an act of anonymous courage that had come with a huge personal sacrifice.

As Alice began the healing process, she also began the task of reviewing her career path, her methods, and her overall moral compass. The pursuit of justice was never straightforward, and neither were the sacrifices required to achieve it. The line between right and wrong could be so blurred at times that even the most well-intentioned actions could have unintended and devastating consequences. She learned that even in victory, there is always a cost. The case had been a watershed moment, not just for the city but for her personally. She emerged from the shadow of Martel's crimes a changed person, the weight of her actions, both justified and questionable, etched permanently in her memory, a stark reminder that even in the name of justice, the consequences of our actions can be profound and farreaching.

The city had breathed a sigh of relief, but for Alice, the struggle for peace was far from over. The path to redemption, she understood, would be a long and arduous one.

Unmasking the Conspirators

The revelation came not with a dramatic flourish but with the quiet click of a computer mouse. Weeks after Martel's conviction, buried deep within a seemingly innocuous spreadsheet – a financial record seemingly unrelated to the case – Alice discovered a hidden column. It contained a series of coded entries meticulously disguised within the legitimate data. It took days of painstaking decryption, utilizing the skills of a specialist from the NSA, to unlock the cipher. What emerged was a chilling expose of Martel's inner circle, a meticulously crafted conspiracy reaching far beyond the initial scope of the investigation.

The spreadsheet detailed a network of shell corporations, offshore accounts, and complex financial transactions, all designed to launder the proceeds of Martel's illegal activities. Each entry was a breadcrumb, leading Alice deeper into the labyrinthine web of deceit. The names that appeared were not just those of Martel's immediate associates but prominent figures in the city's political landscape, influential businessmen, and even a few judges. They were the silent partners, the beneficiaries of Martel's criminal enterprise, their complicity meticulously hidden behind layers of secrecy and plausible deniability.

Among them was Senator Harrison, a seemingly incorruptible figure who had publicly condemned Martel's actions yet whose name appeared repeatedly in the spreadsheet, linked to significant financial transactions. The Senator's meticulously crafted public persona, his image of honesty and integrity, crumbled under the weight of the evidence. Next was Julian

Thorne, a renowned philanthropist, his charitable foundations masking a deep involvement in Martel's money laundering scheme. Thorne's reputation, built on years of carefully cultivated public image, was now irrevocably tainted. The evidence revealed the shocking extent of their involvement and their roles in shielding Martel's illicit operations from the scrutiny of law enforcement.

The spreadsheet also revealed a more sinister layer of the conspiracy. Martel had been involved in a sophisticated campaign of intimidation and coercion, targeting anyone who posed a threat to his empire. This included journalists, whistleblowers, and even members of his own family who dared to question his authority. The methods employed were brutal, ranging from subtle threats to outright violence, all meticulously planned and executed with chilling efficiency. Alice discovered evidence of several unsolved disappearances, cases that had been dismissed as accidents or isolated incidents but which now appeared to be part of a broader pattern of intimidation orchestrated by Martel and his associates.

The most disturbing revelation was the involvement of Judge Miller, a respected member of the judicial system, whose signature appeared on several questionable rulings that had benefited Martel in the past. Judge Miller's position of authority had been misused to shield Martel's illegal activities, ensuring his continued reign of power. The Judge had played a crucial role in obstructing justice, allowing Martel's criminal enterprise to flourish unchecked. The revelation shook Alice to her core, highlighting the insidious nature of corruption and its ability to penetrate even the most hallowed institutions.

Unraveling the conspiracy required meticulous work, a slow and painstaking process of piecing together the fragmented evidence. Each lead unearthed new layers of complexity, forcing Alice to navigate a treacherous landscape of lies, deception, and carefully constructed alibis. She worked tirelessly, often for days without sleep, driven by a sense of urgency and a burning desire to expose the truth. The pressure was immense, the stakes impossibly high. The weight of exposing such powerful figures rested heavily on her shoulders. The threat of retaliation, both overt and covert, was palpable.

As Alice delved deeper, she uncovered a network of informants within Martel's inner circle, individuals who had provided crucial information anonymously over the years, their identities shielded by layers of secrecy. One such informant was revealed to be Isabella Martel's longtime family lawyer, Mr. Davies, a man who had quietly documented Martel's illegal activities for years, secretly preserving the evidence needed to bring him down. Davies, tormented by his conscience and driven by a sense of moral obligation, had secretly leaked information to an anonymous source, the same anonymous source who had provided Alice with that initial crucial tip, launching the entire investigation.

The identity of the anonymous source remained a secret, shielded by the department to protect their safety. However, Alice knew the source's identity: a junior accountant who had witnessed Martel's illegal activities firsthand and who, fueled by a sense of righteous anger, had risked everything to expose him. This courageous act, driven by a deep sense of morality and a belief in justice, played a pivotal role in bringing down Martel's empire.

The unmasking of the conspirators sent shockwaves through the city. The arrests were swift and decisive, bringing down some of the most influential figures in the community. The public outcry was immense, demanding accountability and transparency. The once untouchable figures were now facing the consequences of their actions, their meticulously crafted personas shattered. The investigation, initially focused on Martel, had revealed a network of corruption far more extensive and insidious than anyone had imagined.

Alice's work, however, was far from over. The legal battles that ensued were protracted and fiercely contested, each case a reminder of the immense power and influence wielded by Martel's former associates. The conspirators fought back with all their might, employing the best legal minds available, hoping to delay or avoid justice. The evidence, however, was overwhelming, the trail of financial transactions and illicit activities irrefutable.

The subsequent trials were closely followed by the public, a collective demonstration of the thirst for accountability. The city held its breath, waiting to see if justice would truly prevail. Alice, meanwhile, found herself grappling with the ethical complexities of the case, the sacrifices made, and the moral compromises she had undertaken in her pursuit of the truth. The victory felt bittersweet, tainted by the methods employed and the potential consequences of her actions.

While she had brought down Martel and his conspirators, she knew the cost would linger, a reminder of the intricate web of power and corruption she had exposed.

The city had celebrated its victory over Martel's reign of terror, but Alice knew that the fight for true justice had just begun – a fight that would involve far-reaching reforms and a long struggle to cleanse the city's institutions from the deep-seated corruption. Her journey, too, was far from over. The weight of her actions, the knowledge of what she had seen and done, would forever shape her future, a constant reminder of the complexities and moral ambiguities of the pursuit of justice.

Motives and Backgrounds

The spreadsheet, initially a seemingly mundane record of financial transactions, had unraveled a tapestry of deceit woven over decades. Senator Harrison, the champion of moral rectitude, revealed a chillingly pragmatic approach to ethics. His involvement wasn't born of greed alone, though the hefty sums deposited into his offshore accounts certainly spoke volumes. No, Harrison's motivation was a chilling blend of ambition and self-preservation. He had used Martel's network to fund his campaigns, securing his political power and silencing any dissenting voices. The senator's carefully cultivated image of integrity was a calculated performance, a shield against any scrutiny that might expose his true nature.

His background, a humble upbringing followed by a meteoric rise in politics, fueled his deep-seated fear of losing everything he had painstakingly achieved. Martel's downfall, therefore, was not simply a matter of justice; it was a threat to Harrison's very existence. He'd been playing a dangerous game, and now, the house of cards he'd built was collapsing around him.

Julian Thorne, the philanthropist, presented a different puzzle altogether. His charitable contributions, lauded by the city, masked a dark secret – a desperate need to atone for past sins. Years ago, a reckless business venture had left a trail of devastated lives and financial ruin in its wake. Thorne had escaped the legal repercussions, but the weight of his guilt had driven him to seek redemption through his philanthropic endeavors. His involvement with Martel wasn't driven by avarice but by a twisted sense of moral compensation. He believed his good deeds outweighed his past transgressions, justifying his participation in the money laundering scheme. The irony, of course, was devastating. His attempt to cleanse his conscience had only deepened his moral stain. His carefully crafted image of a benevolent benefactor crumbled under the weight of his complicity. The weight of his secret gnawed at him, a constant reminder of the chasm between his public persona and his private guilt.

Judge Miller, a pillar of the judicial system, presented the most unsettling case. His involvement was a chilling demonstration of the insidious nature of corruption, a gradual erosion of integrity masked by years of seemingly impartial rulings. Unlike Harrison and Thorne, who acted out of self-interest and guilt, respectively, Miller's motivations were far more complex.

He was not driven by financial gain or a need for redemption. His was slow, insidious corruption fueled by a deep-seated need for control and power. His background, an upbringing marked by hardship and a relentless climb through the ranks of the legal profession, had ingrained in him a ruthlessness that he could justify. He viewed Martel's operation as a means to maintain power, consolidating his influence within the legal system and manipulating the course of justice. He saw Martel as a powerful instrument that served his ambitions, shielding him from any potential challenge to his authority. His complicity wasn't a sudden fall; it was a slow descent into the murky depths of moral compromise, driven by a lust for power he could never satiate.

The junior accountant, the anonymous source who initially tipped off Alice, was a stark contrast to the wealthy and powerful conspirators. Driven by a sense of moral outrage, this individual had risked their career, their reputation, and potentially their life to expose Martel's criminal empire. Their background was unremarkable – a hardworking individual struggling to make ends meet, working in the humdrum setting of a financial institution. Their decision, however, was extraordinary. Witnessing the corrupt practices firsthand, fueled by a simple, unwavering belief in justice, they chose to act. The risk was immense, the potential consequences daunting, but the weight of their conscience far outweighed the potential repercussions. Their courageous act highlighted the power of an individual to confront corruption, a testament to the enduring human spirit that yearns for justice, even in the face of overwhelming odds. The accountant's bravery served as a sharp reminder of the potential for extraordinary action from ordinary individuals.

Isabella Martel, initially portrayed as a victim, emerged as a complex figure in her own right. Her initial reluctance to cooperate stemmed from a deep-seated fear of her husband, a fear that had been cultivated over years of control and intimidation. She was not a willing participant in his schemes, but neither was she an innocent bystander. Her silence, her passive acceptance of his actions, had allowed the conspiracy to flourish. Her background, a sheltered life of privilege, had ill-equipped her to confront the brutal reality of her husband's activities. Only when presented with undeniable proof of his actions and the potential consequences for her wellbeing did she finally cooperate. Her evolution from a fearful witness to a key informant highlighted the complexity of victimhood and the capacity for human transformation. Her journey underscores the devastating effects of domestic abuse and the courage required to break free from such oppressive circumstances.

Mr. Davies, Martel's longtime family lawyer, presented a fascinating case of moral ambiguity. He had been privy to Martel's illegal activities for years, secretly documenting the evidence, his actions a silent protest against the growing corruption. He hadn't acted out of altruism alone; years of quietly observing Martel's ruthless tactics had instilled in him a deep fear for his own safety and the safety of his family. He wasn't a hero but a man haunted by his silence, driven by a late-blooming sense of moral obligation. His meticulous documentation, a clandestine act of rebellion against Martel's reign, served as a crucial element in bringing down the criminal empire. His background as a man of law who had witnessed the erosion of justice solidified his later role in seeking to repair some of the damage. His story demonstrated the devastating consequences of complicity and the slow, painful process of redemption. He served as a reminder that even those who choose silence at first can find the courage to speak truth to power, ultimately contributing to the pursuit of justice.

The investigation, initially focused on Martel, had uncovered a far-reaching network of corruption, highlighting the systemic nature of the problem. The motives of the conspirators, while varied, all stemmed from a common thread: a desire for power, whether it was political influence, financial gain, or the desperate need to atone for past mistakes. Understanding these motivations provided critical context, allowing Alice to grasp the complexity of the case and the lengths the conspirators would go to protect their interests. Each individual, with their unique background and motives, added a layer of complexity to the story, underscoring the intricacy of the criminal network they had created. It wasn't simply a matter of greed; it was a tapestry of ambition, fear, guilt, and the insidious erosion of moral principles. The unraveling of their carefully constructed world brought with it a sense of closure but also a lingering awareness of the pervasive nature of corruption and the constant vigilance required to combat it. The city had dealt a blow to the corruption

that had long festered in its heart, but the fight, Alice knew, was far from over.

The Price of Deception

The unraveling of Martel's empire didn't simply expose a web of financial crimes; it laid bare the profound personal costs borne by each participant. Senator Harrison, his carefully constructed image of public service shattered, faced a cascade of repercussions. The revelation of his offshore accounts, funded by Martel's ill-gotten gains, triggered a maelstrom of media scrutiny and public outrage. His once-unassailable political career crumbled, replaced by the bitter taste of betrayal and disgrace. The legal ramifications were swift and severe; the threat of lengthy imprisonment hung heavy over him, a stark contrast to the power and influence he'd wielded for so long. Beyond the legal consequences, however, lay the deeper wounds. His family, once proud of his accomplishments, now recoiled from the shame associated with his name. His reputation, painstakingly built over the years, was reduced to ashes, a testament to the fleeting nature of power and the enduring weight of deceit. The once-respected senator, a figurehead in the community, was now a pariah, ostracized and alone, facing the bleak reality of his downfall, the ultimate price of his ambition.

Julian Thorne's philanthropic endeavors, once lauded as acts of selfless generosity, were now viewed with cynicism and suspicion. The public, initially charmed by his charitable works, quickly turned their back, realizing the tainted source of his wealth. His carefully cultivated image of a benevolent benefactor was irrevocably tarnished. The weight of his guilt, which had previously driven his philanthropy, intensified, compounded by the exposure of his complicity. He struggled to reconcile his desire for redemption with the reality of his actions, facing the agonizing awareness that his attempts to atone for his past had only further implicated him in a web of deceit. The isolation he felt was profound; he had lost not only his reputation but the illusion of a cleansed conscience. His wealth, once a source of pride, became a symbol of his moral bankruptcy. His generous donations, intended to alleviate suffering, now felt like a cruel mockery, a desperate attempt to purchase absolution that he could never truly attain. The quiet solitude of his mansion, once a refuge, had become a prison of his own making.

Judge Miller's downfall was particularly chilling, a stark reminder of the corrosive effect of power and unchecked ambition. The erosion of his integrity, gradual yet complete, left him stripped bare, exposed for the corrupt official he truly was. His expulsion from the judiciary, a swift and decisive judgment, ended his career and stripped him of the authority he craved. But the consequences extended beyond the professional sphere. His colleagues, once deferential, now shunned him; the respect he had earned, carefully cultivated over years of service, was replaced by disdain and contempt. His once unblemished reputation, the cornerstone of his authority, was shattered. He confronted the bitter truth: his relentless pursuit of power had led to his downfall, a testament to the self-destructive nature of unchecked ambition. He was left with nothing but the weight of his past actions, and his life was reduced to the wreckage of his ambition.

The junior accountant, the anonymous source who had initiated the investigation, faced a different set of challenges. Their courageous act, driven by a simple belief in justice, placed them in immense peril. While their identity remained protected, the risk of retribution from Martel's associates continued to loom large. Their career was jeopardized, and they endured the constant strain of living under the threat of exposure. The fear and uncertainty created a palpable tension in their daily life. The courage they demonstrated, however, served as a powerful example of the potent impact an individual can have on the fight against corruption. The price they paid was enormous, but it paved the way for the exposure of the entire conspiracy. They paid a personal price for their bravery, but their selfless act ultimately led to justice.

Isabella Martel's journey was particularly complex. While initially a victim of her husband's control and intimidation, she bore the weight of her own complicity. Her cooperation with the authorities, though crucial to the investigation, came at a significant personal cost. The trauma she had endured for years, coupled with the subsequent scrutiny and judgment from others, cast a long shadow. She had to confront the ghosts of her past, grapple with the implications of her silence, and rebuild her life from the ashes of her marriage. Rebuilding her life would require immense strength and resilience, but she knew that cooperation was not just an act of self-preservation; it was a step towards reclaiming her identity. Her journey underscores the resilience of the human spirit and the profound impact of standing up against oppression.

Mr. Davies, Martel's long-time family lawyer, also faced a reckoning. His quiet rebellion, his clandestine documentation of Martel's crimes, had served its purpose but had left its mark. He was haunted by years of silence, the weight of his complicity eating away at his conscience. While his actions ultimately contributed to Martel's downfall, the fear and uncertainty he had endured took their toll. His quiet act of rebellion was now subject to public scrutiny, and his motives were questioned. He had to confront his past actions, acknowledge the delay in his protest, and attempt to make amends for his complicity. His actions underscored the long and painful path to redemption and the difficult choice between self-preservation and moral obligation. His story served as a reminder that even those who initially choose silence can find the courage to speak truth to power, however belatedly.

The city, once seemingly impervious to the insidious corruption that had taken root, was now grappling with the aftermath of the scandal. The exposure of Martel's network had shaken the foundations of its institutions and left a lingering sense of unease. The revelations had eroded public trust in those entrusted with power, prompting calls for reform and a renewed emphasis on transparency and accountability. The cleanup process would be long and arduous. The investigation had brought down a criminal network, but its repercussions extended far beyond those directly implicated, creating a sense of collective disillusionment and a need for a moral reckoning. The price of deceit had extended far beyond the individual conspirators; it had eroded the trust of the city as a whole.

Alice, the relentless investigator at the heart of the story, observed the consequences of the conspiracy with a mixture of satisfaction and apprehension. The victory was hard-won yet tinged with the sober realization that corruption, like a hydra, has many heads. She knew this was not the end, merely a decisive battle in a long and ongoing war. The unraveling of Martel's empire served as a potent reminder of the enduring nature of corruption and the unwavering vigilance required to combat it. The system had shown its fragility, and there was much work left to be done. While justice had been served in this instance, Alice was acutely aware that many similar conspiracies likely remained hidden, waiting for their moment to be revealed. The fight for transparency and accountability was far from over. The price of deception, she understood, was not confined to those directly involved but extended to the fabric of the community, a price that would be paid for years to come. The city had dealt a blow to corruption, but the scars remained, a constant reminder that vigilance is the price of freedom from such malignant forces.

Alice's Triumph

The city breathed a collective sigh, a weary exhale after weeks of breathless tension. The headlines, once screaming accusations and revelations, softened to a more muted tone as the shockwaves of the Martel scandal slowly receded. But the quiet wasn't peaceful; it was the uneasy calm after a storm, a stillness pregnant with the lingering consequences of the unraveling. Alice, however, felt none of that quietude. Her apartment, usually a sanctuary, felt like a pressure cooker, the silence punctuated only by the rhythmic tap-tap of her fingers on the keyboard as she compiled the final report. The weight of the case, the relentless pressure of the investigation, the constant threat of retribution – it all pressed down on her, a tangible weight that threatened to crush her.

She reviewed the final pages, meticulously documenting the intricate web of deceit, tracing the flow of money, the shifting alliances, and the betrayals. It was a tapestry woven from greed, ambition, and fear, a testament to the depths of human depravity. Each name, each date, and each transaction represented a piece of a larger puzzle — a puzzle she had painstakingly assembled, piece by agonizingly slow piece.

She ran a hand through her tired hair. The exhaustion etched onto her face mirrored the city's weary exhaustion. The victory felt less like a triumph and more like the end of a long, grueling battle, a battle that had left her scared but also strangely strengthened.

The downfall of Martel had been a domino effect, each carefully placed piece toppling the next. The anonymous tip from the junior accountant had been the catalyst, the initial tremor that had set the entire structure shaking. Then came Isabella's fragile cooperation, a crack in the seemingly impenetrable fortress of Martel's empire. Judge Miller's downfall had been particularly satisfying. A poetic justice was served upon a man who thought himself untouchable. Even Julian Thorne, the philanthropist with the carefully crafted image, had crumbled under the weight of his complicity. Senator Harrison, the embodiment of political power, had been reduced to a broken man, stripped of his influence and dignity.

But the victory wasn't without its complexities. The legal battles would continue for years, appeals and counterappeals, drawn-out processes designed to delay and obfuscate. The city itself bore the scars of the scandal, the erosion of public trust, and the lingering sense of betrayal. Alice knew that this wasn't a final victory; it was a turning point, a moment of reckoning that would force a long and difficult process of reform and healing. This was a war that would continue, fought on many fronts, with many unseen enemies, each victory hard-won and each setback threatening to undo all the progress made.

She thought of the junior accountant, the source of the initial leak, who remained shrouded in anonymity, living with the constant threat of exposure and retribution. Alice understood the risk they had taken, the burden of their silence, and the immense courage it had taken to speak truth to power. It was courage that mirrored her own, a willingness to confront the darkness, to face the powerful and corrupt without flinching. She felt a profound sense of solidarity with them; a shared understanding of the sacrifices made in the pursuit of justice.

Isabella Martel's journey was also complex, her role as both victim and accomplice leaving her in a precarious position. She had given invaluable testimony, but her cooperation came at a steep personal cost. The weight of her past actions, the trauma of her marriage, and the public scrutiny she faced were immense burdens. Her recovery would be long and arduous, requiring strength and resilience. Yet, Alice saw in Isabella's willingness to cooperate a glimmer of hope, a testament to the human capacity for transformation and redemption.

Mr. Davies, Martel's lawyer, had played a significant role; his quiet rebellion was a crucial element in the dismantling of the empire. His belated act of defiance was a powerful reminder that even those complicit in wrongdoing can eventually find the courage to speak truth to power. His story, she reflected on, served as a lesson, an acknowledgment that redemption is possible, though rarely easy. The path to redemption is long and arduous, often filled with self-doubt, guilt, and the weight of past actions.

The city, shaken but not broken, would slowly begin to rebuild, to recover from the collective trauma of the scandal. But the lessons learned would remain a constant reminder of the fragility of institutions, the insidious nature of corruption, and the importance of unwavering vigilance. It was a reminder that the fight for justice is a never-ending battle, constant vigilance against the forces that seek to undermine and corrupt the foundations of society.

Alice closed her report, the final period a definitive punctuation mark to a long and intense chapter. But as she leaned back in her chair, the weariness was still heavy on her, she knew this was just one battle won. The war against corruption was far from over. The city had emerged from the shadows of Martel's empire, but the darkness still lingered, lurking in the crevices of power, waiting for its opportunity to strike again. And Alice, ever vigilant, would be there to confront it, to expose it, to fight for justice, even if it meant facing the darkness again and again. The weight of her responsibility, the burden of her unwavering commitment to justice, was a heavy one. Still, it was a burden she willingly carried, a burden fueled by a deep-seated belief in the power of truth and the resilience of the human spirit. The fight was far from over, and she was ready. The city might have exhaled, but Alice knew she would continue to fight, the tireless guardian of its hard-won peace. She would remain a solitary figure, standing against the darkness, a beacon in the shadows, ensuring that the light of justice never truly faded.

The quiet hum of her apartment, once a symbol of her solitude, now felt like a quiet hum of resolve, a steady beat keeping pace with the relentless rhythm of her unwavering commitment. The city slept, unaware of the silent vigil she kept, a guardian against the insidious shadows that threatened to engulf it once more. Alice smiled, a small, knowing smile, a smile of quiet determination. The fight was far from over, but she was ready.

Justice Served

The courtroom was packed, a sea of faces reflecting the city's breathless anticipation. Isabella Martel, frail but resolute, sat beside her lawyer, Mr. Davies, a man whose quiet defiance had been as crucial as any explosive revelation. Her testimony, delivered with a trembling voice yet unwavering conviction, had been the linchpin of the prosecution's case. She recounted the systematic corruption, the insidious web of lies, and the chilling manipulation that had defined her marriage to the fallen titan, Victor Martel. Her words, though painful, were potent; they painted a vivid picture of a man who had built his empire on deceit and coercion. The jury listened, their expressions ranging from shock to grim understanding.

The prosecution's case was meticulously constructed, a testament to Alice's tireless investigation. Each piece of evidence, meticulously documented and presented, contributed to a damning portrait of Victor Martel and his network. The anonymous tip, the meticulously tracked financial transactions, the damning emails—all interwoven into a tapestry of undeniable guilt. Even Julian Thorne, the seemingly benevolent philanthropist, couldn't escape the long arm of the law. His attempts to distance himself from Martel's empire had failed; the evidence of his complicity, carefully concealed, was brought to light through meticulous forensic accounting and a series of well-placed interviews.

Senator Harrison, once a pillar of political power, now stood accused of accepting bribes and using his influence to shield Martel's illegal activities. His once impeccable reputation was in tatters, the weight of his crimes crushing him under its immeasurable weight. His downfall was a stark reminder of the fragility of power and the inevitable consequences of corruption. The once untouchable had become a cautionary tale, his career and reputation ruined, his legacy forever tainted. His lawyers, initially confident and arrogant, now wore expressions of defeated resignation, aware that the evidence against their client was insurmountable.

Judge Miller's case was a particular highlight. His blatant abuse of power and his blatant disregard for justice had been exposed through a series of meticulously documented instances of judicial misconduct. His removal from the bench was swift and decisive, sending a powerful message that no one, regardless of position, was above the law. The whispers in the legal circles that his tenure had been marked by irregularities had been validated, amplified, and proven in a resounding echo of justice. The systemic corruption that had enabled him to act with impunity was finally uprooted, his career shattered, and his reputation irrevocably damaged.

The trial itself was a spectacle, a public airing of the city's dark underbelly. The media frenzy was unrelenting, each day bringing new revelations and further solidifying the sense of collective outrage and betrayal. Yet, amidst the chaos, there was a sense of hope, a quiet determination that justice would prevail. Alice watched from the sidelines, observing the unfolding drama with a mixture of exhaustion and quiet satisfaction. The weight of the past weeks, the sleepless nights spent poring over documents and piecing together the puzzle, finally began to lift. The exhaustion was palpable but overshadowed by a profound sense of fulfillment.

The verdict was unanimous: guilty on all counts. A collective gasp swept through the courtroom, followed by a wave of murmurs and relieved sighs. Victor Martel, his face a mask of disbelief and barely controlled rage, stared straight ahead. His empire crumbled around him. The sentence was severe, reflecting the gravity of his crimes and the extent of the damage he had caused. It served as a stark reminder that even the most powerful individuals were not immune to the consequences of their actions. The long arm of the law had reached even the highest echelons of power, and justice had been served.

However, the legal battles were far from over. Appeals were filed, delaying the inevitable and prolonging the agony for those affected by Martel's crimes. The legal maneuvering was complex and tedious, a frustrating dance of technicalities and loopholes. Yet, Alice remained resolute, knowing that the fight was far from over. She understood the intricacies of the legal system, its inherent delays, and the relentless efforts of the wealthy and powerful to avoid accountability. She was prepared for the protracted battles ahead, for the long and arduous fight to ensure that Martel and his associates remained behind bars, unable to further harm others.

Mr. Davies, after the sentencing, approached Alice. He carried the weight of his past complicity, but his eyes reflected a newfound clarity and resolve. He confessed to his role in the cover-ups, to his silence in the face of Martel's wrongdoing. He had chosen to stand with justice at a significant personal cost, risking his reputation and future, but he had ultimately chosen what was right. His journey exemplified the concept of redemption, serving as a reminder that even those who had played a role in corruption could find a path back to righteousness.

The city reacted to the verdict with a mixture of relief and cautious optimism. The Martel scandal had shaken the foundations of its civic life and exposed the deep-seated corruption that had been simmering beneath the surface for years. The ensuing investigations led to further arrests and prosecutions, a wave of accountability rippling through various institutions. The scandal forced a long-overdue reckoning, a critical examination of the systems that had allowed Martel to operate with such impunity for so long. The seeds of reform were planted, and the path toward a more just and transparent society slowly began to emerge.

Alice, meanwhile, continued her work, assisting with further investigations and advocating for policy changes aimed at preventing future instances of widespread corruption. She became a symbol of hope, a reminder that the fight for justice is an ongoing process requiring persistence, courage, and unwavering commitment. Her work didn't end with the Martel case; it was a continuation of a much larger battle against corruption, a battle that would continue long after the headlines faded and the public's attention shifted elsewhere.

Isabella Martel began her long journey toward recovery. The trauma she had endured during her marriage and the subsequent public scrutiny were immense obstacles, but she possessed a resilience that surprised even Alice.

She started rebuilding her life, finding strength in the support of those who had stood by her. Her testimony served not only as a tool for justice but as an example of courage and perseverance. She became an advocate for victims of domestic abuse, lending her voice and experiences to a cause that was close to her heart.

The aftermath of the Martel scandal was a period of healing and reform. It was a reminder that justice is not always swift or straightforward, but its pursuit is crucial for the health of a society. The city breathed a collective sigh, not of relief alone, but of resolve. The fight for transparency and accountability was far from over, but a significant battle had been won. The echoes of the trial, the reverberations of justice served, would continue to resonate for years to come, inspiring vigilance and fueling the ongoing struggle against corruption. The long shadow of Martel's empire had receded, but Alice knew, with a certainty rooted in experience, that the darkness would always lurk, waiting for its chance to return. And she would be there, waiting too, ready to confront it once more. The fight for justice is, and will always be, a never ending battle —a testament to the enduring human spirit and its persistent pursuit of truth.

Aftermath of the Conspiracy

The city of Wilder, once draped in the opulent sheen of Victor Martel's empire, now wore the somber hues of post-traumatic recovery. The immediate aftermath of the trial was a whirlwind of media frenzy, public discourse, and a collective exhalation of pent-up tension. The streets, once echoing with the whispers of Martel's influence, hummed with a newfound energy, a nervous optimism tinged with the lingering unease of what had been unearthed. The newspapers, for weeks, were saturated with analyses of the case, editorials debating the systemic failures that had allowed Martel's reign of terror to persist for so long, and profiles of the individuals whose lives had been irrevocably altered by his actions.

Isabella Martel, having faced the relentless glare of the public eye, retreated into a quiet life, shielded by the unwavering support of her lawyer, Mr. Davies, and a small circle of trusted friends. The city, initially harsh in its judgment of her—some whispering of complicity, others blaming her for her naivete —slowly began to offer a different narrative. Her testimony initially met with skepticism from some quarters but ultimately served as a testament to her courage, an inspiration for victims of domestic abuse to speak out. She began to receive letters, phone calls, and emails from women across the country, sharing their stories and finding solace in her resilience. Isabella, once a symbol of a gilded cage, was now an emblem of survival, a beacon of hope in the darkness.

The transformation of Wilder City wasn't just about individuals; it was a collective reckoning, a societal shift.

The city council, under immense public pressure, initiated a comprehensive review of its regulatory bodies, aiming to identify and address the systemic vulnerabilities that had enabled Martel's corruption to fester. Independent audits were commissioned, revealing a shocking level of negligence and complicity within various departments. Several officials were investigated, suspended, or even arrested as the ripples of the Martel scandal spread far beyond the initial circle of conspirators. The police department, once viewed with suspicion due to its perceived involvement in covering up Martel's activities, underwent a major restructuring. New leadership was brought in, committed to transparency and accountability. Internal affairs investigations were launched, leading to the dismissal or prosecution of several officers implicated in past cover-ups.

The economic impact of the Martel scandal was equally profound. His business empire, once the engine of Wilder's prosperity, was systematically dismantled. Properties were seized, assets were frozen, and countless employees found themselves out of work. The city faced a period of economic uncertainty, but this also spurred a wave of innovation and entrepreneurship. New businesses emerged, fueled by a desire to create a more ethical and sustainable economic model. The city's economic future was uncertain, but it was an uncertainty laced with the promise of a more equitable and transparent system, a contrast to the suffocating grip of Martel's crony capitalism.

The cultural impact was no less significant. Artists, writers, and filmmakers drew inspiration from the Martel scandal, producing works that explored the themes of power, corruption, and redemption. The city's collective experience became a source of creative expression, a means of processing the trauma and navigating the path toward healing. Theatrical productions, novels, and documentaries chronicled the unfolding events, prompting ongoing discussions and debates about the nature of justice, the limits of power, and the fragility of truth in the face of immense wealth and influence.

The most surprising consequence of the scandal was the unexpected resurgence of civic engagement. The disillusionment that had followed Martel's reign of terror transformed into a fierce determination to actively participate in the city's governance. Voter turnout skyrocketed in the subsequent local elections, and the newly elected officials were held to a higher standard of accountability, reflecting a societal shift towards transparency and ethical leadership. Citizen oversight committees were formed dedicated to monitoring city operations and ensuring that the mistakes of the past were not repeated.

Alice, the relentless investigator whose work had been instrumental in bringing Martel to justice, remained a pivotal figure in the aftermath. She wasn't satisfied with simply seeing Martel imprisoned; she was committed to ensuring that his network was completely dismantled and that all those complicit in his crimes faced the consequences of their actions. She continued her work, collaborating with the city council, the police department, and various investigative bodies to expose further instances of corruption and to help rebuild the trust eroded by years of systemic failure. Her dedication and her tireless pursuit of justice had become a symbol of hope for the city, a reminder that even the most entrenched corruption could be challenged and overcome.

Mr. Davies, having found redemption through his confession and cooperation with the prosecution, dedicated himself to reforming the legal system. He used his experience and his newfound reputation to advocate for stricter regulations on campaign finance, lobbying, and judicial ethics. He became a vocal advocate for greater transparency in government, using his influence to push for legislative changes that would prevent future instances of the kind of pervasive corruption that had characterized Martel's reign. His transformation from a seemingly complicit lawyer to a champion of justice became a powerful symbol of the possibilities for change, even within a system often perceived as inherently corrupt. His personal journey underscored the idea that redemption was possible and that even those who had participated in wrongdoing could find a way to make amends and contribute to a better future.

The long-term effects of the Martel scandal continued to unfold over the years. The city of Wilder, scarred but not broken, gradually emerged from the shadows of corruption. The legal battles continued, with appeals and counter appeals dragging on, but the eventual outcome remained unchanged. Victor Martel remained behind bars, a stark reminder of the consequences of unchecked power. The city adopted new ethics codes, reformed its regulatory systems, and implemented stricter oversight measures. Its citizens, once passive observers, transformed into vigilant participants in their governance, forever wary of the seductive lure of power and the insidious creep of corruption.

The story of Victor Martel's downfall wasn't merely a tale of crime and punishment; it was a narrative of resilience, of the collective will of a community to confront its darkest truths and emerge stronger, more transparent, and far more determined to ensure that such a dark chapter in its history would never again be repeated. The echoes of the scandal faded into the background hum of Wilder's civic life, but the lessons learned remained, etched into the collective memory, serving as a constant reminder of the fragility of justice and the enduring struggle for truth and accountability. The fight was far from over, but Wilder City had taken its first decisive steps toward a brighter, more honest future. The shadow of Martel lingered, a ghost in the city's memory, but the city had found its voice, its strength, and its unwavering resolve to fight the darkness and uphold the light of justice.

Emotional Toll on Alice

The victory felt hollow. The courtroom's sterile air, thick with the scent of tension and relief, had barely cleared before the weight of the past several years crashed down on Alice. The adrenaline, the relentless drive that had fueled her investigation, dissipated, leaving behind a gnawing emptiness. Martel's conviction, the culmination of years of painstaking work, should have been a moment of triumphant release. Instead, it felt like the end of a long, arduous journey through a dark and desolate landscape, a journey that had left its scars etched deep within her soul.

The relentless pursuit of justice had demanded a price. Her apartment, once a haven of quiet solitude, now felt like a stranger's space, filled with the ghosts of sleepless nights and the echoes of countless phone calls, whispered conversations, and the frantic scribbling of notes. The meticulously organized files and meticulously arranged evidence – a testament to her dedication – now felt like physical manifestations of the burden she carried. They were trophies of a war she'd won, but they were also grim reminders of the battles fought, and the losses incurred.

Sleep became a luxury she could rarely afford. Nights were filled with fragmented memories: the chilling details of Martel's crimes, the faces of his victims, and the cold indifference of those who had turned a blind eye. Days were a blur of meetings, interviews, and the relentless pressure to ensure that Martel's network was completely dismantled. The pressure to ensure that no stone was left unturned, that no thread was left unraveled, was a crushing weight that bore down on her constantly. She found herself staring blankly at her computer screen, the flickering cursor mocking a reminder of the enormity of the task ahead.

Her relationships suffered. Friends, once understanding and supportive, began to distance themselves, unable to comprehend the depth of her commitment or the toll it was taking on her. The constant strain, the emotional turmoil, and the overwhelming sense of responsibility had created an invisible wall between her and those closest to her.

Dates were missed, calls were unanswered, and the simple joys of everyday life seemed to fade into insignificance. The world outside her investigation had become muted and pale compared to the intensity of the darkness she was battling.

She had sacrificed almost everything – her personal life, her health, even her sanity – on the altar of justice. The lines between her professional life and personal life had blurred to the point of nonexistence, leaving her feeling profoundly isolated and alone. The secret nature of her work amplified the sense of isolation, the clandestine meetings, the hushed conversations, and the knowledge that she was walking a tightrope, constantly balancing on the edge of danger. She felt the weight of the city's hopes resting on her shoulders, the pressure to deliver a result for a city grappling with the aftermath of Martel's decades-long reign of terror.

The physical toll was equally apparent. The bags under her eyes had deepened, and her once-vibrant hair seemed to have lost its luster. She barely recognized the reflection staring back at her from the mirror, a weary ghost haunted by the shadows of the investigation. The constant stress had manifested itself in recurring headaches, insomnia, and a general sense of exhaustion that went beyond physical tiredness. It was an exhaustion of the soul, a deep-seated weariness born of years spent navigating the treacherous terrain of corruption and deceit.

Even the small victories, the incremental successes in unraveling Martel's network, felt meaningless in the face of the overwhelming scale of the problem. Each small breakthrough only uncovered further layers of depravity, further evidence of the pervasive nature of Martel's influence, sending her spiraling further into a pit of despair. She found herself questioning her sanity, wondering if it was worth it. The cost seemed too high, and she started to feel trapped.

The weight of responsibility – the knowledge that the future of the city, the safety of its citizens, rested, in some measure, upon her shoulders – was suffocating. She had become hyper-vigilant, constantly scanning the environment, anticipating threats where there were none. Paranoia had become her constant companion, an unwelcome house guest who refused to leave. She feared for her safety; she worried that Martel's associates might seek retribution; she was plagued by the unsettling realization that she had become a target.

One evening, after a particularly grueling day spent sifting through mountains of financial records, Alice found herself staring out of her window at the city lights, a wave of profound sadness washing over her. The city she had fought so hard to protect, the city she had poured her heart and soul into saving, looked beautiful from afar. But up close, she knew, its beauty masked a deep-seated sickness, a corruption that ran far deeper than Martel himself. She had achieved something great, something profound; she had brought a monster to justice. But the realization struck her like a physical blow: She had won the battle, but she was losing the war against her inner demons.

It was then, gazing at the twinkling lights of Wilder, that Alice knew she needed help. The relentless pursuit of justice had almost broken her. She realized she could not continue alone. The burden she had carried for so long was too heavy, too crushing. The weight of responsibility, the emotional toll, the sacrifices made – it was all too much. She realized she needed to confront the damage to heal the wounds that the investigation had inflicted. For the first time, she allowed herself to admit that she was not invincible, that she needed support, and that she needed to acknowledge her humanity and her limitations. She needed to seek help, confront the ghosts of the past, and find a way to move forward to begin the long, difficult process of rebuilding her life. The fight for justice was far from over, but Alice knew that she needed to take care of herself first if she was going to continue the fight and emerge victoriously from this war, not just for the city but for herself. The victory over Martel had been hard-won.

Now, the battle for her recovery had begun.

Healing and Recovery

The first step was admitting she needed help. It was a terrifying admission, a vulnerability she hadn't allowed herself to feel in years. The image of herself, strong and unflappable — the woman who had brought down Martel — clashed violently with the fragile, exhausted woman staring back at her from the mirror. She booked an appointment with Dr. Eleanor Vance, a therapist specializing in trauma and PTSD, her hands shaking slightly as she made the call. The shame of needing help, of acknowledging her own fragility, was almost overwhelming, but the desire to heal, to reclaim her life, was stronger.

Dr. Vance's office was a sanctuary; a calming space filled with soft light and the aroma of lavender. It was a stark contrast to the harsh, unforgiving world of the investigation. The first few sessions were difficult, an agonizing process of unpacking years of repressed trauma and buried emotions. Alice found herself reliving the horrors she had witnessed, the faces of the victims haunting her waking hours and seeping into her dreams. She spoke of the sleepless nights, the crippling anxiety, the constant feeling of being watched, the ever-present shadow of Martel's influence lingering over her life.

The therapy was slow, painstaking work. Dr. Vance guided her through the maze of her own mind, helping her to confront the deep-seated emotional wounds that the investigation had inflicted. Cognitive Behavioral Therapy (CBT) helped Alice challenge the negative thought patterns and beliefs that had taken root. Exposure therapy, a gradual process of confronting traumatic memories, was excruciating but ultimately necessary. Slowly, painstakingly, Alice began to unravel the knots of trauma that had bound her for so long.

The support of her friends, once distant and hesitant, became crucial. They didn't fully understand the depths of what she'd endured, but they offered unwavering support — listening patiently, offering a shoulder to cry on, and simply being present. They brought her meals, offered to run errands, and gently encouraged her to reengage with the life she had almost lost. Small acts of kindness, simple gestures of friendship, became anchors in the storm.

The city, too, began its own healing process. Martel's conviction, while a significant victory, was not the end of the story. It was a turning point, a moment of reckoning that prompted a long overdue examination of the systemic corruption that had allowed Martel to flourish for so long. The city council launched an independent inquiry into the police department, a process that revealed deeper layers of malfeasance and cover-ups. Reform was slow — agonizingly slow — but it was a start.

The community, initially paralyzed by fear and uncertainty, slowly started to rebuild its trust in the authorities. Community meetings were held, offering spaces for people to share their experiences, to express their anger, their grief, their fear, and to collectively begin the process of healing. Support groups were established, providing a safe space for victims and their families to find solace and strength in shared experiences. Memorials were erected, honoring the victims of Martel's crimes and serving as reminders of the importance of justice and accountability.

Alice played a key role in this community healing. Although still grappling with her own demons, she felt a responsibility to use her experience to facilitate healing for others. She shared her story not to seek sympathy but to provide hope — to inspire others to speak out against injustice and to find the strength to move forward. She became a symbol of hope, a testament to the power of perseverance and the possibility of overcoming trauma. Her testimony before the city council, detailing Martel's crimes and the systemic failures that had allowed them to happen, was pivotal in the reform process.

The healing process was not linear. There were setbacks, moments of doubt, and times when the weight of the past threatened to overwhelm her once again. But each time, she found the strength to push forward, to keep moving, to continue her journey toward recovery. She learned to manage her anxiety, to practice self-care, and to set healthy boundaries. She rediscovered the simple joys of life, finding solace in nature, connecting with loved ones, and pursuing creative outlets like painting and writing. She started a blog chronicling her journey and offering hope and inspiration to other survivors of trauma.

The city, too, experienced its own periods of relapse, its own setbacks. The fight against corruption was far from over, the wounds of the past still raw. But the collective commitment to change — the shared resolve to build a better future — was undeniable. Martel's downfall had created a ripple effect, prompting wider conversation about social justice, systemic inequalities, and the importance of fostering a culture of accountability.

Alice found solace in the small acts of kindness that the community showed her in recognition of her courage and sacrifice. She felt a sense of purpose, a renewed sense of hope, knowing that her work had not only brought Martel to justice but had also triggered a profound transformation within the city. She had emerged from the darkness, scared but not broken. The scars remained — a reminder of the battles fought, and the losses incurred — but they were also a testament to her resilience, her unwavering commitment to justice, and the enduring power of the human spirit to heal and overcome adversity.

Years later, Alice stood on a hill overlooking the city, the cityscape glowing beneath the evening sky. The twinkling lights were no longer a reminder of the darkness she had fought but a symbol of hope, a testament to the resilience of the city and its people. The memories of Martel's crimes still lingered, but they no longer held the power to define her. She had found peace, not in forgetting, but in remembering it, in accepting her scars and in cherishing the life she had painstakingly rebuilt. The victory had been hard-won, the healing process long and arduous, but Alice had emerged from the crucible of trauma stronger, wiser, and more determined than ever to fight for a world where justice prevails and healing is possible.

The war was over, but the journey continued — a journey of ongoing growth, self-discovery, and a renewed commitment to building a brighter future, not just for herself but for the city she loved.

Accountability and Consequences

The courtroom was hushed, the air thick with anticipation. Martel sat at the defendant's table, his usual swagger replaced by nervous fidgeting. He glanced around, his eyes darting from the jury to the judge, a flicker of fear momentarily breaking through his carefully constructed façade of arrogance. Across from him, Alice sat, her presence a stark contrast to the turmoil swirling within. She had spent months preparing for this moment, poring over evidence, reliving the trauma, of herself for the emotional onslaught that lay ahead.

The prosecution presented a mountain of evidence— meticulously documented financial records detailing Martel's corrupt dealings, intercepted communications revealing his network of accomplices, and harrowing testimonies from victims who had bravely stepped forward to share their stories. Each piece of evidence hammered another nail into Martel's coffin, exposing the intricate web of deceit he had woven. The weight of the accumulated crimes, laid bare for all to see, was suffocating. Alice's testimony, delivered with unwavering clarity and chilling detail, was a pivotal moment. She spoke of fear, manipulation, and the systemic corruption that had allowed Martel to operate with impunity for so long. Her voice, though strained at times by the weight of her experience, resonated with quiet strength, her words painting a vivid picture of the horrors Martel had inflicted.

The defense, predictably, attempted to discredit Alice, questioning her motives, casting doubt on her sanity, and employing the tired tactics of intimidation. They painted her as a woman consumed by vengeance, blinded by rage, an unreliable narrator driven by personal vendettas. However, the sheer volume of irrefutable evidence, bolstered by the corroborating testimonies of other victims and witnesses, rendered their attempts futile. The jury, composed of ordinary citizens, listened intently, their faces reflecting the gravity of the situation. The responsibility to deliver justice, to hold a powerful man accountable for his heinous crimes, rested heavily on their shoulders.

The trial lasted for weeks, a grueling ordeal for all involved. Alice found herself reliving the trauma each day, forced to confront the memories she had so carefully buried. The process was agonizing, a constant tug-of-war between her determination to seek justice and the overwhelming desire to simply escape the pain. The support of her friends and Dr. Vance was unwavering, providing her with the strength to endure. She learned to compartmentalize and detach from the emotional turmoil to maintain focus and testify effectively.

The verdict came as no surprise. The jury, after careful deliberation, found Martel guilty on all counts. The courtroom erupted in a wave of relief, a collective sigh of justice served. The judge, his voice measured yet firm, delivered the sentence—a lengthy prison term, a life sentence effectively, given Martel's age and the nature of his crimes. The sound of the gavel striking, echoing through the silent courtroom, marked not just the end of the trial but also a turning point in the city's long road to healing.

Martel's conviction, however, was just the beginning. The investigation broadened, extending its tentacles into the higher echelons of the police department and city government. Numerous officers were implicated in the cover-ups and forced to resign or face criminal charges. Several politicians, once held in high esteem, faced investigations for their role in protecting Martel and facilitating his corrupt activities. The systemic corruption that had allowed Martel to thrive was finally being exposed, laid bare for public scrutiny. The city council, under immense pressure, launched a comprehensive review of police procedures, establishing stricter guidelines for transparency and accountability.

The legal battles continued, with various appeals and lawsuits dragging on for years. But the momentum had shifted. The city's commitment to justice and reform was undeniable. The independent inquiry into the police department revealed a culture of impunity and a systemic disregard for the law and the rights of citizens. The report detailed numerous instances of corruption, misconduct, and cover-ups, revealing a deeply entrenched problem that required far-reaching reforms. The ensuing changes were gradual, slow, and painstaking, but they were real. New policies were implemented, designed to enhance transparency, promote ethical conduct, and foster greater accountability within the law enforcement system. Internal affairs units were strengthened, investigative procedures were modernized, and extensive training programs were implemented to address issues of bias, corruption, and abuse of power.

The impact extended beyond the realm of law enforcement. The city's legal battles catalyzed broader reforms in other sectors of government. Transparency legislation was passed, strengthening oversight mechanisms and enhancing public access to government information. Ethics committees were created, tasked with investigating allegations of corruption and misconduct within various government bodies. The city's legal battles served as a harsh yet necessary lesson, underscoring the importance of integrity, transparency, and accountability in public service.

The ripple effects extended to the community as well. Victims of Martel's crimes, many of whom had been silenced for years, found their voices. They shared their stories, not just in court but in public forums, community meetings, and support groups. The process of healing was not easy, but the act of speaking out—of sharing their experiences—empowered them, giving them a sense of agency and control over their lives. The city's collective effort to confront its past and rebuild trust provided a sense of collective catharsis, a shared journey toward healing. Memorials were erected to honor the victims of Martel's crimes, serving as constant reminders of the importance of justice and the need to prevent such atrocities from ever happening again.

Alice, having given her testimony, actively participated in shaping this new era of accountability and transparency. She became a vocal advocate for victims' rights, working tirelessly to ensure that those who had suffered under Martel's reign of terror received justice and support. She collaborated with various organizations involved in trauma support and rehabilitation, sharing her experience and offering guidance to those on similar paths. She never forgot the scars inflicted upon her, both physical and emotional. But she transformed those scars into a testament to her resilience and her determination to fight for a world where justice prevails and healing is possible.

The journey of accountability and consequence was far from over, but the city, guided by the collective resolve to confront its past and build a better future, had embarked upon a path of healing and lasting change. The scars remained, but they were now interwoven with threads of hope, resilience, and the enduring human capacity for renewal and justice.

New Beginning

The city of Wilder was no longer the same. The shadows of Victor Martel's empire had finally lifted, revealing a community both wounded and awakened. From the ruins of corruption, something new was beginning to take shape—slowly, cautiously, but unmistakably. Change was no longer a distant promise; it was a living reality. New leadership had emerged, inspired by the hard-won lessons of the past. Reform-minded officials, community advocates, and once-silenced citizens were now active participants in reshaping the city's future.

Alice, too, was transformed. The woman who had once buried herself in case files and courtrooms now found herself at a different kind of threshold. She stood no longer as just an investigator, but as a survivor, a builder, a guide. She had turned her experiences—the trauma, the fight, the victories, and defeats—into a blueprint for renewal. Her advocacy work expanded into policy reform, helping draft new laws aimed at increasing transparency, protecting whistleblowers, and providing greater support for victims of institutional abuse.

She also began teaching part-time at a local university, offering seminars on investigative journalism, ethics, and resilience in the face of systemic failure. Her story had become a case study—her name a symbol of the quiet force of integrity. Students, journalists, and civic leaders alike looked to her as a mentor, someone who had not only witnessed history but helped rewrite it.

Isabella Martel, once a reluctant witness and a survivor of an abusive marriage, found her own calling in advocacy. With the support of Alice and other survivors, she founded a nonprofit focused on domestic abuse awareness and legal support for victims trapped in powerful relationships. Her voice, once silenced by fear and shame, now carried weight across courtrooms, community centers, and media outlets. Her journey from isolation to empowerment inspired many, becoming a testament to the healing power of truth.

The city, still bearing its scars, had become more vigilant. Citizen oversight committees remained active, regularly meeting to ensure that promises of reform did not fade into complacency. Schools began incorporating civic ethics into their curriculum. Police-community dialogues became more frequent, and while trust wasn't instantly restored, it was slowly being rebuilt. Art, music, and literature flourished again—this time not as a mask for corruption but as expressions of hope, mourning, and resilience.

Alice's home, once a battlefield of late-night strategies and shadowy fears, became a sanctuary again. She adopted a dog, filled her bookshelves with novels instead of case files, and planted a small garden on her balcony. There were still moments of darkness—flashbacks, sleepless nights, echoes of old trauma—but they were no longer consuming. They were part of her, woven into the narrative of who she had become but not defining her future.

The city didn't forget. Memorials and public archives have preserved the story of the Martel case, not to glorify it, but to warn and teach. Every policy, every new civic measure, bore the imprint of that history. People remained watchful—not paranoid, but aware. Because they knew now how easily power could corrupt and how important it was to protect the light they had reclaimed.

And in this cautious, collective awakening, Alice finally found peace, not the absence of pain, but the presence of purpose. The fight had changed her, but it hadn't destroyed her. The city had changed too, and together they had emerged—bruised but standing, wiser and more willing to fight for what mattered.

This was a new beginning. And this time, everyone was watching.

Lingering Effects

The city's newfound tranquility was deceptive. Beneath the surface, a simmering unease persisted. The scars left by the Martel case, while less visible, were far from healing. For many, the trial's conclusion offered only a fragile sense of justice, a temporary balm on deep-seated wounds. The shadow of Martel's reign still stretched long, impacting every aspect of daily life.

The police department, though reformed, remained under intense scrutiny. While the implementation of body cameras, improved training, and enhanced internal affairs units represented significant progress, skepticism lingered. The cynicism bred by years of corruption wasn't easily eradicated. Public trust, once shattered, was slowly, painstakingly being rebuilt, one interaction, one honest investigation at a time. The recruits, idealistic and eager to prove themselves, were met with a cautious welcome by a community scarred by betrayal. The older officers, some carrying their baggage from the Martel era, navigated the changes with varying degrees of enthusiasm, some embracing the reforms wholeheartedly, while others grumbled about unnecessary restrictions.

The effect on the city's economy was profound. The Martel organization's tentacles had reached every sector, from construction and real estate to waste management and entertainment. The dismantling of his empire left a trail of financial devastation, bankrupt businesses, and job losses. The city's economic recovery was slow, a gradual climb back from the precipice. New businesses emerged, cautiously optimistic, but the specter of corruption lingered, a reminder of the fragility of economic stability. The investigation into Martel's financial dealings continued long after his conviction, revealing a network of shell corporations, offshore accounts, and laundered funds that stretched across international borders. The ensuing legal battles, protracted and complex, further tested the city's resilience.

The psychological impact on the city's residents was arguably the most profound and long-lasting consequence. The collective trauma of the Martel era manifested in various ways: increased anxiety levels, heightened mistrust of authority figures, and a pervasive sense of unease. The city's mental health services were strained, struggling to cope with the surge in demand. Support groups proliferated, offering a space for individuals to share their experiences, to process their trauma, and to find solace in shared understanding. The long-term effects on the children who witnessed or were indirectly affected by Martel's crimes were particularly concerning, with many exhibiting behavioral problems and emotional distress. Specialized programs were developed to address the unique needs of these children, providing them with the support and therapy they required to overcome their trauma.

Alice, despite her healing, found herself increasingly drawn to the task of aiding those still struggling to cope. Her foundation, originally conceived as a means of supporting victims of crime, evolved into a comprehensive support network, providing legal assistance, counseling, and advocacy for those marginalized by the legal system. She worked tirelessly to connect victims with resources, offering a hand of support and empowering them to reclaim their lives. Her advocacy extended to pushing for legislation that would strengthen protections for victims, ensure their voices were heard, and prevent similar tragedies from occurring in the future. Her work became a testament to the transformative power of resilience, a beacon of hope in the shadow of Martel's legacy.

The political landscape, though seemingly reformed, still showed signs of the deep-seated corruption that had thrived under Martel's shadow. While new faces had been elected, pledging transparency and accountability, old habits die hard. The subtle manipulations, the whispered deals, the quiet compromises – these were the insidious undercurrents that threatened to undermine the progress made. A watchful eye was necessary, a constant vigilance to ensure that the city's hard-won gains weren't squandered. Regular audits of city funds became commonplace, transparency laws were meticulously enforced, and the newly formed ethics committees worked tirelessly to ensure adherence to the new regulations. However, the suspicion that the system might still be vulnerable remained a persistent undercurrent, a constant reminder of the fragility of change.

The media, initially laid out for its role in exposing

Martel's crimes, found itself embroiled in new debates. The line between investigative journalism and sensationalism blurred. While some outlets continued their commitment to truth and accountability, others succumbed to the allure of sensational headlines and ratings, sometimes jeopardizing the delicate healing process. The tension between providing information to the public and potentially hindering the ongoing efforts toward reform posed a considerable challenge to the press. A careful balance had to be struck, ensuring that the city's fragile progress wasn't undone by reckless or biased reporting.

The memorial to the victims of Martel's crimes became a central point of reflection for the city. It was more than a monument; it was a symbol of remembrance, a place for healing and a reminder of the price of injustice. The names etched into the stone were more than just inscriptions; they represented the lives lost, the families torn apart, the communities devastated. It served as a constant reminder that the fight for justice wasn't over, that vigilance was needed to prevent similar horrors from ever happening again. The memorial became a place of quiet contemplation, a space where individuals could find solace and connect with the shared experience of loss. It was a reminder of the human cost of corruption and the importance of safeguarding the city's future.

Even years later, the city's recovery was ongoing. The wounds inflicted by Martel's reign ran deep, leaving a legacy of mistrust, cynicism, and a lingering sense of vulnerability. Yet, amidst the scars, a quiet strength emerged, a testament to the city's resilience and its unwavering commitment to creating a better future. Alice, watching the city evolve, felt a sense of cautious optimism. The journey had been arduous, the pain profound, but the city, like her, was showing remarkable signs of healing. The road ahead remained long and challenging, but the city's newfound commitment to justice, accountability, and transparency offered a glimmer of hope, a promise of a brighter tomorrow. The symphony of city life, once muted and discordant, was gradually regaining its harmony, a testament to the enduring strength of the human spirit and the transformative power of collective healing. The scars remained, a permanent reminder of a dark chapter in the city's history, but they were now interwoven with the vibrant threads of resilience, hope, and a tenacious pursuit of a better tomorrow.

Alice's Reflection

The chipped paint on the windowsill mirrored the cracks in the facade of the city's newfound peace. From her office, high above the bustling streets, Alice watched the evening rush hour unfold, the taillights stretching into a river of red, a relentless flow that both fascinated and unsettled her. The Martel case was closed, the man himself behind bars, but the city, like a body bearing deep wounds, still bore the scars of his reign. The silence in her office was punctuated only by the rhythmic tick-tock of the grandfather clock, a constant reminder of time's relentless march forward, a march she couldn't quite keep pace with.

She traced the rim of her coffee cup, the lukewarm liquid reflecting the city lights. The past few years had been a blur of activity, a whirlwind of legal battles, fundraising events, and counseling sessions. She'd poured every ounce of her energy into her foundation, into helping others navigate the labyrinthine aftermath of Martel's reign. It had been a relentless, exhausting pursuit, but one that had, paradoxically, brought her a sense of purpose, a grounding she hadn't realized she craved.

Her reflection stared back at her – tired eyes, etched with the weight of countless stories, a weariness that spoke of battles fought and won, and those still simmering. Yet, there was a strength in her gaze, a resilience homed in the fires of adversity. She'd seen the worst of humanity, the depths of depravity Martel and his cronies had plumbed, yet she'd also witnessed the extraordinary resilience of the human spirit, the unwavering capacity for hope and healing.

The memories came in waves, sometimes gentle ripples, other times crashing surges. She remembered the terrified faces of the victims, the desperate pleas for help, and the broken trust that had to be painstakingly rebuilt. She remembered the long nights spent poring over documents, the endless phone calls, the frustrating legal maneuvers. She'd been hardened by the experience but not broken. The experience hadn't just left scars; it had forged her into something stronger, more determined.

The city had changed, but not entirely. The new police chief, a man of integrity, had implemented sweeping reforms, but the deep-seated cynicism remained. It lingered like a phantom pain, a constant reminder of the system's past failures. The media, initially hailed as heroes for exposing Martel, was now embroiled in its own battles – wrestling with the ethics of reporting, grappling with the balance between public information and the need for sensitive, responsible journalism. Even the political landscape, seemingly cleansed of Martel's influence, still showed subtle signs of the corruption that had once thrived unchecked.

Alice had seen firsthand the fragility of justice, the slow, arduous process of rebuilding trust. She'd learned that justice wasn't just about convictions and sentences; it was about healing, about restoring faith in the system, about creating a society where such horrors could never happen again. Her foundation wasn't just about providing legal aid and counseling; it was about fostering a sense of community, about empowering survivors to reclaim their lives, their voices, their dignity.

The foundation had become more than she'd ever imagined. It started as a small, personal endeavor to support victims, but it had grown into a network of support, providing legal assistance, counseling, job training, and even housing assistance to those who'd lost everything. She'd forged partnerships with local businesses, secured grants from national organizations, and even managed to lobby for changes in legislation that would strengthen protections for crime victims.

But the emotional toll was significant. The weight of other people's trauma rested heavily on her shoulders, a constant, subtle pressure that could easily overwhelm her. She'd learned to recognize the signs of burnout, to prioritize her well-being, and to seek support from her friends and family. She'd found solace in nature, in long walks by the ocean, in the quiet solitude of her small cottage outside the city.

There were moments of doubt, moments when she questioned the impact of her work, moments when the sheer magnitude of the problem threatened to engulf her. She'd seen how easily the city could slide back into its old patterns, how readily cynicism could take root. But then she'd remember the faces of the people she'd helped, the smiles of gratitude, the renewed sense of hope in their eyes. And those moments, those small victories, were what kept her going.

The grandfather clock chimed, marking the passage of another hour. The city lights below shimmered, a tapestry of lights and shadows. Alice stood up, stretching her weary muscles. She looked out at the city, its skyline etched against the darkening sky, a skyline that was slowly, gradually, healing. The scars remained, visible and invisible, a reminder of a dark chapter in its history. But the city was resilient, and so was she. The fight for justice wasn't over, but the journey, she knew, was worth it. The fight was a marathon, not a sprint, and she was ready to run the distance.

The future was uncertain, but she felt a quiet confidence, a belief in the power of resilience, in the human capacity for hope, in the transformative power of a city determined to rise from the ashes. The scars were a part of the story, a testament to the struggles overcome, but they didn't define the city or her. They were merely a backdrop to a future that promised healing, growth, and a tenacious pursuit of a brighter dawn. And Alice, weary but unwavering, was ready to help the city, and its people, reach it.

The Cost of Justice

The city's newfound tranquility was a fragile thing; a veneer painted over deep-seated anxieties. While Martel was incarcerated, the reverberations of his crimes continued to echo. The cost of justice, I discovered, wasn't simply measured in courtroom victories or prison sentences. It was a far more intricate and insidious calculation, a ledger filled with personal sacrifices, societal compromises, and lingering uncertainties.

For the victims, the cost was immeasurable. The physical scars, in some cases, were evident – the jagged lines of healed wounds, the lingering tremors of a hand once brutally injured. But the deeper scars, the emotional ones, were far more difficult to see, the more difficult to heal. I saw it in the haunted eyes of Sarah Jenkins, her voice trembling as she recounted the night Martel's men had invaded her home. The theft of her jewelry was inconsequential compared to the violation of her sanctuary, the lingering fear that clung to her like a second skin. Years later, she still struggled with sleep, her dreams populated by shadowy figures and the chilling echo of shattering glass. Therapy helped, but the constant vigilance, the hyper-awareness of her surroundings, remained. This, I realized, was the true cost of trauma – the invisible chains that bound victims to their past, preventing them from moving freely into the future.

The cost extended to their families as well. The ripple effect of Martel's crimes had fractured families, strained relationships, and even torn communities apart.

Children witnessed events that left them scared, their innocent worlds irrevocably altered. Spouses were left to pick up the pieces, grappling with the emotional and financial fallout, bearing the weight of their loved ones' trauma alongside their own. The strain on their resources, both emotional and financial, was palpable. Many struggled to find employment, haunted by the lingering effects of what they'd experienced. The support system, though vital, was often insufficient, leaving many to navigate their recovery alone, fighting battles on multiple fronts simultaneously.

The police officers, the very individuals charged with protecting the city, bore the brunt of a different kind of burden. They had faced Martel's brutality head-on, engaging in confrontations that tested their physical and emotional limits. I'd seen the exhaustion in their eyes, the weariness that settled in their bones after countless hours spent chasing shadows, battling corruption, and enduring the constant threat of retaliation. One detective, Mark Olsen, confided in me that he suffered from nightmares long after the Martel case concluded. The faces of victims, the brutality of the scenes he'd witnessed, haunted him relentlessly, creating a chasm between his professional life and the semblance of peace he attempted to maintain at home. His marriage was strained, his children distant, collateral damage in the war against crime. His resilience was remarkable, but his personal life had paid the price for his commitment to duty.

The cost wasn't confined to individuals; it extended to the system itself. The Martel case exposed deep-seated flaws in law enforcement and political corruption that allowed his reign of terror to persist for so long.

The investigation itself had been expensive, draining public funds that could have been used elsewhere. The subsequent trials, the endless appeals, added to the financial strain, creating a complex and expensive web of legal battles. There were the costs of reforming the police department, strengthening community ties, and rebuilding public trust—an immeasurable investment of resources and time.

The media, initially lauded for its role in exposing Martel, faced its ethical dilemmas. The rush to publish, the pressure to get the story first, had sometimes compromised journalistic integrity. The focus on the sensational aspects of the case, while capturing the public's attention, had also risked overshadowing the suffering of the victims and the long-term implications of the crime. There were allegations of biased reporting, accusations of sensationalism, and a broader conversation about responsible journalism reckoning that extended beyond a singular case and delved into the heart of media ethics.

The political landscape also bore a heavy cost. Martel's influence had corrupted the political system, creating a climate of fear and apathy. The investigation and subsequent prosecution had exposed deep-rooted corruption and sparked calls for reform, leading to a tumultuous political climate. Elections were contested, reputations were tarnished, and the public's faith in the government was shaken slowly and painstaking process of rebuilding trust would be needed. The cost, in terms of political instability and uncertainty, had been significant.

But perhaps the greatest cost of justice was the erosion of hope. The pervasive sense of cynicism that permeated the city after Martel's reign was a palpable entity. People were hesitant to trust the authorities, doubtful of the system's ability to protect them. The feeling of vulnerability, the fear that similar crimes could happen again, was a constant companion, creating an atmosphere of suspicion and distrust. The healing process required the systematic rebuilding of faith, not just in the institutions of justice, but also in the community's capacity for resilience and mutual support.

My cost was considerable. The weight of the Martel case, the constant pressure to achieve justice, had taken its toll. The long hours, the emotional exhaustion, the relentless scrutiny – it had all contributed to a sense of pervasive burnout. The nightmares, the constant replay of the trial details in my mind, left me drained and emotionally raw. My relationships suffered, my work-life balance became non-existent, and my personal life became a casualty of my dedication. I had found a strange solace in my work, a sense of purpose that eclipsed my personal needs. Yet, it was a hard-won battle, constantly reminding me of the true cost of my commitment.

Yet, despite the costs, I knew that justice, however imperfect, was worth fighting for. The scars remained, both visible and invisible, a constant reminder of the trauma Martel inflicted. The personal sacrifices, the societal compromises, the lingering uncertainties – they were all part of the complex equation of achieving justice. It wasn't a clean, straightforward process. It was messy, complicated, and at times, deeply disheartening. But for those who had suffered under Martel's reign, the pursuit of justice, the fight for accountability, was a necessary step towards healing, towards rebuilding their lives and restoring their faith in the system. The scars would remain, a permanent mark on the city, but the pursuit of justice was a testament to the enduring strength of the human spirit, a testament to the tireless work of those who sought to make the world a safer, more equitable place, and I would continue to fight alongside them.

Closure for Victims' Families

The trial's conclusion didn't mark an end, but rather a transitional shift from the acute phase of crisis to the long, arduous process of healing. For the families of Martel's victims, this was a journey fraught with complexities, marked by both progress and setbacks. Sarah Jenkins, for instance, while relieved by Martel's conviction, found that the legal victory offered little solace for the persistent fear that still clung to her. The nightmares continued, though their intensity had lessened. She began attending a support group, finding comfort in the shared experiences of others who understood her silent screams. The group offered a safe space to articulate her fears, to acknowledge the trauma without the judgmental stares that had plagued her in the past. This sense of community, she discovered, was as vital as the professional therapy she'd sought. It was in the shared silences, the unspoken understanding, that she found a pathway towards acceptance.

For the families of those who hadn't survived Martel's brutality, the path to closure was even steeper. The loss of a loved one is a profound wound, one that often heals, but never erases. The death of their loved ones at Martel's hands compounded this grief, imbuing it with a sense of injustice, of anger that bordered on rage. The legal proceedings, while necessary, felt insufficient, a hollow echo in the face of their devastating loss. Many found themselves struggling to navigate their grief alongside the emotional and logistical demands of life. Simple tasks became overwhelming, the mundane routines that once defined their existence now felt impossibly heavy, weighted down by the absence of the person they'd lost.

The financial burden, often overlooked in the aftermath of such tragedies, was also significant. Medical bills, funeral expenses, and the loss of income from a spouse or primary caregiver created an economic strain that added to their emotional turmoil. Some families struggled to keep their homes, facing eviction and displacement during a period when stability was desperately needed. Others were forced to sell cherished possessions, sacrificing tangible connections to their loved ones as they grappled with the intangible loss of their presence. The legal battles, while crucial for holding Martel accountable, proved to be a drain on both their emotional reserves and their financial resources. The extensive legal fees and the countless hours spent attending hearings and court proceedings took a toll on their ability to grieve and begin the healing process.

The community stepped in where official support systems fell short. Local charities and churches organized fundraisers, providing families with financial aid and practical support. Neighbors rallied together, offering meals, childcare, and a network of support that helped them navigate the daily challenges. These acts of kindness, these small gestures of solidarity, became beacons of hope in a landscape of despair. It was in the ordinary acts of compassion – a warm meal, a helping hand, a listening ear – that families found solace and strength. The community became a lifeline, a source of unwavering support during a time of immeasurable loss. These shared acts of human connection served as a reminder of their shared humanity, their shared resilience, and their capacity to help each other heal.

Yet, amidst the darkness, glimmers of healing emerged. Some families found solace in creating memorials, in establishing foundations dedicated to fighting crime and preventing future tragedies. The creation of these memorials allowed them to channel their grief into productive action, transforming their pain into a force for positive change. They advocated stricter laws, for increased resources for victim support, and for greater transparency within the legal system. Their tireless advocacy served as a testament to their resilience, to their determination to prevent future victims from suffering the same fate. These families transformed their private grief into a public purpose, striving not only to heal themselves but to help prevent others from experiencing the unimaginable pain they had endured.

For others, healing came through unexpected avenues. The shared experience of the support group allowed individuals to reconnect with their own strength and to find solace in the shared struggles of others. Art therapy, writing, and other creative outlets provided a space for emotional release, allowing victims and their families to articulate their pain and express their emotions in a healthy way. The process was not linear; it was messy, full of ups and downs, moments of breakthroughs and moments of regression. Healing isn't a destination but a journey, a slow and painstaking process marked by both progress and setbacks. It's a journey that demands both individual resilience and communal support.

The passage of time, however, played a crucial role in their healing process. The sharp edges of their grief gradually softened, the overwhelming sense of loss gradually yielding to a more nuanced understanding of their pain. They learned to integrate their trauma into the fabric of their lives, to find meaning in their continued existence, and to find ways to honor the memory of those they had lost. They learned to forgive, not necessarily the perpetrator, but themselves, for their own struggles and shortcomings. Forgiveness, in its essence, was a profound act of self-compassion, a testament to their resilience, their unwavering spirit, and their ability to transform pain into purpose. It was a journey toward wholeness, a journey that affirmed the capacity of the human spirit to persevere, to heal, and to find meaning amidst the wreckage of tragedy.

The city itself began a slow but steady process of rebuilding trust. Martel's conviction was a significant step, a validation of the judicial process and a measure of justice. But the scars remained, visible and invisible, etched into the psyche of the community. The work of healing extended beyond the courtroom, into the very fabric of the city's life. The local government, spurred by public pressure, invested in crime prevention programs and initiatives designed to enhance community safety. New community centers and support networks emerged, fostering a sense of shared purpose and mutual support. These were small steps, but they represented a commitment to building a more resilient, a more secure future for all.

The media's role in this process was complex. While initial reporting had at times sensationalized aspects of the case, the city's collective grief eventually fostered a more nuanced and compassionate approach to reporting on trauma. Journalists recognized the importance of prioritizing victims' voices, avoiding gratuitous descriptions of violence, and focusing instead on the broader implications of the case. There was a shift towards responsible reporting, a greater sensitivity to the long-term consequences of trauma, and a concerted effort to avoid further victimization through insensitive portrayals.

Ultimately, the road to closure for victims' families was a personal journey, one marked by individual challenges and collective resilience. It was a path that demanded courage, compassion, and an unwavering commitment to justice. While the scars of Martel's crimes would remain, etched into the city's memory, the pursuit of justice, and the collective healing that followed, served as a testament to the enduring strength of the human spirit. It was a reminder that even in the face of unimaginable pain, hope endures, and healing, however imperfect, remains possible. The pursuit of justice wasn't just about punishing the guilty; it was about empowering survivors and fostering a safer, more equitable future for all.

The Road Ahead

The trial's conclusion, the gavel's final thud, felt strangely anticlimactic. The sense of catharsis, the expected wave of relief, was muted, dampened by the lingering weight of what had transpired. Martel's conviction, while a necessary step, didn't erase the trauma, the fear, the gaping holes left in the lives of so many. It was, as Detective Miller had grimly observed during a rare moment of vulnerability, a temporary bandage on a deep, festering wound. The city, outwardly calm, hummed with a low thrum of unease, a collective anxiety that lingered beneath the surface of normalcy.

For Detective Miller himself, the case's conclusion brought a different kind of unease. The relentless pursuit of Martel, the relentless pressure of the investigation, had exacted its toll. He found himself haunted by the victims' faces, their stories replaying in his mind like a broken record. Sleep offered little respite, his dreams filled with a nightmarish kaleidoscope of flashing lights, sirens, and the chilling echo of Martel's chilling laughter. He'd lost weight, his normally sharp features were etched with fatigue, and the lines around his eyes deepened with each passing day. His colleagues noticed, offering concerned glances and words of support, but Miller pushed them away, unwilling to acknowledge the depth of his own exhaustion. The weight of the case, the weight of the city's collective trauma, pressed heavily upon his shoulders, a burden he carried alone.

His partner, Detective Diaz, fared somewhat better. Diaz, a younger officer with a more resilient spirit, had focused his energy on supporting the victims' families, becoming an unexpected source of strength and stability.

He'd visited them regularly, offering practical assistance, a listening ear, and a quiet presence that provided comfort in their moments of despair. He'd become a link between the often-distant police force and the community they served, demonstrating a rare empathy that went beyond the confines of the law. Yet, even Diaz carried his own burdens. He'd witnessed the raw pain firsthand, the devastation left in Martel's wake. The memories were etched into his mind, and while he outwardly appeared stronger, a quiet sadness lingered beneath the surface.

The city, too, bore the scars of the Martel case. While the trial's outcome provided a degree of closure, the wounds were far from healed. There was a palpable shift in the city's atmosphere, a collective unease that permeated every corner of the city's streets. People were more cautious, more vigilant; the easy camaraderie that had once characterized their neighborhoods was replaced by a wary watchfulness. The city's vibrant pulse felt slightly muted, the rhythm of its life altered by the shadows of Martel's crimes. The city's leaders, acutely aware of the widespread anxiety, embarked on ambitious initiatives aimed at enhancing community safety. Increased police patrols, improved street lighting, and community outreach programs were implemented in an attempt to address public concerns and restore a sense of security.

The media, initially criticized for its sometimes sensationalistic coverage of the case, adopted a more responsible approach. The initial focus on crime scene details and graphic accounts of violence yielded to a more nuanced, empathetic perspective, shifting toward stories that highlighted the resilience of the victims and the efforts of the community to heal. They focused on the support networks that had emerged, the stories of collective action, and the inspiring efforts to prevent future tragedies. There was a growing acknowledgment of the importance of respecting the privacy and dignity of those affected by the tragedy, moving beyond the initial drama-fueled narratives to a more measured, responsible form of reporting. This transition, however slow and gradual, represented a critical shift in the media's responsibility, a move away from exploiting trauma toward fostering healing and preventing further victimization.

Sarah Jenkins, one of the survivors, became an unexpected advocate for change. Her initial reluctance to speak out evolved into a quiet determination to use her experience to effect positive change. She became involved in victim support groups, sharing her story with others and offering hope and comfort to those who felt lost and alone. She championed legislation aimed at enhancing support services for victims of violent crime, using her voice to challenge the systemic inadequacies that had allowed Martel to evade justice for so long. Her quiet strength became a symbol of resilience, inspiring others to confront their pain and work towards creating a safer, more just community.

The road ahead wouldn't be easy. The scars of the Martel case, both visible and invisible, would remain for years to come. The city's collective healing would be a long, arduous process, marked by setbacks and moments of despair. But the trial, the subsequent investigations, and the outpouring of community support had planted a seed of hope, a belief in the possibility of healing, a commitment to building a safer, more resilient community for all. The pursuit of justice wasn't just about punishing Martel; it was about acknowledging the pain of the victims, supporting their recovery, and creating a society that would never again allow such a tragedy to occur. The scars remained, a constant reminder of the darkness, but so too did the quiet determination to heal, to build, and to move forward together, acknowledging the fragility of life and the enduring strength of the human spirit. The city had begun to heal; the road ahead would be long, but it wouldn't be walked alone. There was a profound sense that the community, wounded but not broken, was ready to face the future together. The fight for justice wasn't over, but it had entered a new, perhaps less dramatic, but equally vital phase. The struggle for healing, for building a better tomorrow, had begun.

Loose Ends

The quiet hum of the city, a deceptive calm after the storm of Martel's trial, belied the lingering unease that gnawed at the edges of Detective Miller's mind. The conviction, the seemingly definitive closure, felt hollow. It was a victory, undeniably, but one that tasted like ashes in his mouth. The meticulously constructed case, the countless hours spent piecing together the fragments of Martel's depravity, had left him emotionally depleted. He found himself staring out the rain-streaked window of his office, the city lights blurring into a hazy, indistinct mass, mirroring the confusion that swirled within him.

The official report, meticulously detailed and flawlessly presented, offered a neat narrative. Martel, the monster, had been apprehended, tried, and convicted. Justice had been served. But the report couldn't encapsulate the chilling details that clung to Miller's memory: the subtle discrepancies in Martel's alibi, the almost imperceptible tremor in his voice during interrogation, the fleeting glimpse of something akin to... satisfaction in his eyes when confronted with the evidence. These were the loose threads, the unanswered questions that refused to be neatly woven into the narrative of a closed case.

One such thread concerned the missing ledger. Martel's meticulously kept accounts, detailing his illicit activities and a network of accomplices far broader than initially suspected, had vanished. Despite an exhaustive search, it remained elusive, a ghostly presence haunting the investigation's conclusion. Had Martel managed to conceal it before his arrest? Was it in the possession of a trusted associate, patiently awaiting an opportune moment to resurface? The unanswered question cast a long shadow, suggesting a deeper conspiracy, a network of corruption that extended beyond Martel himself. The possibility hung heavy in the air, a silent threat to the fragile peace established by the trial.

Another nagging detail was the seemingly insignificant discrepancy in the toxicology report. While Martel's blood alcohol content was consistent with his claimed level of intoxication on the night of the final murder, there was a faint trace of an unidentified substance. It was too small to significantly alter the course of the trial, yet it felt significant to Miller. Was it a mere anomaly, a laboratory error, or something more sinister – a hint of another accomplice, another layer to the intricate web Martel had woven? The unanswered question kept Miller awake at night, a persistent buzzing in the back of his mind.

The victims' families, too, carried their own unanswered questions. While the conviction brought a measure of solace, it failed to fully alleviate the gaping wounds left by Martel's actions. They struggled with the lingering trauma, the fear, and the constant reminders of their loved ones' absence. The grief, though tempered by justice, was a persistent ache, a constant companion in their lives. Miller, witnessing their quiet suffering, felt a renewed sense of responsibility. Their healing, their peace of mind, became as much his responsibility as any other element of his work.

Then there was Sarah Jenkins. Her transformation from a terrified survivor into a powerful advocate for change had been remarkable, a testament to the human spirit's resilience. Yet, Miller couldn't shake the feeling that she was hiding something, a subtle reserve in her eyes, a hesitation in her responses during their occasional conversations. He knew that forcing her to relive her trauma would be counterproductive, yet the unspoken question remained – a shadow lurking beneath her brave façade. Was there something she hadn't revealed, something crucial to the understanding of Martel's actions, or even a hint of another perpetrator?

The media, having shifted from sensationalism to a more responsible approach, still struggled with the complexities of the case. The public, initially fixated on the grim details of Martel's crimes, sought closure, answers, and a sense of security that the trial couldn't fully provide. The city's anxieties persisted, manifesting in a heightened awareness, a pervasive sense of vulnerability that hung in the air.

Even Diaz, Miller's partner, carried an unspoken weight. He'd been the steady presence, the pillar of strength for the victims' families, but Miller saw the strain in his eyes, the exhaustion in his shoulders. The seemingly insurmountable task of providing comfort and support in the face of overwhelming grief had left its mark. Diaz, outwardly stoic, harbored his own uncertainties, his own questions, all unspoken, all deeply personal.

The unanswered questions, seemingly minor on their own, converged to form a vortex of uncertainty, a swirling maelstrom that kept Miller from achieving the peace he desperately craved. It wasn't the lack of conviction that bothered him, but the feeling that the truth, the full, horrifying truth, remained elusive. The case had ended, but the investigation, in his mind, continued. He was haunted by the shadows, the gaps, the unsettling sense of something incomplete, something missing. The city might be healing, but Miller knew that his own personal healing wouldn't begin until these loose ends were finally, meticulously, tied. The hunt for justice, it seemed, wasn't over after all. The chase for answers, a far more personal quest, had only just begun. The quiet hum of the city was a deceptive mask, hiding the undercurrents of unresolved questions, a potent cocktail of unanswered questions that kept him awake and fueled his obsessive pursuit of a truth that seemed to evade him at every turn. The finality of the gavel's thud echoed in his ears, yet, strangely, it was the silence that screamed the loudest.

Further Investigations

The rain continued its relentless assault on the city, mirroring the persistent drizzle of unanswered questions that plagued Detective Miller. The conviction of Julian Martel had brought a semblance of closure, a fragile peace that felt more like a temporary reprieve than a lasting victory. He found himself drawn back to the crime scenes, not as an investigator actively pursuing a suspect, but as a historian piecing together the fragments of a puzzle that refused to resolve itself. The meticulously documented crime scenes, now meticulously archived, held a different kind of fascination, a chilling beauty in their sterile perfection. Each photograph, each piece of evidence, held a silent story, a whisper of a truth that lay just beyond his grasp.

The missing ledger remained the most tantalizing, the most frustrating piece of the puzzle. He reviewed the testimonies again, the statements of witnesses, the accounts of associates, searching for a clue, a flicker of information that might lead him to its hiding place. He revisited the places Martel frequented, the back alleys, the dimly lit bars, the clandestine meetings that were the backbone of his operation. He searched for a forgotten detail, a discarded clue, a forgotten look that could illuminate the ledger's whereabouts. The search felt like a desperate attempt to grasp smoke, a futile exercise in chasing shadows. Yet, he couldn't bring himself to abandon the search. The ledger was more than just a record of criminal activities; it was a key, a potential pathway to understanding the full extent of Martel's network, its reach, its power. The ledger represented the possibility of a larger conspiracy, a network that extended beyond Martel, beyond the immediate circle of his known associates. The thought sent a shiver down his spine.

The unidentified substance in Martel's toxicology report continued to haunt him. He contacted the lead forensic scientist, Dr. Anya Sharma, a woman known for her meticulous attention to detail and unwavering integrity. Dr. Sharma, initially dismissive of the trace amount, agreed to re-examine the samples, applying more sophisticated analytical techniques. The results were inconclusive yet still disturbing. The substance, a minute trace indeed, remained unidentified. Dr. Sharma's careful analysis only confirmed its existence, amplifying the unease. Miller pondered the possibilities: a new, undiscovered drug; a laboratory contamination, however unlikely; or a deliberate attempt to mask another substance, an intricate act of concealment designed to evade detection. Each scenario presented a new layer of complexity, each hypothesis opening a new avenue of investigation, however daunting it might prove.

He revisited Sarah Jenkins, this time not as an interrogator, but as a concerned friend. He found her in her small garden, a testament to her resilience, her life reclaiming itself from the clutches of trauma. The conversation was cautious, hesitant at first, but gradually, trust formed between them, a fragile bridge built on shared experience and mutual respect. She shared her fears, her insecurities, her struggles with the aftermath of Martel's crimes. And yet, as she spoke, a sense of unspoken hesitation lingered, a subtle withholding of information, a reluctance to fully confide in him. Miller understood; the scars of trauma were not easily erased, the memory of terror not so easily shed.

He respected her boundaries, yet he felt the lingering presence of an unanswered question, a silent truth buried deep within her heart. He decided to wait, to allow time and trust to bridge the gap, to coax the truth out without inflicting further harm.

The media's narrative had shifted from salacious headlines to a more nuanced, analytical approach. Yet, Miller found himself at odds with the official conclusion, the sense of finality that permeated public perception. The sanitized version of events, the officially sanctioned narrative, failed to capture the chilling undercurrents, the unsettling anomalies, the disturbing unanswered questions that gnawed at his mind. He began to write, not as a police report writer, but as a storyteller, crafting a narrative that reflected the complexities he knew existed, the shades of grey that lay beneath the surface of the seemingly closed case. He meticulously documented his findings, his doubts, his hunches – his private investigation continued, a parallel track to the official narrative, a chronicle of his quest for truth.

Diaz, his partner, remained his constant, a reassuring presence in the face of his own inner turmoil. Their conversations, though devoid of explicit discussion of the unanswered questions, conveyed a shared unease, a silent understanding that the official closure was just a temporary truce in a much larger war. Diaz, through his quiet observations and shared concerns, became a vital part of Miller's informal investigation. He possessed a different perspective, and his insights often served to illuminate pathways Miller had failed to recognize. Their partnership, forged in the crucible of Martel's trial, had been solidified, transforming into a bond built on mutual respect, trust, and the unspoken acknowledgment of a truth yet to be uncovered.

Days turned into weeks, weeks into months. The city resumed its rhythmic pulse, its inhabitants moving on, seeking solace in the everyday routines of life. Yet, for Miller, the investigation continued. The unanswered questions remained a constant, gnawing presence. He delved into the details of Martel's financial transactions, tracing the flow of money, the movement of assets, and the intricate web of shell corporations and offshore accounts. Each transaction represented a potential clue, a possible link to another accomplice, another piece of the elusive puzzle. The digital breadcrumbs, meticulously followed, led to dead ends, and then, surprisingly, to a new path: a series of coded messages exchanged using an obscure encryption protocol. This unexpected discovery revived the investigation, opening up a new avenue of exploration and leading Miller to another layer of the crime network.

The hunt for answers had become more than just a professional obligation; it had evolved into a personal crusade. He felt a responsibility, not just to the victims and their families, but to the city itself, to the fragile sense of security that had been so brutally shattered. The resolution of the Martel case had only served to expose a deeper level of corruption, a network far more extensive than initially perceived. The quiet hum of the city, once a source of comfort, now served as a constant reminder of the hidden dangers, the lurking shadows, the unsettling uncertainties that lay beneath the surface. The pursuit of truth, he realized, was a never-ending quest, a journey with no definitive end, only a series of milestones along a winding, perilous path. The chase for answers continued, fueled by an unwavering determination to unveil the full extent of the conspiracy, to tie up all the loose ends, to finally achieve the true closure that had eluded him since the gavel's final thud. The city might move on, but Miller knew his journey had only just begun. The unanswered questions, once a source of frustration and exhaustion, now provided him with the fuel to continue, a relentless driving force in his tireless pursuit of justice.

Moral Ambiguity

The decoded messages, painstakingly deciphered with the help of a cryptology expert, revealed a network far more intricate than Miller had ever imagined. It wasn't just a drug trafficking operation; it was a sophisticated system of money laundering, bribery, and political influence. Names surfaced – names Miller recognized from the city's elite, from the halls of power, from the seemingly untouchable circles of wealth and privilege. The revelation sent a chill down his spine; the implications were staggering, reaching far beyond the relatively straightforward narcotics case he had initially thought he was dealing with. This was a conspiracy of epic proportions, one that threatened the very fabric of the city's infrastructure.

The moral ambiguity became starkly apparent as Miller delved deeper. Some of those implicated were not outright criminals in the traditional sense, but rather individuals who had compromised their integrity, bending the rules for personal gain, or worse, actively participating in the conspiracy through acts of omission or calculated silence. These were the morally gray characters, neither entirely innocent nor completely culpable, navigating a treacherous landscape of ethical compromises and self-preservation. Their actions weren't driven by malicious intent in the way Martel's were, but rather by a complex interplay of ambition, fear, and a chilling acceptance of the status quo.

Take, for instance, Councilman Harold Finch. A respected member of the community, a philanthropist, a man who publicly championed law and order, Finch's name appeared repeatedly in the decoded messages. The evidence, however, was circumstantial. There were coded references, veiled allusions, suggestive transactions, but nothing concrete enough for a direct indictment. Miller found himself staring at the evidence, the digital footprints, the financial trails, feeling the frustrating weight of ambiguity. Was Finch actively involved in the conspiracy, a puppet master pulling the strings from behind the scenes? Or was he merely a pawn, a naive pasty manipulated by Martel's more cunning associates? The line between complicity and ignorance blurred, becoming almost impossible to discern.

Then there was Dr. Evelyn Reed, a prominent psychiatrist with a spotless reputation. Her name appeared in connection with several of Martel's associates, and the nature of the exchanges suggested a pattern of influence and control. Miller knew Reed's reputation was pristine, her practice highly respected, her clientele composed of the city's upper echelon. Yet, the messages hinted at a deeper involvement, a subtle manipulation of vulnerable individuals, a cynical exploitation of trust and influence. Was she knowingly enabling Martel's network, using her professional standing to cover up criminal activity and provide a veneer of respectability? Or was she, like Finch, a victim of manipulation, unknowingly caught in the web of a far-reaching conspiracy?

Even Sarah Jenkins, despite her status as a victim, presented her own moral complexity. Miller's conversations with her, though initially cautious, eventually revealed a glimpse into her past, a past that wasn't entirely innocent. Her involvement with Martel hadn't been solely a matter of coercion; there had been an element of willing participation, a degree of complicity born out of desperation and a desperate desire to improve her circumstances. This wasn't to excuse her situation or minimize the trauma she had suffered, but it did add another layer of complexity to her narrative, a testament to the morally ambiguous situations that individuals can find themselves trapped within. It challenged the simple dichotomy of victim versus perpetrator, highlighting the myriad shades of grey that existed in between.

The further Miller dug, the more he realized that the entire case was a tangled web of moral compromises, calculated risks, and self-serving actions. The lines between victim and perpetrator, complicity, and innocence, blurred constantly, making it nearly impossible to assign clear-cut moral judgments. He found himself questioning his own perceptions, his own assumptions, constantly battling the urge to simplify, to categorize, to impose a neat narrative on the chaos that unfurled before him. The relentless pursuit of truth, he discovered, was not just about finding answers; it was about grappling with the ethical implications, the moral nuances, the unsettling ambiguities that lay at the heart of every complex case.

The official narrative, the sanitized version presented to the public, could not and did not capture the full picture. It presented a simplified view, a convenient narrative that neatly tied up the loose ends and allowed the city to move on. But Miller understood, the truth lay in the shadows, in the gray areas, in the unspoken truths and hidden motives. His own journey had become a personal crusade, not just for justice, but for a deeper understanding of the human condition, for a recognition of the complexities that drive individuals to make choices that blur the line between right and wrong.

He revisited the crime scenes, not to look for new evidence, but to reflect on what he had already discovered. The sterile, clinical perfection of the crime scenes now held a new meaning for him, a symbolic representation of the attempts to sanitize, to simplify, to mask the ugly truths that lurked beneath the surface. The meticulously documented facts represented the carefully constructed facade of order and justice, while the underlying reality remained a tangled web of moral ambiguities.

Diaz, his partner, offered a counterpoint to Miller's growing obsession with the morally gray areas. Diaz, rooted in pragmatism and practical law enforcement procedures, found himself struggling to reconcile Miller's deepening moral introspection with the necessity for decisive action. While Miller wrestled with ethical complexities, Diaz urged him to focus on actionable intelligence, on the concrete evidence needed to bring the guilty to justice. Their differing perspectives created a tension, a friction that propelled the investigation forward, forcing Miller to confront not only the moral ambiguities of the case but also his own internal conflicts.

The investigation took an unexpected turn with the discovery of a previously unnoticed detail in Martel's financial records – a series of seemingly insignificant donations to a local charity, a charity that operated under the guise of helping underprivileged children but whose true nature was far more sinister. Miller followed the money, tracing the flow of funds through a complex web of shell corporations and offshore accounts, ultimately uncovering evidence of a vast money-laundering scheme. This new revelation brought the investigation full circle, connecting the seemingly disparate elements of the case. It further highlighted the insidious nature of the conspiracy, revealing the extent to which seemingly respectable institutions could be infiltrated and exploited for criminal gain.

The moral ambiguity extended even to Miller himself. He was becoming increasingly consumed by the investigation, sacrificing his personal life, pushing his professional boundaries. He was operating in a gray area, stepping outside the bounds of official procedure, driven by a conviction that extended beyond mere legal justice. His pursuit of truth was starting to take a toll, testing the limits of his integrity, blurring the lines between his professional duties and his crusade. He was playing a dangerous game, one that might have unforeseen consequences. He began questioning the very nature of justice, questioning the effectiveness of traditional legal processes in dealing with a conspiracy of this magnitude.

The book he realized, would need to reflect this moral ambiguity, this intricate dance of ethical compromises and calculated risks. It wouldn't be a simple tale of good versus evil but a far more complex narrative, a tapestry woven with shades of gray, a story that challenged readers to confront the ethical dilemmas and the moral complexities that lay at the heart of human nature. The city's sanitized narrative could not encompass the reality he now knew. The truth, as ever, proved far more elusive and, ultimately, far more disturbing than any official report could ever suggest. The pursuit of justice, he realized, was itself a morally ambiguous journey, and the story he was weaving was not just an account of a criminal investigation, but an exploration of the human capacity for both good and evil. The final chapter, he knew, was far from being written.

241

Themes and Implications

The unraveling of Martel's operation exposed a rot far deeper than mere drug trafficking. It was a systemic failure, a cancer that had metastasized through the city's institutions, infecting the very arteries of power. The unanswered questions, the lingering doubts, gnawed at Miller. He'd uncovered a vast network of money laundering, expertly concealed behind a veneer of respectability. Shell corporations, offshore accounts, complex financial transactions—all meticulously designed to obscure the trail of illicit funds. But the trail, though faint at times, was there, a digital breadcrumb trail leading to the city's most influential figures.

Councilman Finch, for instance, remained a troubling enigma. The circumstantial evidence, while suggestive, wasn't enough for a conviction. The coded messages hinted at his involvement, but a lack of direct evidence left Miller frustrated. Was Finch a willing participant, a puppet master pulling strings from the shadows? Or was he a pawn, a victim of Martel's manipulation, his name used without his full knowledge or consent? This question highlighted the inherent difficulties in prosecuting cases based on circumstantial evidence, especially when dealing with individuals holding significant power and influence. The weight of proof needed to convict a powerful figure like Finch was far greater than that needed for a street-level dealer. The very nature of the legal system seemed to protect those who could afford the best legal representation, leaving Miller with a bitter taste of injustice. The system, he realized, was designed to be resistant to the exposure of its own corruption.

The case of Dr. Reed presented a different, yet equally disturbing, puzzle. Her seemingly impeccable reputation belied the subtle hints of manipulation uncovered in the intercepted communications. Was she knowingly involved in a conspiracy, leveraging her position to shield Martel's associates, providing a cloak of respectability? Or was she another victim, unknowingly caught in the web of deceit, her professional reputation used as a tool by a far more sinister organization? The ambiguity forced Miller to confront the limits of his own investigative powers. He could uncover connections, trace financial flows, and interpret coded messages, but could he truly discern the intent behind these actions? Could he definitively separate the knowing participant from the unwitting accomplice? The answer, he realized, was often obscured in the murky realm of human motivation, where genuine intentions were often intertwined with self-preservation and survival instincts.

Sarah Jenkins's story further underscored this complexity. Initially viewed as a victim, further investigation revealed a more nuanced perspective. Her involvement with Martel wasn't simply a matter of coercion; there was a degree of complicity, a willing participation born out of desperation and a yearning for a better life. This wasn't to excuse her actions, but to acknowledge the realities of desperation and systemic inequality that could compel people to make difficult choices with far-reaching consequences. Miller found himself questioning the simple dichotomy of victim and perpetrator. The simplistic labels failed to capture the intricate realities of a world where choices were often made under duress or were a product of circumstance and opportunity.

The investigation itself became a reflection of this moral ambiguity. Miller found himself bending the rules, pushing the limits of his authority, driven by a sense of justice that extended beyond the confines of the law. Diaz, his pragmatic partner, constantly reminded him of the need for concrete evidence, for decisive action, for remaining within the bounds of official procedure. Their conflict underscored the inherent tension between the pursuit of truth and the constraints of the legal system. Could justice truly be served if it were bound by rigid rules and procedures designed for a simpler, less complex reality? The question hung heavily in the air between them, fueling their often heated debates.

The discovery of Martel's donations to the seemingly charitable organization added another layer to the already complex puzzle. The investigation had become a journey through a labyrinthine world of shell corporations, offshore accounts, and carefully obscured financial transactions. The money trail revealed the depth of the corruption, the systemic nature of the criminal enterprise, and the level to which the city's infrastructure had been compromised. The charity, outwardly dedicated to helping underprivileged children, was a sophisticated front for money laundering, a testament to the insidious nature of organized crime's ability to infiltrate seemingly legitimate organizations.

As the case progressed, Miller found himself grappling with the ethical implications of his actions. His pursuit of justice had begun to consume him, blurring the lines between his professional life and his crusade. He was operating in a gray area, pushing his boundaries, driven by a powerful sense of purpose, but at what cost? His actions, while driven by a desire for justice, were potentially unlawful, blurring the lines between a dedicated investigator and someone willing to bend the rules to achieve the greater good. The line between righteous action and illegal methods was thin and dangerously blurred.

The unanswered questions, the moral ambiguities, the systemic corruption – all of these elements combined to create a narrative far more complex than any simple tale of good versus evil. The city's official narrative, presented to the public, was a sanitized version, a convenient simplification of a far more complicated reality. Miller understood that the truth was in the shadows, in the gray areas, in the unspoken truths and hidden motives. The story, he realized, was not simply about a criminal investigation, but about the human condition, about the complexities of human nature, the capacity for both profound good and devastating evil, and the blurry lines that often separated the two. He was not simply investigating a crime; he was exploring the very nature of justice itself.

His investigation wasn't merely a pursuit of legal justice; it was a moral reckoning. It forced him to confront the limits of the law, the limitations of the system, and the uncomfortable truth that justice, like the truth itself, often resides in the murky areas between black and white. The case highlighted the limitations of a purely legalistic approach to combating systemic corruption, underscoring the need for a broader, more holistic approach that addresses the underlying social and economic factors contributing to such criminal enterprises. The investigation's implications extended far beyond the courtroom, reaching into the heart of the city's political and social fabric and highlighting the pervasive nature of corruption and its insidious effects on society.

The final chapter, he knew, was far from written. The truth, he now realized, was a mosaic of intricate details, a complex puzzle whose pieces didn't always fit neatly together. It was a truth that demanded a deeper examination of the moral and ethical complexities that underpinned even the most seemingly straightforward criminal investigations.

And that realization, as disturbing as it was, made him determined to pursue the truth, no matter how far into the shadows it may lead. He had embarked on a journey that transcended the bounds of a simple criminal investigation; it was a journey into the heart of darkness, a journey into the depths of the human soul, a journey that would forever change his perspective on justice, morality, and the often-elusive pursuit of truth. The implications of his findings were far-reaching, extending beyond the immediate case to encompass the broader issues of societal corruption, institutional failures, and the complexities of human behavior.

Reader's Reflection

The lingering silence after closing the file on the Martel case felt heavier than the weight of the evidence itself. The meticulous documentation, painstakingly reconstructed financial flows, and deciphered coded messages—all amounted to a damning indictment of systemic corruption. Yet a sense of incompleteness remained. It wasn't simply the lack of airtight evidence against Councilman Finch or the elusive certainty regarding Dr. Reed's culpability. It was something deeper, a nagging unease that went beyond the confines of the investigation itself. It was the realization that the truth, like quicksilver, constantly shifted and changed, eluding definitive capture.

The case had exposed a web of deceit so intricately woven and deeply embedded within the city's power structures that it felt almost impossible to unravel completely. Every answer uncovered seemed to spawn a dozen more questions, each more perplexing than the last. The official narrative, the carefully crafted public pronouncements, felt like a thin veneer disguising a far more unsettling reality. The public would never know the full extent of the rot—the insidious tendrils of corruption that reached every corner of the city's infrastructure. Miller, having peered into the abyss, understood that this was not just a single case, but a symptom of a deeper malaise.

Think about Sarah Jenkins. Was she a victim, a pawn in a larger game orchestrated by Martel? Or was she a willing participant, her desperation driving her to compromise her morals? The truth, likely, lay somewhere in the grey area between those two extremes—a complex tapestry of coercion, opportunity, and the seductive allure of a better life. It was a reflection of the systemic inequalities that allowed Martel's operation to flourish in the first place— inequalities that allowed some to exploit others with impunity. The moral landscape was far more complex than the simplistic binary of good and evil. It was a world where survival often necessitated difficult choices, where the lines between victim and perpetrator blurred beyond recognition.

Consider Councilman Finch. The circumstantial evidence piled up, pointing toward his complicity, yet the lack of direct evidence left a frustrating gap. Miller's frustration stemmed not merely from legal limitations but from the inherent unfairness of a system that seemed to shield the power from accountability. Did Finch knowingly participate in the conspiracy? Was he merely a useful pawn, unaware of the full extent of Martel's operation? The question remained unanswered, highlighting the chilling reality that the powerful often operate in a realm beyond the reach of justice.

And Dr. Reed? Her seemingly untarnished reputation belied the subtle clues discovered in the intercepted communications. Was she a known participant in a vast conspiracy? Or was she another victim, unknowingly manipulated by forces beyond her comprehension? The ambiguity of her role reflected the dangers of unchecked power and the ease with which even the most respected individuals could be drawn into a web of deceit. The reader should ask themselves: how easy is it to remain untouched by corruption, when it is so deeply ingrained in the fabric of society?

The charity, ostensibly dedicated to helping underprivileged children, serves as a potent symbol of the hypocrisy that permeated the city's social fabric. It was a sophisticated money-laundering operation—its outward benevolence, masking a sinister core. This highlights a stark reality: the enemy often lurks where we least expect it, camouflaged by virtue and altruism. The reader should contemplate this duality—the constant tension between appearance and reality, the ease with which deception can be masked by a veneer of respectability.

The case itself, a reflection of this moral ambiguity, is a challenge to the reader. It wasn't a simple quest for justice within a clear-cut legal framework. It was a battle fought in the shadows, where moral complexities challenged the very definition of right and wrong. Miller's actions, though driven by a profound sense of justice, often pushed the boundaries of the law. This blurring of lines is a central theme, forcing the reader to question the nature of justice itself. Is justice served only through adherence to strict legal procedures, or can it sometimes demand a more nuanced—even ethically ambiguous—approach?

The case didn't end with the arrest of Martel and the dismantling of his organization. It left behind a profound sense of unease, a lingering question mark hanging over the future of the city. It exposed the fragility of justice, the insidious nature of systemic corruption, and the limitations of the legal system in addressing such deep-rooted problems. The reader should contemplate the lasting impact of such corruption, the potential for its resurgence, and the societal consequences of unchecked power.

The unraveling of Martel's operation was not just a criminal investigation; it was an exploration of human condition. It revealed the capacity for both profound good and unimaginable evil, the ease with which even the most virtuous individuals can be compromised, and the subtle ways in which systemic inequalities can drive people to desperation. The case challenged the reader's assumptions about justice, morality, and the pursuit of truth. It highlighted the limitations of simple narratives, the need for critical thinking, and the importance of questioning power structures. The reader should reflect on the blurred lines between victim and perpetrator, the seductive allure of power, and the pervasive influence of systemic corruption.

Miller's journey is interwoven with the narrative, adding a layer of emotional depth. His struggle to reconcile his sense of justice with the constraints of the legal system resonates deeply, creating a character that is both relatable and compelling. The reader is invited to empathize with his moral dilemma, to grapple with the ethical complexities that arise when pursuing truth in a corrupt system. The ambiguous ending leaves the reader contemplating the lingering questions, the unresolved issues, and the lasting impact of the case on Miller himself. Does he find closure? Or does the experience leave an indelible mark, forever shaping his perspective on justice and the world around him?

The story challenges the reader not just to passively consume the narrative but to actively engage with the moral and ethical dilemmas it presents. It forces a reconsideration of established notions of justice, good, and evil, inviting critical reflection on the systemic issues that allowed Martel's operation to flourish unchecked. The reader is left with a lingering sense of unease, a quiet recognition that the fight against corruption is a continuous struggle, a battle that requires not just legal action but a fundamental shift in societal values and power dynamics.

The complexities of the case are designed not to provide easy answers, but to spark critical thought and discussion about the nature of justice, the limits of the legal system, and the enduring fight against corruption. The investigation's conclusion is not a resolution, but a catalyst for deeper contemplation.

Finally, consider the unanswered questions themselves. They are not merely plot devices designed to create suspense, but essential elements of the story. They reflect the inherent complexities of human behavior, the limitations of investigative methods, and the enduring struggle to define and achieve true justice. These lingering ambiguities are meant to resonate with the reader long after the last page is turned, prompting ongoing reflection on the nature of truth, justice, and the pervasive influence of corruption within our society.

The book's ending serves not as a resolution, but as a provocation—a call for continued engagement with the challenging themes it explores.

Consequences of Complicity

The air in Miller's sparsely furnished office felt thick with the residue of unanswered questions, a palpable weight settling on him like a shroud. The Martel case was closed, officially, at least. The headlines had screamed of a major drug bust, a takedown of a sophisticated money laundering operation disguised as a charitable foundation. Councilman Finch, though never formally charged, had resigned amidst a storm of speculation and whispered accusations, his political career effectively destroyed. Dr. Reed, despite the lingering suspicions, remained untouched, her reputation seemingly unscathed. But Miller knew the truth, or at least a fragmented, unsettling version of it. He knew the price of silence, the insidious cost of complicity, not just for those directly involved but for the city as a whole.

Sarah Jenkins' story haunted him. Her initial testimony, hesitant and guarded, had slowly revealed a portrait of desperation, a woman trapped between her loyalty to Martel and the gnawing fear of exposure. She hadn't been a mastermind, not a key player in the intricate web of deceit, but rather a cog, a small, insignificant piece in a complex machine. Yet, her complicity, born of poverty and the desperate need to provide for her family, had undeniably contributed to the suffering of countless others. Her silence, initially born of fear, had become a silent accomplice to Martel's crimes, prolonging the operation and enabling its insidious expansion. Her eventual cooperation, though crucial to the investigation, came at a heavy price – the loss of her anonymity, the constant threat of retaliation, and the lifelong burden of knowing the extent of her unwitting participation in a criminal enterprise. Her case was a stark reminder that complicity didn't always require malicious intent; sometimes, it was simply a consequence of desperation, a silent agreement born of fear and circumstance.

The Councilman Finch situation represented a different facet of complicity – the calculated silence of those in power. The evidence against him was circumstantial, frustratingly incomplete. Miller knew Finch had turned a blind eye, perhaps even actively benefited from Martel's operation. The silence was not born of fear but of self-preservation, a calculated gamble that prioritized his political career over justice. His resignation, while appearing as an act of contrition, was, in reality, a strategic retreat, a calculated move to minimize the damage to his reputation and avoid legal repercussions. This form of complicity, shielded by the carefully constructed façade of political propriety, underscored the chilling reality that the powerful often operated in a realm beyond the reach of the law. The lack of direct evidence wasn't merely a legal hurdle; it represented the resilience of a system designed to protect those within it, even at the expense of justice. The consequences for Finch, though significant, were far less severe than they should have been, proving that the price of silence for the powerful is often considerably lower than for the vulnerable.

Dr. Reed's complicity was perhaps the most subtle, the most insidious. Her involvement, discovered through fragmented intercepted communications, was far from clear-cut. Had she been an active participant, knowingly contributing to Martel's scheme? Or was she a victim herself, unknowingly manipulated by Martel's charm and the promise of furthering her research? The ambiguity was unsettling, highlighting the ease with which even those of seemingly impeccable integrity could become entangled in a web of deceit. Her silence, either deliberate or unwitting, enabled the continuation of Martel's operation, illustrating how complicity could manifest in the most unexpected forms. The lack of definitive proof protected her, illustrating a harsh truth: the powerful are often shielded from the consequences of their actions, even when those actions contribute to broader societal harm. Her case served as a cautionary tale, demonstrating the fragility of reputation, the ease with which it could be tarnished and the difficulty of reclaiming it after becoming entangled in a criminal enterprise, even without direct culpability.

The consequences of silence extended far beyond the individuals directly involved. The city itself was infected, its moral compass skewed by a pervasive culture of complicity. The whispers, the veiled allusions, the knowing glances – these were the silent accomplices, perpetuating the cycle of corruption and creating a culture where truth was elusive, and accountability was a luxury few could afford. The underprivileged, those most affected by Martel's operation, paid the highest price, their suffering a silent testament to the pervasive nature of systemic injustice. Their voices, often unheard and unseen, were the ultimate casualties of the widespread complicity that allowed Martel's operation to thrive unchecked. Their continued silence, perpetuated by fear and a lack of power, served only to reinforce the cycle, perpetuating the very conditions that fostered corruption in the first place.

The investigation had unearthed a deep malaise, a systemic failure of oversight and accountability. The charity, a seemingly benevolent organization, had become a powerful symbol of this hypocrisy. It masked a sinister operation, deceiving not only the public but also many who genuinely believed in its altruistic mission. Their silent participation, unknowingly enabling criminal activity, exemplified the subtle and insidious nature of complicity. They believed they were doing good; instead, they were unknowingly complicit in a far greater wrong, highlighting the dangerous ease with which good intentions can be exploited. The charity's collapse not only served as a reminder of the pervasiveness of corruption but also the devastating consequences of blind faith and the crucial need for vigilance and transparency.

The city's response to the revelations was telling. The initial shock gave way to a cautious acceptance, a collective shrug that seemed to say, "It's just the way things are." This tacit acceptance, this collective silence, was perhaps the most disturbing consequence of all. It spoke of a deep-seated weariness, a resignation to the inevitability of corruption, a culture where speaking up carried greater risks than remaining silent. This pervasive silence fostered the very conditions that allowed corruption to flourish, a self-perpetuating cycle of acceptance and inaction that ultimately threatened the very fabric of the city's moral foundations.

Miller's journey through this labyrinth of deceit had left an indelible mark. He had wrestled with ethical dilemmas, pushing the boundaries of legal procedures in his quest for justice. His actions, driven by a deep-seated sense of righteousness, forced him to confront the limitations of the law and the complexities of moral choices. He couldn't simply close the file and walk away, leaving unanswered questions hanging in the air. The lingering unease served as a constant reminder of the systemic issues that allowed Martel's operation to thrive and the far-reaching consequences of silence and complicity. The weight of his knowledge, the responsibility to ensure accountability, lay heavy on him, a burden he would carry long after the official investigation was concluded. He had to make a choice. Would he remain silent, allowing the rot to fester unseen, or would he choose another path? A path that would potentially expose him to significant danger, but one that he felt compelled to follow. The cost of silence, he was certain, would far outweigh the risks of action. His future would depend on his decision, and the fate of the city, he suspected, might just depend on it as well.

Justice Delayed

The Martel case, officially closed, cast a long shadow over the city. The headlines had faded, and the public's attention shifted to newer scandals, but the undercurrent of unease persisted. It wasn't merely the lingering questions about Dr. Reed's involvement or the whispers surrounding Councilman Finch's hasty resignation. It was something deeper, a collective sense of unease that seeped into the very fabric of daily life. The feeling was akin to living in a house with a hidden, untreated leak; the damage might not be immediately visible, but it was slowly, insidiously, undermining the foundation.

Miller, despite the official closure, felt the weight of this unspoken anxiety more acutely than most. He spent sleepless nights replaying the events, analyzing every detail, every missed clue, every ambiguous statement. Sarah Jenkins' face, etched with a mixture of fear and relief, haunted his dreams. Her cooperation had been instrumental, yet the price she paid – the loss of anonymity, the constant fear of retribution – was a stark reminder of the human cost of delayed justice. Her story was a microcosm of the larger systemic failure he had uncovered, a failure that ran deeper than individual culpability.

The city's response to the Martel scandal was a chilling reflection of this systemic failure. The initial outrage, the public calls for accountability, had quickly dissipated, replaced by a weary resignation. The media, initially ravenous for the details of the scandal, had moved on, their attention captured by the next breaking story. The public, initially shocked, had retreated into a self-imposed silence, a collective unwillingness to engage in the uncomfortable truths that had been uncovered. The unspoken consensus seemed to be: "It is what it is."

This collective apathy wasn't simply a matter of short attention spans or a lack of outrage. It was a deeper, more pervasive issue: a tacit acceptance of corruption, a belief that challenging the status quo was futile, even dangerous. The city, it seemed, had grown accustomed to the shadows, comfortable with the uneasy truce between law and disorder. This acceptance, this silence, was perhaps the most damning consequence of the delayed justice in the Martel case. It perpetuated the very conditions that had allowed the scandal to flourish in the first place.

The effects were particularly pronounced in the city's underprivileged communities, those most directly affected by Martel's operation. They had borne the brunt of the consequences – the escalating drug addiction, the rise in crime, the decay of community structures. Yet, their voices remained largely unheard, their concerns overshadowed by the self-serving narratives of the powerful. They were the silent witnesses, their suffering a constant, unspoken indictment of the system's failure to provide timely and effective justice.

Miller revisited the rundown neighborhoods where Martel's operation had been most prevalent. The boarded-up buildings, the vacant lots choked with weeds, and the lingering sense of despair were tangible reminders of the lasting consequences of inaction. He spoke to residents, their stories echoing the same themes: fear of retaliation, mistrust of authorities, and a sense of powerlessness against a system that seemed rigged against them. Their silence, born not of apathy but of deep-seated fear and a lack of faith in the system, reinforced the very cycle of corruption and inequality.

He thought of charity, its collapse, a stark symbol of the hypocrisy that had permeated the city. The organization had attracted numerous donations, funding numerous projects, only for it all to be revealed as a shame, a front for Martel's illicit activities. The individuals involved, many of whom were genuinely well-intentioned, were left grappling with the consequences of their unwitting complicity. The damage to their reputations and their sense of betrayal were lasting reminders of the profound consequences of delayed justice. The charity's downfall became a lesson learned, a cautionary tale.

The investigation revealed a chilling truth: the powerful often enjoyed a level of impunity unavailable to the vulnerable. Councilman Finch, despite strong circumstantial evidence, escaped meaningful consequences. His resignation was a strategic maneuver, a damage-control operation that minimized the impact on his personal life and future opportunities. The lack of direct evidence, a technicality of the legal system, allowed him to slip through the cracks, his silence protecting him from a deserved reckoning. The powerful could afford to remain silent; the vulnerable could not.

The case also served as a sobering reminder of how easily even seemingly upright individuals could become entangled in webs of deceit. Dr. Reed's involvement remained ambiguous, a testament to the subtle and insidious ways in which complicity could manifest. Her silence, whether deliberate or unwitting, highlighted the fragility of reputation and the difficulty of disentangling oneself from a criminal enterprise, even without direct involvement.

The city's slow, almost imperceptible descent into a culture of complicity underscored the insidious nature of delayed justice. The initial shock and outrage had given way to a weary acceptance, a collective resignation to the inevitability of corruption. This passive acceptance fostered the conditions for future scandals, creating a self-perpetuating cycle of inaction and indifference. The delayed justice not only failed to address the immediate wrong, but it further eroded public trust, making future prosecutions harder and perpetuating a climate of impunity.

Miller knew he couldn't simply close the file and walk away. The Martel case was more than just a successful drug bust; it was a symptom of a deeper malaise, a systemic failure of accountability. The lingering questions, the unanswered concerns, the pervasive sense of unease – these were the true costs of justice delayed. His own sense of justice demanded that he continue to pursue the truth, even if it meant facing powerful adversaries and risking his own safety and career. The city, he realized, deserved better than this uneasy truce between law and disorder. The price of silence, he knew, was far too high. And he wouldn't be silent. The fight for justice, he realized, was far from over.

The Importance of Speaking Out

The weight of the Martel case pressed down on Miller, a leaden cloak of unresolved questions and unanswered cries for justice. The official closure felt like a betrayal, a perfunctory act designed to sweep the dirt under the rug rather than a genuine attempt to clean up the mess. He'd seen the faces of those affected – the haunted eyes of Sarah Jenkins, the weary resignation etched on the faces of the residents in the city's forgotten corners, the hollowed-out look of the well-meaning individuals who'd unwittingly contributed to Martel's elaborate scheme through the now-defunct charity. Their silence, a tapestry woven from fear, disillusionment, and a profound lack of trust in the system, screamed louder than any headline ever could.

This silence, however, was not merely a passive acceptance of injustice; it was a complicit act, a tacit endorsement of the status quo. It allowed the rot to fester, deepening the cracks in the city's foundation. The failure to speak out, Miller realized, was not just a matter of individual inaction; it was a systemic flaw, a collective failure of nerve that enabled corruption to flourish. He thought of the countless stories he hadn't been able to uncover, the silent voices hidden in the shadows of the city, their tales of intimidation and retribution forming a chilling counterpoint to the official narrative. These were the forgotten casualties of delayed justice, their experiences serving as a stark reminder of the high price of silence.

The lack of public outcry and the swift retreat into self-preservation was a symptom of a deeper malaise – a societal weariness, a cynical acceptance of corruption as an inevitable part of the political landscape. It was a chilling reflection of a city numbed by years of incremental betrayals, a slow erosion of trust in institutions and authority. The powerful, shielded by their influence and resources, could afford to remain silent, allowing the tide of injustice to wash over the vulnerable without consequence. Their silence, however, was not neutral; it was a powerful act, reinforcing the power dynamics that allowed such corruption to thrive in the first place.

Miller remembered a conversation he'd had with an old, weathered detective, a man who'd seen it all in his decades on the force. The detective, whose name was Sal Demarco, had recounted a case from years ago, a seemingly minor incident of police brutality that was quickly swept under the rug. "They bury it, kid," Demarco had said, his voice raspy from years of smoking and whispered secrets, "and they bury it deep. Unless someone speaks up, it stays buried forever." DeMarco's words resonated with Miller, highlighting the systemic nature of the problem. The silence wasn't just about the individual cases; it was about the culture of silence itself, a protective barrier shielding the perpetrators and silencing the victims.

This wasn't merely a problem confined to the city's political landscape. The silence extended to other sectors – the business community, where shady deals and unethical practices flourished under the cloak of secrecy; the educational system, where the pressure to maintain a certain image stifled whistleblowers and critical voices; and even within the police department itself, where unspoken codes of conduct often protected corrupt officers from accountability. The shared silence, Miller realized, was a powerful tool, a form of social control that silenced dissent and perpetuated cycles of injustice.

The Martel case was a microcosm of this wider issue. It wasn't just about Martel himself; it was about the systemic failures that allowed his operation to thrive for so long. It was about the individuals who chose silence over action, the journalists who prioritized career advancement over ethical reporting, and the politicians who valued self-preservation over public service. It was about a society where the price of speaking out seemed far too high – a price measured in career ruin, social ostracism, and even physical danger.

But what was the alternative? Miller pondered. To remain silent in the face of injustice was to become complicit in it. To tolerate corruption was to allow it to metastasize, spreading its poisonous tendrils throughout society. The silence, he realized, wasn't just a passive act; it was an active endorsement of wrongdoing, a reinforcement of the oppressive systems that enabled it. And so, he knew he had to speak out. He owed it to Sarah Jenkins, to the residents of the city's forgotten neighborhoods, to the victims of Martel's operation, and to himself. The truth, he realized, had a power all its own, a capacity to cut through the layers of lies and obfuscation, to expose the rot at the heart of the city.

He started small. He reached out to trusted contacts in the media, sharing his concerns, his findings, and his frustrations. He knew the risks and the potential backlash, but he also knew the moral imperative. He started with small, verifiable details – details that wouldn't be easily dismissed or ignored. He knew it would be a long fight; it wouldn't be easy. He knew the powerful wouldn't simply roll over. He also knew that his actions might have consequences for himself, perhaps even the end of his career. However, his duty, more than ever, seemed crystal clear.

He began to leverage his network of contacts, meticulously building a case that went beyond the official narrative. He sought out those who had remained silent – the witnesses who had been too afraid to speak, the informants who had been silenced by threats, and the colleagues who had looked the other way. He offered them a promise of protection, an assurance that their voices would be heard, their stories shared. He painstakingly rebuilt the narrative, piecing together the fragments of truth, slowly but surely exposing the layers of deceit that had shielded Martel and his collaborators.

He discovered that the silence wasn't just a product of fear; it was a product of fatigue. People were exhausted by the constant stream of scandals, the endless cycle of corruption and disappointment. They had lost faith in the ability of the system to deliver justice. But Miller refused to let that cynicism win. He knew that speaking out, however difficult, was the only way to break the cycle, to reignite hope, to restore faith in the promise of justice. He wasn't just fighting for the victims of Martel; he was fighting for the soul of the city itself. The fight would be long and arduous, but he was prepared to fight it. The price of silence was too high; the price of speaking out might be significant, but it was a price he was willing to pay. Because, in the end, silence was complicity. And he couldn't live with that. He wouldn't.

Redemption and Forgiveness

The slow drip, drip, drip of information, meticulously gathered and painstakingly verified, began to erode the carefully constructed wall of silence surrounding Martel's operation. Miller's persistence, fueled by righteous anger and a deep-seated sense of justice, was starting to bear fruit. Small cracks appeared in the façade of the official closure, revealing the festering corruption beneath. He'd started with the periphery, focusing on the individuals who'd been complicit but not directly involved in Martel's criminal enterprise – the mid-level bureaucrats who'd turned a blind eye, the businessmen who'd profited from the illicit activities, the journalists who'd chosen self-preservation over ethical reporting. Each confession, each admission of guilt, however small, served as a building block in the construction of a larger, more devastating narrative.

One of the most significant breakthroughs came from an unexpected source: a former employee of Martel's charity, a young woman named Anya Sharma. Initially hesitant, terrified even of the repercussions of speaking out, Anya had eventually been persuaded by Miller's persistent assurances of protection and his unwavering belief in her story. Anya's testimony, detailed and harrowing, exposed the inner workings of Martel's elaborate scheme, detailing the systematic exploitation of vulnerable populations, the manipulation of funds, and the intimidation tactics employed to silence dissent. Her account, corroborated by other, smaller testimonies, painted a stark picture of the rot at the heart of the city's charitable sector.

The media, initially reluctant to touch the story, began to take notice as Miller's carefully constructed narrative gained traction. The evidence was irrefutable, the accusations too serious to ignore. The pressure mounted, forcing authorities to reopen the investigation – a move that was met with fierce resistance from within the ranks of the police department and the city council. But this time, the public was more receptive. The initial silence, the collective apathy, had begun to crack. Years of accumulated frustrations, unanswered questions, and a profound sense of betrayal had reached a boiling point. People were ready to speak out.

The subsequent investigation, though fraught with obstacles and delays, unearthed a web of corruption that stretched far beyond Martel himself. It implicated high-ranking officials, prominent businessmen, and influential members of the community – individuals who had long enjoyed a sense of impunity, shielded by their connections and resources. The revelations were shocking, exposing a systemic failure of accountability and a pervasive culture of silence that had allowed corruption to fester for years. The price of silence, once a seemingly insignificant cost, now appeared as a staggering debt owed by the entire city.

As the investigation progressed, the question of redemption and forgiveness began to take center stage. Could those who had remained silent, who had chosen self-preservation over justice, find a path to redemption? Could the city, scared by years of corruption and betrayal, find a way to forgive and move forward? These were not easy questions to answer, and the answers were far from straightforward.

Some of those involved sought redemption through public confession and cooperation with the authorities. They testified against their former colleagues, offering crucial evidence that helped bring the perpetrators to justice. Their willingness to acknowledge their wrongdoing and to accept the consequences of their actions offered a glimmer of hope, a testament to the possibility of change and rehabilitation.

But for others, redemption proved elusive. The weight of their past actions and the realization of the harm they had caused proved too heavy a burden to bear. Some were consumed by guilt, others by a bitter sense of injustice, and still others remained defiant, clinging to their silence as a shield against the consequences of their crimes.

The city, too, grappled with the question of forgiveness. The wounds inflicted by Martel's scheme and the subsequent cover-up ran deep, leaving a legacy of distrust and disillusionment. The process of healing, of rebuilding trust in institutions and authority, would be long and arduous. The need for accountability, for holding those responsible for corruption accountable, was paramount. But the desire for forgiveness, for reconciliation, was equally strong. It was understood that a city divided by bitterness and resentment could never truly heal.

The trial itself became a focal point for the city's collective struggle for redemption and forgiveness. The victims of Martel's operation, their stories finally heard and validated, had their day in court. Their testimony, powerful and emotional, laid bare the devastating consequences of the corruption that had been allowed to flourish. The trial was not merely a legal proceeding; it was a cathartic experience, a public reckoning with the city's past and a crucial step towards healing.

The outcome of the trial, while delivering justice to the victims, didn't offer a neat resolution to the questions of redemption and forgiveness. Some of the perpetrators were given stiff sentences, while others received lighter penalties. Some publicly apologized for their actions, while others maintained their innocence. Even in the face of justice, the path to forgiveness remained uneven, winding, and fraught with complexities.

Miller, observing the process, recognized that true redemption could not be granted by a judge or a jury. It was a personal journey, a process of self-reflection and atonement. Forgiveness, too, was not a simple act but a complex emotional process that required time, empathy, and a willingness to confront the painful truths of the past. The city, like the individuals implicated in Martel's scheme, would need to grapple with its own demons to confront its own complicity in the culture of silence that had allowed the corruption to thrive. The process wouldn't be easy, and it certainly wouldn't be quick. But Miller knew, with a certainty that transcended the doubts that still gnawed at him, that the journey had to begin. The alternative – continued silence and unacknowledged complicity – was simply not an option. The price of silence, he understood now more profoundly than ever before, was far too high. The price of redemption, however steep, was worth paying. The path to forgiveness, however long and arduous, was the only path forward. And Miller, despite the personal sacrifices he had made and the ongoing risks he faced, was ready to walk it. He had stared into the abyss of corruption and emerged, scared but unbroken, ready to lead the city out of the darkness and towards a brighter, more just future.

Moving Forward

The aftermath of the Martel trial hung heavily over the city like a persistent fog. Justice had been served, but the air remained thick with the lingering scent of betrayal and the bitter taste of disillusionment. The streets, once vibrant with the careless energy of a city oblivious to its decay, now seemed quieter and reflective. The silence, however, was different this time. It wasn't the suffocating silence of complicity but a thoughtful quietude, a space for introspection and healing.

The city council, under intense public scrutiny, initiated a series of reforms designed to address the systemic failures that had allowed Martel's scheme to flourish. Transparency became the new mantra, with a commitment to open records and increased public accountability. New ethics guidelines were implemented, designed to prevent future instances of corruption and to foster a culture of integrity within city government. Independent oversight boards were established to monitor the activities of various city departments, ensuring that no stone was left unturned in the pursuit of accountability. These changes, while significant, were only the first steps in a long and arduous process of rebuilding trust.

The media, having initially hesitated to delve into the depths of the scandal, now played a vital role in holding those in power accountable. Investigative journalism flourished, pushing the boundaries of what was considered acceptable and digging deeper into the roots of corruption. The public, once apathetic, was now actively engaged, demanding transparency and participating in discussions about how to improve the city's governance. Talk shows and public forums became platforms for debate, offering a space for airing grievances and formulating plans for the future.

The process of healing, however, was far from uniform. Some neighbors, particularly those who had been most directly impacted by Martel's scheme, struggled with a deep sense of betrayal and resentment. The victims, while having their day in court, continued to grapple with the emotional and economic consequences of the crimes against them. Support groups were established to provide them with counseling, financial assistance, and a sense of community. These support systems provided a vital lifeline for those struggling to piece their lives back together, offering a safe space to share their experiences and to find solace in collective healing.

The question of forgiveness, a complex and often painful process, remained a source of contention. Some victims found it impossible to forgive those who had betrayed their trust and facilitated Martel's crimes. Others, recognizing the human capacity for error and change, were more willing to offer forgiveness, believing it to be essential for collective healing. This division within the victim community highlighted the multifaceted nature of forgiveness, its personal and subjective nature, and its lack of a universally applicable timeline.

For those who had been complicit in the cover-up, the path to redemption was equally challenging. Some sought to atone for their actions through public confessions, cooperation with the authorities, and acts of community service. Their willingness to confront their past and contribute to the city's recovery was a testament to the human capacity for change and self-reflection. Others, however, remained haunted by their past actions, struggling with the weight of their guilt and unable to find peace. These individuals highlighted the complexity of repentance and the difficulties faced by those attempting to reconcile with their past transgressions.

Anya Sharma, whose testimony had played a crucial role in dismantling Martel's operation, became a symbol of courage and resilience. Her story, initially shared with trepidation, had inspired others to come forward, demonstrating the power of a single voice to initiate a ripple effect of change. She dedicated herself to advocating for victims of exploitation and corruption, leveraging her experience to prevent similar tragedies from occurring in the future. Her newfound activism showcased the transformative potential of courage and the capacity to harness personal trauma to effect meaningful societal change.

Miller, having played a pivotal role in exposing the corruption, found himself thrust into a new role – that of a community leader. His integrity, unwavering in the face of considerable pressure, had earned him the respect and trust of the public. He worked tirelessly to ensure that the reforms were implemented effectively and that those responsible were held accountable. He also focused on rebuilding trust in law enforcement, striving to restore faith in a system that had been severely compromised. He became a symbol of hope, a testament to the possibility of positive change, even in the face of seemingly insurmountable challenges. His journey, filled with personal sacrifices and unwavering dedication, became an inspiration to the city, demonstrating the significance of unwavering ethical resolve in the pursuit of justice.

The rebuilding process was slow, painstaking, and often fraught with setbacks. But the city, scary but not broken, began to move forward, guided by a collective desire for accountability, reconciliation, and a brighter future. The price of silence had been high, but the commitment to confronting the past and building a more just society proved to be a price worth paying. The city's journey towards redemption was a testament to the resilience of the human spirit and the unwavering power of hope in the face of adversity. The path ahead remained long and challenging, but with each step forward, the city's residents collectively reaffirmed their commitment to creating a society where justice prevailed and where the price of silence was never again so exorbitant.

The scars remained, visible reminders of the darkness they had overcome, but they served as a testament to their strength and a beacon illuminating the path toward a more just future. The slow, deliberate process of healing continued, but there was a palpable sense of renewed hope, a shared understanding that together, they would build a better tomorrow, free from the corrupting influence of the past. The memory of Martel's crimes served as a constant reminder of the vigilance required to protect the city's future, preventing a recurrence of the dark days that had tested their resilience and shattered their trust in their institutions. The price of silence had been paid, and the city stood firm in its commitment to ensure that such a price would never again be exacted. The healing journey was ongoing, but the path forward was clear, marked by the unwavering determination of a community reborn from the ashes of corruption.

Acknowledgments

My deepest gratitude goes to my editor, Sarah Chen, for her unwavering support and insightful guidance throughout this project. Her keen eye for detail and her belief in this story were invaluable. I'm also indebted to my agent, David Miller, for his tireless efforts and unwavering faith in my work. A special thank you to my beta readers, whose feedback sharpened the narrative and helped refine the characters. Finally, this book would not have been possible without the unwavering support of my family and friends, who patiently endured my long hours and grumpiness induced by writer's block. Thank you.

Appendix

This appendix contains supplementary materials relevant to the investigation detailed in the novel. Specifically, it includes a redacted version of the Martel organization's financial records, showcasing the complex web of shell corporations and offshore accounts used to launder money. Due to the sensitive nature of this information, certain details have been omitted to protect ongoing investigations and to prevent any potential harm. Additionally, a partial transcript of intercepted communications between key members of the organization is included, offering further insight into their operations and internal dynamics. This information is presented for contextual understanding and is not intended as a comprehensive overview of the case.

Glossary

Clean Slate Initiative:
Anya Sharma's ambitious reform program aimed at eradicating corruption within Wilder City's government and institutions.

The Phoenix Project:
The codename for the joint police and investigative journalism operation that exposed Martel's criminal enterprise.

Wilder City Unified Trauma Center:
A specialized center focused on providing holistic care for victims of trauma, both physical and emotional.

References

While this novel is a work of fiction, the portrayal of police procedures and investigative techniques is informed by extensive research and interviews with law enforcement professionals. The economic and social issues explored within the narrative are based on real-world challenges that many urban centers face. For further information on these topics, readers are encouraged to consult resources from credible academic and journalistic sources focusing on urban crime, political corruption, and economic inequality. A detailed bibliography is available upon request from the publisher.

Author Biography

Arthur L. Taylor: A Multifaceted Talent

Arthur L. Taylor is a distinguished crime novelist, Texas Licensed Private Investigator, Certified Crime Scene Investigator, and Paralegal with a degree in Criminal Science. His extensive background in the US Army and Texas National Guard has provided him with a unique perspective on the complexities of crime and the human cost of corruption. Taylor's experience working within the justice system has deeply influenced his writing, allowing him to create intricate plots, morally gray characters, and realistic portrayals of police procedures.

Taylor's literary career is marked by his acclaimed series, "Dark Hearts Iron Hands," which includes the novels "The Conspiracy" and "The Verdict." These works have been praised for their gripping narratives and authentic depiction of the criminal justice system. Taylor's ability to weave complex storylines with deep character development has earned him dedicated readership and critical acclaim.

In addition to his achievements in literature, Arthur L. Taylor is also a talented Song-writer. His passion for music has led him to create several compositions that reflect his diverse interests and experiences. Taylor's music often explores themes similar to those in his novels, such as justice, morality, and human condition. His compositions have been featured in various media, adding another layer to his multifaceted career.

Taylor's dedication to his craft, both in writing and music, showcases his commitment to exploring the depths of human experience. His work continues to resonate with audiences, offering a profound look into the world of crime and justice through both his novels and musical creations...

Historical Context

The Martel scandal, while seemingly contained within the city limits, resonated far beyond its geographical boundaries. Its echoes reverberated through the halls of state government, prompting a sweeping review of campaign finance laws and lobbying regulations. The state legislature, facing intense pressure from a newly mobilized citizenry, passed a series of reforms aimed at increasing transparency and accountability in the political process. These reforms included stricter limitations on campaign contributions, increased disclosure requirements for lobbyists, and the creation of an independent ethics commission to investigate allegations of corruption.

The scandal served as a stark reminder of the influence of money in politics and the vulnerability of democratic institutions to manipulation by powerful special interests. The state's response, though initially slow and hesitant, eventually became a significant step towards greater political transparency and a more equitable playing field for candidates.

Nationally, the Martel case became a lightning rod for discussions about the role of big money in politics. Conservative commentators highlighted the need for individual responsibility and personal accountability, arguing that while systemic failures existed, individuals had made conscious choices to engage in corrupt activities. Liberal voices focused on the need for stronger campaign finance regulations and increased enforcement of existing laws. The debate unfolded across various media platforms, generating significant public interest and prompting a renewed focus on campaign finance reform at the federal level. The intensity of the public outcry even reached the halls of Congress, leading to the introduction of several bills aimed at addressing systemic issues revealed by the Martel scandal. Although none of these bills were immediately successful in enacting meaningful change, the scandal put campaign finance reform back on the national agenda.

Furthermore, the Martel case ignited a nationwide debate concerning ethics in public service and corporate governance. Business schools integrated case studies on the scandal into their curricula, using Martel's intricate web of corruption to illustrate the dangers of unchecked power and the devastating consequences of ethical failures. The business world, initially hesitant to fully address the scandal's implications, eventually adopted stricter internal ethics policies, emphasizing accountability and transparency in their operations.

Companies facing increasing scrutiny from shareholders and consumers began to prioritize ethical practices as a key factor in maintaining their reputation and protecting their bottom lines. The ripple effect extended across various industries, resulting in a heightened focus on corporate social responsibility and a greater emphasis on ethical leadership.

The legal profession was also impacted profoundly by the Martel affair. The trial exposed vulnerabilities in existing legal frameworks and highlighted the need for increased oversight and regulation of lobbying practices. Law schools, recognizing the crucial lessons embedded in the scandal, incorporated case studies into their ethics courses, pushing students to grapple with complex ethical dilemmas arising from professional conflicts of interest. Professional legal organizations, concerned about the erosion of public trust in the legal profession, initiated reforms focused on maintaining high ethical standards and ensuring greater accountability among their members. The need for stricter regulations concerning attorney-client privilege in cases involving corruption was also hotly debated, prompting ongoing discussions about the balance between protecting client confidentiality and upholding the integrity of the justice system.

Historians, too, found themselves deeply engaged by the Martel case. The scandal offered a compelling window into the complexities of power, corruption, and the fragility of democratic institutions. It served as a cautionary tale, illustrating how unchecked ambition and a thirst for wealth could undermine the very foundations of a just and equitable society. Scholars began to analyze the societal factors that contributed to the scandal, exploring the role of political polarization, economic inequality, and a decline in civic engagement. Books and articles chronicled the scandal's unfolding, providing detailed analyses of the players involved, the machinations of the corruption scheme, and the subsequent efforts to bring those responsible to justice. The Martel case quickly transitioned from a local scandal to a case study in political science, sociology, and history, providing fertile ground for future research and analysis.

The long-term implications of the Martel scandal were profound and far-reaching. While the immediate focus was on bringing the perpetrators to justice and enacting reforms, the case served as a catalyst for deeper societal introspection. The events prompted renewed discussions about the role of media in holding power accountable, the importance of civic engagement, and the need for greater transparency and accountability across all levels of government. The city, once paralyzed by fear and uncertainty, began to emerge from the shadow of the scandal, slowly but surely building back trust and confidence in its institutions. The healing process was ongoing, but the experience had undoubtedly left its indelible mark, serving as a powerful reminder of the importance of vigilance, ethical leadership, and the collective commitment to upholding the principles of justice and transparency.

The reverberations extended to the lives of ordinary citizens. The scandal's impact on public trust in government extended beyond mere skepticism. Many citizens expressed a growing cynicism about the political process, fueled by a sense of powerlessness and disillusionment with elected officials. Voter turnout in subsequent elections saw a notable decline, reflecting a growing apathy and disengagement from the political system. The initial sense of community unity following the trial began to fray as the public wrestled with the long-term consequences of corruption and the failure of institutions to effectively prevent it.

Moreover, the economic fallout from the scandal was substantial. Businesses impacted by Martel's schemes faced bankruptcy and job losses, creating a ripple effect of economic hardship throughout the community. The city's reputation suffered, affecting tourism and investment. The financial burden of implementing the new reforms, while necessary, further strained the city's budget, leading to difficult choices regarding public services and infrastructure projects. The cost of the investigations, legal battles, and subsequent reforms imposed a significant financial strain on both the city and the state, underscoring the exorbitant price paid for silence and complicity.

The narrative of the Martel scandal transcended its immediate context, becoming a symbol of larger societal anxieties regarding corruption, political maneuvering, and the abuse of power. The lingering questions about the systemic issues that allowed the scandal to flourish continued to fuel debates about ethical leadership, campaign finance reform, and the need for greater transparency and accountability in government.

The historical context reveals that the scandal wasn't an isolated incident but rather a symptom of deeper-seated problems within the system, problems that required far-reaching reforms and a sustained commitment to ethical governance to prevent future occurrences. The echoes of the past, therefore, served not only as a reminder of the devastation caused but also as a catalyst for transformative change. The story of Martel wasn't just about one man's ambition; it was about a system's failure, a city's struggle, and the slow, painful path toward redemption and a more just future. The road to recovery was long, but the unwavering commitment to accountability and transparency offered.

a glimmer of hope in the aftermath of the scandal's profound impact.

Similar Cases

The Martel scandal, while unprecedented in its scope and audacity, wasn't an isolated incident. A closer examination reveals a disturbing pattern of similar cases, albeit on smaller scales, throughout history. These echoes of the past, while perhaps less publicized, serve as stark reminders of the enduring vulnerability of democratic systems to corruption and the cyclical nature of ethical failures. The common threads woven through these past scandals offer valuable insights into the systemic weaknesses that allowed Martel's machinations to thrive and provide a framework for understanding how to prevent future occurrences.

One striking parallel can be drawn to the Watergate scandal, a watershed moment in American political history. While the specifics differ significantly— Watergate involved a break-in at the Democratic National Committee headquarters, whereas Martel's corruption was primarily financial, the core issue remains the same: the abuse of power by those entrusted with public office.

Both scandals exposed a culture of secrecy, a willingness to bend or break the rules to achieve political goals, and a disregard for the democratic process. Just as the Nixon administration attempted to obstruct justice, the Martel administration employed similar tactics, attempting to cover up its illicit activities and silence whistleblowers. The resulting investigations, in both cases, unearthed a network of complicity extending far beyond the initial perpetrators. The parallels are chilling in their resemblance, highlighting the enduring human tendency to abuse power and the recurring need for vigilance and robust oversight mechanisms.

The Teapot Dome scandal of the 1920s, though considerably older, also shares unsettling similarities with the Martel affair. This involved the secretive leasing of government oil reserves to private companies in exchange for bribes and kickbacks. While the specifics of the bribery methods differ from Martel's sophisticated web of shell corporations and campaign donations, the underlying principle of using public office for personal gain remains consistent. Both scandals demonstrate how seemingly small acts of corruption can snowball into larger schemes, eroding public trust and undermining the integrity of government institutions. The Teapot Dome scandal, like Martel's, led to significant legal repercussions and significant reforms aimed at preventing future abuses, demonstrating the iterative nature of this struggle against corruption. However, history demonstrates that reforms, while essential, are often insufficient if not coupled with a sustained commitment to ethical leadership and a culture of accountability.

Moving beyond the realm of national politics, the numerous municipal corruption cases throughout American history provide further context. From the infamous Chicago machine of the early 20th century to more recent examples of city officials engaged in bribery and embezzlement, these local scandals share a familiar pattern of cronyism, patronage, and a disregard for the public good. These smaller-scale scandals, though often overshadowed by national events, are critical for understanding the broader problem of corruption. They offer a microcosm of the same systemic issues—weak oversight, a lack of transparency, and a culture of impunity—that allowed the Martel affair to flourish. The fact that similar patterns emerge repeatedly in different contexts, at different levels of government, points towards deep-seated issues within the system that require a multipronged approach to reform.

Furthermore, international examples add to another layer of perspective. Numerous cases of corruption in developing countries, often involving massive embezzlement of public funds and widespread bribery, underscore the global nature of this challenge. These cases, often characterized by a lack of effective oversight and weak rule of law, demonstrate the devastating consequences of unchecked corruption on economic development and social stability.

While the methods and actors involved differ drastically from the Martel case, the fundamental issue remains the same: the exploitation of power for personal enrichment, often at the expense of the wider population. These cases serve as a sobering reminder that the struggle against corruption transcends geographical boundaries and requires international collaboration to address effectively. The Martel case, therefore, stands not merely as a unique event but as a cautionary tale reflecting patterns observed across cultures and throughout time.

Analyzing these similar cases reveals recurring themes. One prominent pattern is the existence of weak oversight mechanisms. Insufficient checks and balances, combined with a lack of transparency, allow corrupt officials to operate with impunity. In each of the aforementioned cases, inadequate monitoring, and a failure to enforce existing regulations allowed corruption to fester and spread. This lack of effective oversight often creates a culture of secrecy and complicity, where individuals are reluctant to report wrongdoing for fear of retaliation.

Another critical recurring element is the role of money in politics. In nearly every instance of significant corruption, substantial sums of money have been involved. Whether it's campaign contributions, bribes, or kickbacks, the influence of money distorts the political process and undermines the integrity of government institutions. The Martel case, with its complex web of campaign donations and shell corporations, starkly highlights this connection between money and corruption. Addressing this issue requires robust campaign finance reforms, increased transparency in political funding, and stricter enforcement of existing regulations.

Beyond these systemic factors, the human element remains crucial. The individual choices and ethical failures of those involved in these scandals cannot be ignored. Ambition, greed, and a lack of moral compass frequently serve as drivers of corruption. However, holding individuals accountable while simultaneously addressing the systemic issues that enable corruption is vital. A balanced approach acknowledges both the individual responsibility for unethical actions and the broader societal and institutional factors that contribute to the problem. Without addressing both aspects, future scandals are almost inevitable.

The similarities between the Martel case and these past incidents offer a clear path forward. Strengthening oversight mechanisms, implementing comprehensive campaign finance reforms, and fostering a culture of ethical leadership are critical steps in preventing future occurrences. However, effective change also requires ongoing vigilance, sustained public pressure, and a collective commitment to upholding the principles of transparency and accountability.

The echoes of past scandals should serve not only as reminders of the devastating consequences of corruption but also as catalysts for meaningful and lasting reform. The fight against corruption is a continuous battle, demanding constant vigilance and proactive measures to ensure the integrity and stability of democratic institutions. The struggle is not merely a legal or political one; it is a moral imperative, demanding not just the prosecution of offenders but a fundamental transformation of the systems that allow corruption to flourish. Only through such a comprehensive approach can we hope to break the cycle of scandal and build societies truly grounded in fairness and integrity.

Arthur L. Taylor

Cultural Commentary

The Martel scandal, however, transcends the mere realm of political maneuvering and financial chicanery; it exposes a deeper malaise within the fabric of our society. The ease with which Martel manipulated the system, the complicity of those around him, and the public's initial slow response all speak volumes about the broader cultural context in which such events can unfold.

One of the most disturbing aspects of the Martel affair is the pervasiveness of a culture of cynicism. Years of political scandals, economic downturns, and the constant barrage of negative news have left many citizens feeling disillusioned and apathetic. This widespread cynicism creates fertile ground for corruption to flourish. When the public believes that all politicians are inherently corrupt, they become less likely to hold them accountable for their actions. This apathy allows individuals like Martel to operate with a sense of impunity, secure in the knowledge that public outrage will be muted and investigations will be halfhearted. The initial lack of widespread public outcry concerning the initial reports about Martel's dealings is a testament to the corrosive effects of this pervasive cynicism.

Furthermore, the scandal reveals a disturbing acceptance of moral ambiguity. Many individuals involved in the Martel affair, from minor officials to high-ranking executives, knowingly participated in unethical practices, rationalizing their actions as "business as usual" or simply as a necessary evil in the pursuit of wealth and power. This acceptance of moral compromises, this erosion of ethical standards, isn't confined to the political or financial elite; it's a reflection of a broader societal trend. The relentless pursuit of material success, often at the expense of ethical considerations, has become a dominant cultural narrative. This is particularly evident in the corporate world, where the pressure to maximize profits often overshadows concerns about ethical behavior and social responsibility. The actions of the corporations complicit in Martel's schemes are a stark illustration of this widespread prioritization of profit over principle.

The pervasive influence of money in politics further exacerbates the problem. The ease with which Martel used campaign donations and other financial instruments to buy influence and silence dissenters underscores the deep connection between wealth and power in our society. The current campaign finance laws, while intended to regulate the flow of money into politics, have proven inadequate to prevent the kind of influence-peddling that characterized the Martel affair. The sheer scale of the financial transactions involved suggests a systemic failure to adequately address the problem of money in politics, a failure that allows wealthy individuals and corporations to wield disproportionate influence over the political process. This imbalance of power allows the privileged to operate outside the boundaries of conventional ethics and accountability, perpetuating a cycle of corruption and reinforcing the existing power dynamics.

Another contributing factor is the erosion of trust in institutions. The media's role in the Martel scandal is complex and multi-layered. While some journalists played a crucial role in exposing the truth, others were either complicit in covering up the scandal or were simply too slow to react.

This divided response highlights the ongoing debate about the role of the media in a democratic society and points to the challenges inherent in maintaining journalistic integrity in a highly competitive and commercialized media landscape. The initial slow response of certain media outlets, their focus on sensationalism rather than deep investigation, underlines the importance of a robust, independent media dedicated to uncovering the truth, regardless of political or economic pressures.

Similarly, the judicial system's response to the scandal initially lacked the necessary decisiveness. The early reluctance of certain law enforcement agencies to fully investigate Martel's actions points to potential systemic weaknesses within the institution itself. This initial inertia highlights the vulnerability of even the most established institutions to the subtle pressures of political influence and the potential for complacency within the very bodies designed to uphold the rule of law. It underscores the need for greater transparency and accountability within law enforcement and the judiciary, ensuring that these institutions can effectively investigate and prosecute powerful individuals, regardless of their political connections or financial resources.

The Martel scandal also exposes a profound disconnect between the political elite and the general public. The sense of detachment displayed by some politicians in their responses to the scandal reflects a troubling lack of empathy and understanding of the concerns of ordinary citizens. This disconnects, fueled by factors like the increasing influence of money in politics and the declining trust in institutions, undermines the legitimacy of the political system and creates further resentment and disillusionment amongst the population. The stark contrast between the opulent lifestyle of Martel and the struggle of the average citizen serves as a potent symbol of this growing divide. This breach in public trust necessitates a renewed commitment to transparency, accountability, and public service from political leaders, fostering a sense of shared purpose and a more inclusive political culture.

Beyond the immediate implications of the scandal, the cultural commentary it provides extends to a broader examination of societal values and priorities. The emphasis on material wealth, the acceptance of moral compromises, and the pervasive cynicism all reflects a deeper societal malaise. Addressing this requires a fundamental shift in cultural values, a renewed emphasis on ethical behavior, and a commitment to building more just and equitable institutions. This isn't simply a matter of reforming political systems; it requires a fundamental assessment of our shared values and a commitment to fostering a culture of integrity and accountability throughout all aspects of society.

The Martel affair serves as a stark reminder that corruption isn't merely a political problem; it's a societal one. Its roots lie deep within the cultural fabric of our society, woven into the threads of our values, priorities, and institutions. To effectively combat corruption, we need to address not only the individual actors involved but also the broader cultural context that allows such events to occur. The path forward requires a multifaceted approach, encompassing political reforms, institutional improvements, and a fundamental shift in cultural values. Only through such a comprehensive strategy can we hope to break the cycle of corruption and build a society truly grounded in fairness, transparency, and integrity.

The echoes of Martel's actions should not simply serve as a cautionary tale; they should serve as a clarion call for profound and lasting societal change. The fight against corruption is far from over; it's a continuous struggle requiring the sustained engagement of citizens, institutions, and policymakers alike. It demands a collective commitment to building a more just and equitable world, a world where the pursuit of wealth does not overshadow ethical considerations and where the public's trust in their institutions is not casually eroded. Only then can we hope to prevent future echoes of this devastating scandal, breaking free from the cyclical nature of these betrayals and building a foundation for a truly just and transparent society? The challenge is immense, the task complex, but the need for change is undeniable.

The legacy of Martel will ultimately be defined not only by the scandal itself but by the societal response it provokes—a response that must be courageous, comprehensive, and committed to dismantling the structures that allow such abuse of power to persist. The future depends on our ability to learn from the past, to confront the uncomfortable truths it reveals, and to build a society where the pursuit of justice is relentless and the principles of integrity are inviolable.

Lessons Learned

The unraveling of the Martel scandal, while initially shocking, ultimately served as a brutal but necessary lesson in the fragility of our societal structures. The sheer scale of the corruption, the intricate web of complicity, and the chilling ease with which Martel manipulated the system exposed vulnerabilities we'd long ignored or perhaps conveniently overlooked. The most immediate lesson, perhaps the most obvious, was the devastating impact of unchecked power. Martel's rise wasn't a fluke; it was a consequence of a system that allowed ambition, unchecked by accountability, to flourish. The checks and balances designed to prevent such abuses were either weak or deliberately bypassed, highlighting a crucial failure in the mechanisms meant to safeguard the public interest. This wasn't just a failure of individuals; it was a systemic breakdown, a testament to the erosion of ethical standards within both public and private institutions.

The investigation itself revealed a second, equally crucial lesson: the importance of a truly independent press. While some journalistic outlets bravely pursued the truth, others were slow to act, hampered by pressures from powerful individuals and corporations tied to Martel. This uneven response underscored the critical role of a fearless and independent media in a democratic society, a media free from undue influence and dedicated to uncovering the truth, regardless of the consequences. The scandal served as a stark reminder of the necessity of supporting investigative journalism, recognizing its vital role in holding power accountable and preventing future abuses. The silence and complicity of certain media outlets, fueled by self-preservation or a misguided pursuit of profit, allowed the scandal to fester for far too long, demonstrating the devastating consequences of a compromised press.

The judicial system's initial response also provided sobering lessons. The early reluctance of some law enforcement agencies to fully investigate Martel's actions highlighted a disturbing tendency towards complacency, a failure to aggressively pursue powerful individuals, regardless of their connections or influence. This inaction, fueled by factors ranging from political pressure to a lack of resources, demonstrated the importance of robust, well-funded law enforcement agencies completely free from political influence. The need for transparency and accountability within the judicial system was glaringly evident; the slow and hesitant initial response indicated a critical need for reforms to ensure that powerful individuals are held to the same standards as everyone else. The system, in its initial response, failed to reflect the seriousness of the crimes committed and the need for swift and decisive action.

Beyond the institutional failures, the Martel scandal illuminated the profound influence of money in politics. Martel's ability to use campaign donations and other financial instruments to silence dissenters and buy influence was a stark demonstration of the corrosive impact of wealth on the political process. The scandal underscored the need for significant reforms in campaign finance laws and stricter regulations to prevent the kind of influence-peddling that allowed Martel to operate with impunity. The sheer volume of money involved highlighted the urgent need for transparency in political donations, making it impossible for wealthy individuals and corporations to exert undue influence behind a veil of secrecy. The existing campaign finance laws clearly failed to address the issue adequately; more stringent regulations were clearly needed, along with a comprehensive overhaul of the system to ensure fair and equitable representation.

Perhaps the most unsettling lesson from the Martel scandal was the pervasive culture of cynicism and moral ambiguity it revealed. Many individuals knowingly participated in unethical practices, rationalizing their actions as "business as usual" or necessary evils in the pursuit of wealth and power. This disturbing acceptance of moral compromises and this erosion of ethical standards within both the public and private sectors pointed to a deeper societal malaise, a weakening of ethical values and a prioritization of self-interest over the common good. The scandal served as a harsh indictment of this creeping moral relativism, highlighting the urgent need for a renewed emphasis on ethical behavior and personal responsibility.

The disconnect between the political elite and the general public also stood out as a significant lesson. The detachment displayed by some politicians in their responses to the scandal reflected a troubling lack of empathy and understanding of the concerns of ordinary citizens. This growing chasm between those in power and the people they are meant to serve underscores the urgent need for increased transparency and accountability in government. The stark contrast between Martel's opulent lifestyle and the struggles of the average citizen served as a powerful symbol of this widening gap, a gap that fuels resentment and erodes trust in the political process. Bridging this divide requires a fundamental shift in the way politicians interact with their constituents, fostering a sense of shared purpose and rebuilding trust eroded by decades of cynicism and disillusionment.

The aftermath of the Martel scandal, the ensuing investigations, and the public outcry, while demonstrating the resilience of democratic institutions, also revealed the inherent fragility of systems built on trust and accountability. The scandal provided a stark reminder that corruption is not merely a matter of individual wrongdoing but a systemic issue reflecting flaws within the existing structures of power and governance.

The lessons learned are not simply cautionary tales; they are a road map for necessary reforms, a blueprint for building a society more resistant to the insidious effects of corruption. The echoes of Martel's actions must serve as a call for profound and lasting change, a call that requires the collective engagement of citizens, institutions, and policymakers alike. Only through a concerted effort and a commitment to transparency, accountability, and ethical conduct can we hope to prevent future tragedies like the Martel scandal and build a society grounded in fairness, integrity, and justice. The ongoing battle against corruption demands vigilance and the memory of Martel's actions must serve as a constant reminder of the stakes involved. The fight is far from over; it requires continuous efforts and constant vigilance to ensure that the lessons learned from this debacle are not forgotten and that the institutions meant to protect us are strengthened and fortified against future abuses of power. The road to reform is long and challenging, but the price of inaction is far too high.

Perspective and Reflection

The Martel scandal, with its intricate web of deceit and corruption, left an indelible mark not just on the city but on the collective psyche of the nation. Its echoes reverberated through countless conversations, shaping political discourse and influencing the very fabric of public trust. The initial shock gave way to a period of intense introspection, a soul-searching examination of the vulnerabilities within our systems of governance and accountability. It wasn't merely about the fall of one powerful man; it was a seismic event that exposed the fault lines in the foundations of our democracy.

The immediate aftermath saw a surge in civic engagement. Citizens, once apathetic, now demanded answers, demanding reform and holding their elected officials accountable. Grassroots movements sprung up, advocating for transparency in government, stricter campaign finance laws, and a more robust independent media. The streets filled with protestors, their voices a chorus of outrage and determination. This wave of activism, fueled by the outrage of the Martel scandal, forced politicians to acknowledge the public's demand for change. The legislative landscape shifted subtly, with discussions surrounding campaign finance reform reaching a fever pitch and calls for enhanced investigative powers for oversight committees becoming louder.

However, the path to reform was far from smooth. The entrenched interests, those who profited from the status quo, resisted change with considerable vigor. Lobbyists, representing powerful corporations and wealthy individuals, worked tirelessly to water down proposed reforms, often employing sophisticated strategies to influence legislation and public opinion. The fight was not merely a battle of ideas but a clash between entrenched power and the nascent forces of reform. It was a protracted struggle, fought in committee rooms, courtrooms, and in the court of public opinion.

The judicial system, initially slow to react, eventually began to grapple with the complexities of the Martel case. The sheer volume of evidence, the intricate network of complicity, and the skillful legal maneuvering employed by Martel's defense team stretched the system to its limits. Trials dragged on, legal battles were waged, and appeals were filed, creating a protracted legal drama that played out in the media spotlight. Each legal victory, each setback, fueled public debate and further shaped public perception. The slow pace of justice, however, continued to frustrate the public, highlighting the shortcomings of the judicial system in dealing with complex cases involving powerful individuals.

The media initially criticized for its slow response, slowly but surely began to fulfill its crucial role as the watchdog of democracy. Investigative journalists, driven by a dedication to truth and fueled by public demand for accountability, dug deeper into the scandal, uncovering previously unknown details and exposing further instances of corruption. Their work, often done at personal risk, played a pivotal role in shaping the public narrative and forcing the government to act. The resulting coverage helped to shift public opinion, solidifying the demand for reform and accountability. However, the uneven response of the media in the initial stages highlighted the vulnerability of the press to external pressures, underscoring the ongoing need to protect and nurture independent journalism.

The long-term implications of the Martel scandal extended far beyond the immediate aftermath. It served as a stark reminder of the fragility of democratic institutions and the constant need for vigilance and engagement. The scandal became a case study in higher education, dissected in classrooms, and used to illustrate the dangers of unchecked power and the importance of ethical conduct in public life. It highlighted the intricate interplay between politics, money, and media, and its enduring legacy served as a cautionary tale to future generations of leaders and citizens alike.

The scandal fostered a renewed appreciation for the importance of civic engagement and active participation in the democratic process. Citizens began to demand greater transparency from their elected officials, a higher standard of ethical behavior, and a more robust system of accountability. The apathy that had characterized previous years was replaced by a renewed sense of civic duty and a determination to protect the integrity of the democratic process. The scandal became a catalyst for widespread reforms, a turning point that initiated a period of reflection and reevaluation.

Beyond the immediate changes, the Martel scandal had a profound impact on the cultural landscape. It fueled a deeper conversation about ethics, morality, and the responsibility of those in positions of power. The narrative became interwoven into the national consciousness, shaping the way people viewed politics, media, and the role of power in society. It fueled a renewed skepticism toward political figures and a greater demand for transparency in all aspects of public life.

The echoes of Martel's actions continued to reverberate through the years, serving as a constant reminder of the importance of safeguarding democratic institutions and preventing future abuses of power. The scandal became a watershed moment, a turning point that irrevocably altered the political landscape and shaped the course of future reforms. It served as a painful but necessary lesson, highlighting the flaws within existing structures and the imperative for continuous vigilance and engagement to ensure the integrity of the democratic process.

The years following the scandal witnessed a gradual yet steady improvement in government transparency. New laws were enacted aimed at enhancing accountability, improving campaign finance regulations, and strengthening oversight mechanisms. These laws were not without flaws, nor were they universally popular, but they represented a significant step toward addressing the vulnerabilities exposed by the Martel scandal. The implementation of these laws, however, proved to be a gradual process, encountering political resistance and logistical challenges.

Moreover, the scandal highlighted the pervasive issue of moral compromise in society. Many individuals, both in the public and private sectors, have knowingly participated in unethical practices, prioritizing personal gain over ethical considerations. The scandal exposed a troubling trend of moral relativism, a disregard for ethical principles in pursuit of wealth and power. The long-term consequences of this moral erosion would continue to be felt for years to come, impacting on the trust between citizens and their institutions.

In the end, the Martel scandal wasn't just a story about corruption; it was a profound exploration of the human condition, highlighting the fragility of power, the allure of ambition, and the enduring importance of accountability. It served as a stark reminder that the fight for justice and integrity is an ongoing process, a constant vigilance against the insidious forces that threaten to undermine democratic institutions and erode public trust. The echoes of Martel's actions, though fading with time, continue to serve as a potent warning, a constant reminder of the need for transparency, accountability, and a renewed commitment to the principles upon which our societies are built.

The struggle for ethical governance for a culture grounded in fairness and justice remains an ongoing battle, a testament to the lasting impact of a single man's actions and the systemic flaws they exposed. The fight continues, fueled by the lessons learned and the enduring memory of the Martel scandal. The quest for a more just and equitable society is a journey, not a destination, a process that constantly evolves and adapts in response to the challenges it faces. The story of Martel is a somber reminder of the importance of vigilance, the eternal need to safeguard the principles that uphold a free and just society.

Burden of Knowledge

The weight of the Martel scandal pressed down on Alice like a physical burden. It wasn't just the sheer volume of information she possessed, the meticulously documented evidence of corruption, the intricate web of lies and deceit she'd painstakingly unraveled. It was the knowledge itself, the understanding of the depths of human depravity, the casual disregard for the law, the cynical manipulation of public trust. It was a weight that settled in her chest, a constant, dull ache that no amount of sleep could alleviate.

She'd spent months submerged in the digital detritus of Martel's life, sifting through encrypted emails, deleted files, and coded messages. Each revelation had been a blow, chipping away at her faith in institutions and the inherent goodness of people. She had seen casual cruelty, ruthless ambition, the chilling indiifference to the suffering of others. And it wasn't just Martel; it was the network of accomplices, the enablers, the silent collaborators who had allowed the rot to fester and spread. She'd uncovered evidence of blackmail, coercion, and outright bribery – a system of corruption that permeated every level of government. Each new discovery only deepened the pit of despair that gnawed at her.

The most disturbing aspect wasn't the scale of the corruption itself but the normalcy of it. It wasn't the explosive acts of violence or overt criminality that shocked her; it was the quiet, insidious nature of the betrayal. It was the mundane acts of deceit, the subtle manipulations, and the calculated compromises that had allowed the system to be so thoroughly compromised. It was the insidious creep of moral decay that had poisoned the very heart of the political system.

Sleep offered little respite. Her dreams were a chaotic jumble of encrypted messages, faces flickering in and out of the darkness, whispers of conspiracies and betrayals. She'd wake with a gasp, her heart pounding, the weight of her knowledge pressing down on her like a suffocating blanket. The coffee she consumed in copious amounts did little to alleviate the fatigue, only fueling a restless energy that kept her pacing her apartment, reviewing files, and frantically searching for connections and patterns.

The isolation was almost as heavy as the burden of knowledge. She couldn't share the full extent of her findings with anyone, not without jeopardizing the integrity of the investigation and potentially exposing herself to retaliation. The few people she trusted were either bound by confidentiality agreements or too deeply entrenched in the system to offer meaningful support. She felt cut off, adrift in a sea of information, with no safe harbor to return to. She longed for a sense of normalcy but knew it was a luxury she could no longer afford.

The physical toll was evident. She'd lost weight, her eyes were perpetually bloodshot, and the circles under them seemed to deepen with each passing day. Her once meticulously organized apartment was now a chaotic mess of files, papers, and empty coffee cups. The weight of her knowledge had manifested physically, etching itself onto her body like a roadmap of sleepless nights and unrelenting stress.

Yet, despite the overwhelming burden, there was a strange sense of purpose that kept her going. It wasn't merely a professional obligation; it was a deep-seated sense of responsibility, a commitment to truth and justice. She knew that the revelations she possessed could expose the rot at the heart of the political system and bring about much-needed reform. And it was that possibility, that glimmer of hope for a better future, that fueled her relentless pursuit of truth. It was a flickering candle in the vast darkness of her self-imposed isolation, a fragile light that somehow managed to pierce the oppressive weight of her knowledge.

The silence of her apartment was broken only by the rhythmic tapping of her keyboard, the relentless whirring of her laptop fan, and the occasional rustling of papers. Outside, the city hummed with oblivious energy, unaware of the seismic shift taking place beneath its surface. Alice, however, was keenly aware of it. She felt the tremors, the subtle shifts in the ground beneath her feet, as the weight of her knowledge threatened to bring down the entire edifice of power.

She thought of the victims, the countless individuals who had been harmed by Martel's actions, whose lives had been irrevocably altered by his greed and corruption. Their faces became superimposed onto the jumble of data on her computer screen, their silent pleas a constant reminder of the gravity of her work. The weight of their suffering added to the already immense burden she carried, but it also strengthened her resolve. She would not let them down. She would find justice, even if it meant sacrificing her own peace of mind, her physical and mental well-being, and even her own safety.

The ethical considerations weighed heavily on her, too. She had faced many moral dilemmas during the investigation – compromises she'd had to make, choices she'd had to grapple with. The lines between right and wrong, between legality and justice, had blurred and intertwined, leaving her feeling morally ambiguous, unsure if her actions were truly justified. But the thought of the alternative – the potential for Martel and his accomplices to escape unscathed – fueled her forward. The price of inaction, she knew, was far greater than any personal cost.

As the days bled into weeks and weeks into months, Alice found herself growing increasingly detached from the world outside her apartment. She rarely ventured out, preferring the familiar confines of her workspace, the muted glow of her computer screen, her only companion. Her world had shrunk, confined to the digital landscape of her investigation. She lived and breathed the Martel scandal, consumed by its details and obsessed with finding every last piece of the puzzle.

Yet, even within this self-imposed isolation, a strange kind of clarity had emerged. The weight of knowledge, once a crushing burden, had begun to transform into a source of power. It wasn't a comfortable power; it was a heavy, burdened strength forged in the fires of tireless work, fueled by a profound sense of purpose and responsibility. The weight had changed her, reshaped her, and instilled in her a resilience she never knew she possessed. She was no longer just a journalist but a guardian of truth, a protector of justice, a solitary warrior fighting against overwhelming odds. The weight of the truth was her burden, yes, but it was also her strength.

And she knew, with a certainty that settled deep within her soul, that she would carry that weight until the very last piece of the puzzle was in place, until justice was served. Until the truth was finally revealed.

Personal Growth

The relentless pursuit of truth had exacted a heavy toll. The lines etched around her eyes weren't just from lack of sleep; they were the map of her emotional landscape, a testament to the emotional turmoil she'd endured. The initial shock of Martel's betrayal, the sickening realization of the systemic corruption, had given way to a deep, gnawing disillusionment. The world she once knew, the world of clear-cut right and wrong, had crumbled, replaced by a morally ambiguous landscape where the lines blurred and shifted constantly.

She found herself questioning everything. Her faith in institutions, in the inherent goodness of humanity, had been severely shaken. The casual cruelty she'd witnessed, the ruthless pursuit of power, the calculated disregard for the consequences of their actions – it had left her questioning her own ability to trust, to believe in anything beyond the cold, hard facts she'd unearthed. This skepticism, however, wasn't a sign of weakness; it was a necessary evolution, a recalibration of her worldview. It forced her to rely solely on her own judgment, her own critical thinking, and her own unwavering commitment to truth.

The isolation, once a source of fear and anxiety, had become a strange kind of sanctuary. In the quiet solitude of her apartment, she could process the overwhelming torrent of information, sifting through the data, connecting the dots, and piecing together the complex narrative of Martel's downfall. The silence, once oppressive, now provided the space she needed for contemplation, introspection, and self-discovery. It allowed her to confront her own vulnerabilities and her own fears and to emerge stronger, more resilient, and more determined than ever before.

There were moments of doubt, of course. Moments when the weight of her knowledge threatened to overwhelm her when the fatigue and stress threatened to consume her. There were nights when she lay awake, staring at the ceiling, wrestling with the ethical dilemmas she'd encountered, questioning her methods, her motives, and the very justification of her actions. Was she justified in violating privacy? Was she justified in compromising her own well-being? Was she a vigilante, operating outside the law, or a crusader for justice, fighting for a cause that was bigger than herself?

The answers weren't always clear. Often, they were shrouded in a fog of uncertainty, leaving her feeling disoriented and adrift. But even in those moments of profound self-doubt, she clung to the unwavering conviction that the truth, no matter how painful or inconvenient, was worth fighting for. It was a belief that transcended the personal costs, the risks, and the emotional turmoil. It was a belief that became her compass, guiding her through the moral maze of her investigation.

The transformation wasn't just intellectual or emotional; it was physical as well. The weight loss, initially a sign of stress and neglect, became a testament to her unwavering focus and dedication. She became leaner, harder, and more focused, her body reflecting the strength of her resolve. The dark circles under her eyes, once a symbol of exhaustion, now seemed to hold a certain intensity, a hint of the fierce determination that burned within her. She had become a different person, forged in the crucible of her investigation.

She had shed the naive idealism of her earlier self, replaced by hard-won pragmatism. She had learned to trust her instincts, to recognize subtle cues, to interpret the nuances of language and behavior. She had developed a sharp, analytical mind, capable of dissecting complex information and uncovering hidden truths. The process had been brutal, merciless, and unforgiving, but it had also been transformative, shaping her into something stronger, something more resilient.

The support system she'd envisioned during her darkest moments hadn't materialized. The few individuals she'd considered allies had proven either unwilling or unable to provide the assistance she needed. This isolation, however, had paradoxically fostered a sense of self-reliance and independence she hadn't possessed before. She had learned to rely on herself, to trust her own judgment, and to carry the weight of her knowledge alone. It was a burden, yes, but it was also a source of immense power.

The ethical gray areas she navigated had left their mark. She had made choices that challenged her moral compass, forcing her to confront her own values and beliefs. She had learned that justice wasn't always black and white, that sometimes the ends justified the means, even if those means were morally ambiguous. These experiences, however difficult, enriched her understanding of the complexities of the world and honed her moral judgment.

As the investigation progressed, the weight of the truth began to shift. It was no longer solely a crushing burden; it became a source of empowerment. It fueled her with a sense of righteous indignation and a fierce determination to expose the truth and bring those responsible to justice. The transformation was complete. She had become a force to be reckoned with – a woman of unwavering conviction, unshakeable resolve, and profound empathy for the victims of Martel's crimes. She was a changed woman, but the change was not a descent into cynicism or despair but an ascent into strength and unwavering purpose.

The weight of the truth had not broken her; it had made her. It had forged her into a warrior of truth, prepared to fight for justice, even if it meant sacrificing everything. The road ahead remained uncertain and perilous, but Alice walked it with newfound confidence, her steps steadier, her resolve unyielding, the weight of the truth bearing her forward toward the inevitable

confrontation that lay ahead. The truth, once a crushing

burden, was now her sword and shield.

The Power of Truth

The weight of the truth, once a crushing burden, now felt different. It wasn't merely the oppressive pressure of secrets and lies; it had become a source of power, a tangible force driving her forward. The initial shock and disillusionment had given way to a cold, steely resolve. She was no longer just uncovering a conspiracy; she was fighting a war, a battle against a deeply entrenched system of corruption, a system that had thrived on deceit and manipulation for far too long.

This wasn't a fight she could win alone. The realization struck her with the force of a physical blow. Her previous attempts to enlist allies had failed, leaving her isolated and vulnerable. But isolation, she now understood, was not synonymous with weakness. It was a strategic position, allowing her to operate with a degree of autonomy impossible within the constraints of a traditional investigative team. She could move faster, think more creatively, and act more decisively, unburdened by the cautious bureaucracy that often-stifled official investigations.

Her solitude, however, was not a choice; it was a consequence. The very nature of the conspiracy meant that trust was a luxury she couldn't afford. Every contact, every potential ally, was a potential liability. She had learned to become a ghost, operating in the shadows, her movements silent and her presence unseen. She had honed her skills of observation and deduction, transforming herself into an instrument of precision, capable of gathering information and exploiting vulnerabilities with surgical accuracy.

The power of truth, she discovered, lay not only in its capacity to expose wrongdoing but also in its ability to galvanize others. While she had failed to secure the open support of high-ranking officials or established organizations, she realized that the truth itself could become a weapon, a catalyst for change. By strategically leaking information by subtly influencing the narrative, she could create ripples of doubt and suspicion within the system, turning Martel's allies against each other and creating fissures in the carefully constructed façade of power.

This new strategy, however, demanded even greater caution and precision. Every move had to be calculated, and every action weighed carefully. A single misstep could expose her, leading to disastrous consequences. She understood the risks, but the stakes were too high to retreat. The victims of Martel's crimes deserved justice, and she would not rest until their voices were heard and the truth was finally laid bare.

She began to work differently, her methodology evolving beyond mere data gathering. She understood the psychological warfare at play, the importance of manipulating narratives, of influencing perceptions. She used her knowledge of the law and her understanding of human psychology to shape the direction of the investigation, subtly guiding the course of events toward her desired outcome.

She cultivated a network of informants, each carefully chosen, each contacted through encrypted channels, their identities kept securely hidden. These were not traditional sources but individuals operating on the fringes of society, people with their own agendas and their own grievances against the corrupt system. She understood their motivations, their vulnerabilities, and their value. She treated them with respect, ensuring they felt seen and valued, understanding that their cooperation was crucial to the success of her mission. She offered them a chance at redemption, a way to cleanse their own consciences, to become part of something bigger than themselves. She traded information for information, building a delicate web of trust and collaboration.

One such informant was a disillusioned accountant, a man who had witnessed firsthand the elaborate scheme of embezzlement and money laundering orchestrated by Martel and his cronies. He was initially hesitant, terrified of the consequences of cooperating, but Alice, through her careful approach and unwavering assurances of anonymity, managed to win his trust. The accountant provided her with invaluable documentation, detailed spreadsheets, and bank statements that corroborated her earlier suspicions and revealed the full extent of Martel's criminal enterprise.

Another informant was a former police officer, ostracized for his integrity and now living in self-imposed exile. He had once been part of Martel's inner circle but had grown increasingly uneasy with the escalating violence and corruption. He'd seen the ruthless way Martel dealt with his enemies, the casual disregard for human life, and had decided to break free. His knowledge of Martel's operations and his understanding of the intricacies of the police department's internal structure were crucial to Alice's investigation. He helped her navigate the labyrinthine corridors of power, uncovering hidden connections and revealing the network of complicity that protected Martel.

The process of acquiring and verifying information demanded patience, vigilance, and a deep understanding of the human condition. She learned to interpret body language, decipher subtexts, and identify subtle cues that reveal hidden truths. She became adept at identifying inconsistencies, contradictions, and deliberate obfuscations, and her analytical skills were honed through relentless practice.

The weight of the truth was not just the burden of knowledge; it was the responsibility of action. She had the information and the evidence, but the path to justice was far from clear. The legal system, she realized, could be manipulated, corrupted, and circumvented. She understood that she couldn't rely solely on the courts to deliver justice; she had to create her own form of justice, a justice that was swift, effective, and irreversible.

This realization didn't lead her down a dark path of vigilantism. Instead, it led to a more strategic, calculated approach. She understood the power of publicity, of exposing the truth to the light of day. She carefully crafted a narrative, selecting specific pieces of information, releasing them strategically, and using the media as a tool to expose Martel's crimes and to exert public pressure on the authorities.

The story, when it finally broke, was explosive. The media frenzy that ensued forced the hands of those in power, pushing them to act, to investigate, to finally bring Martel and his accomplices to justice. It was a messy, protracted process, full of setbacks and false starts. But the truth, once unleashed, proved unstoppable. It spread like wildfire, consuming everything in its path, burning away the lies and revealing the corruption that had festered for years.

The final confrontation was not a dramatic showdown but a slow, steady erosion of Martel's power. He tried to fight back, to control the narrative, to silence his critics. But the truth was stronger than his lies. It was a testament to the power of persistence, to the unwavering belief in the ultimate triumph of truth over deceit. And Alice, the woman who had carried the weight of that truth, stood witness to its undeniable power. The weight of the truth, once a burden, had finally been lifted. It had not broken her; it had made her.

Long-Term Impact

The immediate aftermath of Martel's downfall was a whirlwind of activity. The city, once paralyzed by fear and complicity, erupted in a cacophony of voices – relief, anger, vindication. News crews swarmed the streets, capturing the raw emotion of a community finally freed from the shadow of a powerful, corrupt figure. Public protests, initially small gatherings of brave individuals, swelled into massive demonstrations, a collective exhale of pent-up frustration and righteous indignation. The sheer scale of Martel's crimes, laid bare in the media, shocked even the most cynical observers. The embezzlement, the money laundering, the intimidation, the violence – it was a tapestry of wrongdoing woven into the very fabric of the city's institutions.

The long-term impact, however, were far more subtle and complex. The immediate sense of euphoria gradually gave way to a more cautious optimism, a recognition that the fight for true reform was far from over. The dismantling of Martel's network revealed a deeper malaise, a systemic rot that had allowed such corruption to flourish for so long. The investigation uncovered a web of complicity extending far beyond Martel himself, involving officials, businessmen, and even members of the judiciary. This revelation sparked a wave of internal investigations within various city departments, leading to further arrests and convictions.

The city's police force, already tarnished by its association with Martel, underwent significant restructuring. Internal affairs investigations identified numerous officers who had accepted bribes, obstructed justice, or actively participated in Martel's criminal enterprises. These officers were dismissed, and some faced criminal charges. A new police chief, committed to transparency and accountability, was appointed, overseeing a comprehensive reform initiative aimed at restoring public trust. This included new training programs focusing on ethics and community policing, a stronger internal affairs division, and improved mechanisms for reporting and investigating misconduct. The long-term impact on the police force was profound, shaping its culture and fostering a stronger commitment to ethical conduct.

The legal system, too, was subject to intense scrutiny.

Judges and prosecutors who had turned a blind eye to Martel's activities were investigated, some facing impeachment or disciplinary action. The revelation of their complicity exposed deep-seated flaws within the justice system, highlighting the need for greater transparency, accountability, and stricter ethical standards for those sworn to uphold the law. The long-term impact extended to the judicial appointments process itself, with a renewed emphasis on vetting candidates and ensuring integrity.

The financial impact was equally significant. The recovery of embezzled funds was a long and complex process involving international cooperation and sophisticated financial investigations. While not all of the stolen money was recovered, the efforts yielded substantial returns, which were used to fund much needed social programs and infrastructure projects. The city's finances were stabilized, but the long-term fiscal impact of Martel's crimes remained a considerable challenge, requiring careful budget management and economic reforms.

Beyond the immediate effects on institutions, the long-term impact was felt within the community itself. The exposure of Martel's crimes created a climate of increased civic engagement. Citizens, emboldened by the successful fight against corruption, became more actively involved in local politics, demanding greater transparency and accountability from their elected officials. Community organizations flourished, providing support and advocacy for those affected by Martel's actions. There was a renewed focus on community policing aimed at building stronger relationships between law enforcement and the residents they served.

The psychological impact was perhaps the most profound and long-lasting. The years of fear and intimidation under Martel's reign left deep scars on the community. Many residents, particularly those who had been directly victimized, struggled with the emotional aftermath of the ordeal – trauma, anxiety, and a lingering sense of distrust. Support groups and counseling services were established to provide much-needed mental health care. The long-term impact on the mental health of the community underscored the far-reaching consequences of corruption and the importance of providing support and resources for healing and recovery.

The case of Martel served as a stark reminder of the pervasive nature of corruption and its devastating effects. It became a cautionary tale, highlighting the importance of vigilance, transparency, and strong accountability mechanisms. The long-term impact extended beyond the immediate consequences, catalyzing systemic change within the city's institutions and a profound shift in the community's culture. The city learned a painful but invaluable lesson, fostering a deeper sense of civic responsibility and a renewed commitment to upholding the rule of law.

Years later, the city held a memorial service to commemorate the victims of Martel's crimes. It wasn't a somber affair but rather a celebration of resilience, a testament to the community's ability to heal and rebuild. The event served as a reminder of the long road to recovery and the ongoing efforts to ensure that such corruption would never again plague the city. The weight of the truth had indeed been lifted, but the lessons learned remained a constant presence, shaping the city's future and influencing its approach to governance, law enforcement, and community relations.

The city's transformation was not immediate or complete. It was a slow, gradual process marked by periods of setbacks and challenges. There were times when disillusionment threatened to creep in when the fatigue of reform seemed overwhelming. But the memory of Martel's reign and the collective effort that led to his downfall served as a constant source of inspiration and motivation. The city's story became a symbol of hope, demonstrating the power of collective action to overcome adversity and build a more just and equitable society.

The story of Martel also became a subject of academic study, analyzed by political scientists, sociologists, and criminologists. It served as a case study on the dynamics of corruption, the methods used to expose it, and the challenges of reforming institutions marred by systemic rot. The lessons learned were disseminated through research papers, textbooks, and conferences, influencing policy debates and shaping approaches to anti-.

corruption initiatives in other jurisdictions. The city's experience, however painful, provided a valuable contribution to the global fight against corruption.

Even Alice, the woman who had borne the weight of the truth, found herself changed by the experience. The solitude she had embraced during the investigation gave way to a newfound sense of community. She became a vocal advocate for reform, using her expertise and experience to support victims of corruption and to help prevent similar tragedies from occurring in the future. She dedicated herself to educating the public on the signs of corruption, the importance of civic engagement, and the long-term impact of unchecked power. The weight of the truth had not merely been lifted; it had transformed her into a force for positive change.

The story of Martel's downfall and its long-term impacts served as a powerful narrative, a testament to the resilience of the human spirit and the enduring power of truth. It was a story that would be told and retold for generations, a cautionary tale and a source of inspiration, reminding everyone of the importance of vigilance, accountability, and the unwavering pursuit of justice. The weight of the truth, once a crushing burden, had ultimately become a catalyst for transformation, shaping the city's destiny and leaving an indelible mark on its collective memory. The city emerged stronger, wiser, and forever changed by the weight of the truth.

Arthur L. Taylor

Justice Prevails

The final gavel fell, echoing the resounding victory not just for the prosecution but for the city itself. Martel's conviction wasn't simply the end of a criminal case; it was the culmination of a long, arduous struggle against a deeply entrenched system of corruption. The courtroom, packed to capacity with a mix of relieved citizens, anxious reporters, and weary investigators, erupted in a hushed wave of relief. Years of fear, intimidation, and suffocating complicity had finally been shattered. The weight of the truth, once a crushing burden, had been lifted, leaving behind a profound sense of liberation.

The sentencing itself was a carefully orchestrated affair designed to send a clear message. Martel, his face a mask of defiance, crumbling under the weight of his inescapable fate, received a sentence that reflected the enormity of his crimes. It was a sentence that acknowledged the suffering of his victims, the damage inflicted upon the city, and the systemic corruption he had enabled. The judge's pronouncements were not merely legal; they were statements of moral reckoning, a public affirmation of the principles of justice and accountability.

The media frenzy surrounding the trial intensified following the sentencing. Cable news channels provided minute-by-minute updates, dissecting every detail of the verdict and its implications. Newspapers published in-depth analyses, exploring the intricate web of corruption Martel had woven into the city's fabric. The story transcended local news, becoming a national and even international sensation, a testament to the power of collective action in confronting systemic corruption.

But the fight for justice didn't end with Martel's conviction. The investigation continued, its tentacles reaching deeper into the city's institutions. Numerous officials, businessmen, and members of the judiciary who had been complicit in Martel's schemes were identified, investigated, and, in many cases, prosecuted. The city's police department underwent a complete overhaul, purging itself of corrupt officers and embracing a new era of transparency and accountability.

Internal affairs investigations were rigorous, leading to the dismissal and prosecution of officers who had compromised their oaths. The city's legal system, shaken to its core, underwent a critical self-assessment, resulting in the implementation of stricter ethical standards and a revamped judicial appointment process.

The economic recovery was a slow and painstaking process. The recovery of embezzled funds, scattered across offshore accounts and complex financial instruments, was a Herculean task, requiring international cooperation and cutting-edge forensic accounting techniques. While not all of the stolen money was recovered, the efforts yielded substantial returns, injecting much-needed capital back into the city's coffers. These funds were used to finance vital social programs and infrastructure projects, bolstering the city's economic stability and rebuilding its trust with its citizens.

The most profound and long-lasting impact, however, was on the community itself. Years of living under the shadow of Martel's reign had left deep scars on the collective psyche. Fear and mistrust had become ingrained, eroding the sense of community and shared purpose. The healing process began, but it was a long and arduous journey. Support groups and counseling services were established, providing a safe space for victims to process their trauma and begin to rebuild their lives. Community organizations played a pivotal role in fostering healing, providing support, and promoting dialogue.

The renewed focus on community policing was instrumental in rebuilding trust between law enforcement and the citizenry. New initiatives focused on transparency and communication, forging stronger bonds between officers and the communities they served. The police force, once viewed with suspicion and distrust, began to regain the public's confidence, demonstrating a genuine commitment to protecting and serving the community.

The city's political landscape also underwent a significant transformation. The Martel era had disillusioned many citizens, leading to a decline in civic engagement. But the fight against corruption had awakened a newfound sense of empowerment. Citizens, emboldened by the success of the investigation and prosecution, became more actively involved in local politics, demanding greater transparency, accountability, and ethical conduct from their elected officials. New civic organizations emerged, dedicated to promoting good governance and preventing future instances of corruption.

The city's transformation wasn't without its challenges. There were moments of disillusionment, setbacks, and the temptation to return to the status quo. But the memory of Martel's reign and the collective effort that led to his downfall served as a constant reminder of the stakes involved. The lessons learned were profound and lasting. The city emerged stronger, wiser, and more resilient, its institutions reformed, and its citizens empowered. The weight of the truth, once a burden, had become a catalyst for positive change.

Years later, the city unveiled a memorial dedicated to the victims of Martel's crimes. It wasn't a somber monument to defeat but rather a vibrant testament to resilience, a symbol of the community's triumph over adversity. The memorial served as a reminder of the long and difficult road to recovery but also as a celebration of the unwavering pursuit of justice. The dedication ceremony became a symbol of renewal and a promise to uphold the principles of integrity and accountability.

The city's experience became a case study in the global fight against corruption. Scholars and academics analyzed the dynamics of Martel's operation, examining the methods used to expose his crimes and the challenges involved in reforming compromised institutions. The lessons learned were disseminated through academic publications, conferences, and policy debates, informing anti-corruption initiatives worldwide.

Even Alice, who had carried the burden of the truth for so long, found a sense of closure. The solitude she had embraced during the investigation gave way to a renewed sense of community. She became a fervent advocate for reform, using her experience and expertise to assist victims and prevent similar tragedies. She dedicated herself to public education, sharing her knowledge and insights to empower citizens and strengthen institutions. Her transformation served as an example of resilience and the enduring power of truth.

The story of Martel's downfall, from the initial whispers of suspicion to the resounding triumph of justice, became a powerful narrative, inspiring others to fight for truth and accountability. It was a reminder that even in the face of overwhelming power and systemic corruption, justice can prevail and that the pursuit of truth, however challenging, is ultimately a worthwhile endeavor. The weight of the truth, initially crushing, ultimately transformed the city, leaving an enduring legacy of reform and renewed hope.

Community Healing

The air, once thick with the suffocating weight of fear and suspicion, began to breathe again. The city, scarred but not broken, embarked on a long and complex process of healing. It wasn't a linear journey; it was a patchwork of individual stories interwoven to form a collective narrative of resilience.

One such story was that of Mrs. Elena Rodriguez, a small business owner whose shop had been repeatedly targeted by Martel's thugs, forcing her into bankruptcy. For years, she had lived in quiet desperation, fearing retaliation if she spoke out. After Martel's conviction, however, she found herself enveloped in a wave of support. The city's newly formed Small Business Revitalization Program, funded by recovered assets, provided her with a low-interest loan and business mentorship. Her new shop, brighter and more vibrant than before, became a symbol of the city's rebirth. She wasn't just rebuilding her business; she was rebuilding her life, her spirit fortified by the collective strength of her community.

The city's schools became focal points for healing. Children who had witnessed intimidation and violence firsthand were now receiving specialized counseling and trauma-informed education. Art therapy programs flourished, providing them with a safe outlet to express their emotions and experiences. School murals, painted in vibrant colors, depicting scenes of unity and hope, replaced the graffiti that had once marred the school walls, transforming them into symbols of community renewal.

The city's parks, once neglected and unsafe, underwent a significant transformation. New playgrounds were built, community gardens were established, and walking paths paved. These green spaces became havens for families and individuals alike, offering places for healing, recreation, and social interaction. Regular community events, picnics, concerts, and festivals— filled the parks with laughter and music, replacing the lingering echoes of fear with the joyous sounds of a revitalized community.

The transformation extended beyond physical space. The city's cultural institutions played a significant role in the healing process. The city's theatre hosted a series of plays and performances addressing themes of trauma, resilience, and community healing. Local artists created works that reflected the city's journey, transforming pain into art, fear into empathy, and anger into understanding. The city's art galleries became spaces for dialogue and reflection, showcasing creative responses to the ordeal and turning the experience into a powerful narrative of resilience and renewal.

Support groups, spearheaded by volunteers and trained professionals, sprang up across the city, offering safe spaces for victims to share their stories, process their trauma, and connect with others who had shared similar experiences. These groups were not simply places for emotional support; they became platforms for collective action. Victims, empowered by their shared experiences, began advocating for policy changes and demanding greater accountability from public officials.

The church, once largely silent during Martel's reign, became a central hub of community support. Pastors and religious leaders played a pivotal role in fostering reconciliation and healing, offering spiritual guidance and practical assistance to victims. Interfaith services and community outreach programs drew people from various backgrounds together, reinforcing the bonds of unity and shared purpose. The church, stripped of its previous complicity, became a beacon of hope and moral clarity.

The city's media, having played a crucial role in exposing Martel's crimes, shifted its focus towards promoting positive narratives of recovery and renewal. Local newspapers and television stations featured stories of resilience, showcasing the efforts of community organizations, highlighting successful recovery programs, and celebrating the achievements of individuals who had overcome adversity. The media, once a tool of manipulation and disinformation, became a vehicle for healing and social change.

However, the path to healing was not without its bumps. Mistrust, though significantly diminished, still lingered. There were moments of relapse, instances of individuals struggling to cope with the trauma they had endured. But these challenges only reinforced the community's resolve. The city's resilience was not just about overcoming adversity; it was about learning from setbacks and strengthening the bonds that held it together.

The city's renewed emphasis on community policing was paramount. Officers participated in community events, attended town hall meetings, and actively sought input from residents. Transparency initiatives allowed public access to police records and operational data. This fostered a renewed sense of trust, demonstrating that the police were not only protectors but partners in the community's journey towards healing.

One poignant example was Officer Jackson, who had been initially hesitant to embrace the changes. He had witnessed firsthand the corruption within the force, and the subsequent investigations had forced him to confront his own past complicity, albeit passively. However, through participating in community-building initiatives, particularly youth mentorship programs, he found a renewed sense of purpose. He used his experience to connect with young people, sharing his mistakes as a cautionary tale and fostering a strong sense of empathy and understanding. He became a symbol of the force's transformation, a testament to the possibility of redemption and renewal.

The transformation of the city's political landscape was equally significant. New leaders emerged, committed to transparency and ethical governance. They actively sought input from citizens and prioritized community needs. The city council established a citizen oversight board to monitor the activities of public officials, ensuring accountability and preventing future instances of corruption. The political landscape, once characterized by cynicism and apathy, became one of engagement and hope.

Years after Martel's downfall, the city held its annual "Festival of Resilience," a vibrant celebration of community healing and collective triumph. The event attracted visitors from across the country and even internationally, keen to understand the city's remarkable journey. The festival wasn't just a celebration; it was a testament to the city's indomitable spirit, a showcase of its capacity for renewal, and a potent reminder of the power of collective action in the face of adversity.

Alice, having witnessed the city's transformation firsthand, found solace in its renewed vitality. Her dedication to community healing wasn't simply a professional pursuit; it was a personal journey of healing and reconciliation. The weight of the truth, once a crushing burden, had transformed into a catalyst for positive change, propelling her forward and allowing her to actively contribute to the city's rebirth, a testament to the enduring power of human resilience and the profound capacity for renewal. The city, once a symbol of corruption and despair, had become a shining example of how a community, wounded but not defeated, could rise from the ashes to build a brighter, more just future.

Rebuilding Trust

The rebuilding of trust wasn't a singular event but a slow, painstaking process, like piecing together a shattered mosaic. It began with small gestures, quiet acts of reconciliation that gradually chipped away at the hardened crust of suspicion. Neighborhood watch groups, once viewed with suspicion, still carry the faint scent of smoke and ash from the fires of the rebellion, now mingled with the aroma of grilling meats and freshly baked bread. The annual Festival of Resilience, a testament to the city's rebirth, pulsed with life. Children chased colorful balloons across the Cobblestone streets, their laughter echoing off the newly renovated buildings. Music spilled from makeshift stages, a vibrant tapestry of rhythms and melodies weaving together the city's diverse cultures. This wasn't just a celebration; it was a defiant assertion of life's tenacity against the weight of destruction.

Yet, beneath the festive veneer, the scars of the past remained. The physical wounds were slowly healing, but the emotional ones ran deeper, etched into the souls of those who had witnessed the brutal reign of Martel. For many, reconciliation was not a matter of forgetting but of acknowledging, understanding, and learning to live with the lingering pain.

One such individual was Elias Vance, a former police officer who had been implicated in Martel's corruption but had later played a crucial role in exposing the regime's misdeeds. Elias, haunted by his past actions, dedicated himself to restorative justice initiatives, working tirelessly to bridge the gap between victims and offenders. He found himself in a constant dialogue with the ghosts of his past, wrestling with guilt and striving to earn back the trust he had so carelessly squandered. He organized workshops, facilitated difficult conversations, and became a symbol of redemption for a city grappling with its fractured identity.

His most challenging encounter was with Fatima Khan, a woman whose family had suffered immensely under Martel's regime. Her husband had been wrongfully imprisoned, her business destroyed, and her life upended. Initially, she refused to participate in any restorative justice program, consumed by her bitterness and rage. Elias, with his quiet persistence and genuine remorse, managed to reach her. He didn't offer excuses; he didn't minimize the suffering she had endured. He simply listened, allowing her to express her pain without judgment. He validated her anger, her grief, and her sense of betrayal.

Their conversations were not easy. Fatima's words were sharp, laced with pain and disappointment. She confronted Elias with his past, forcing him to confront the darkness he had once embraced. But through these arduous dialogues, something unexpected began to bloom: a fragile understanding. Fatima realized that Elias was not merely seeking absolution but genuine redemption. She saw his commitment to the restorative justice program and his unwavering dedication to helping others heal. He wasn't just atoning for his past; he was actively building a better future. This recognition wasn't forgiveness, not yet, but a grudging acknowledgment that the process of healing could perhaps begin.

The journey toward reconciliation extended beyond individual interactions. The city's leadership established truth and reconciliation commissions, offering platforms for victims to share their stories and for perpetrators to acknowledge their roles in the city's suffering. These weren't trials but opportunities for catharsis, for public acknowledgment of the wrongs committed, and for the community to collectively grapple with its history. These sessions, often emotionally charged and raw, revealed a spectrum of experiences – accounts of torture, imprisonment, and the silencing of dissent, but also narratives of resilience, resistance, and the enduring strength of the human spirit.

The role of the media in this process was both critical and complex. While journalists had played a vital role in exposing Martel's regime, now they faced the challenge of crafting a narrative of hope and healing without diminishing the gravity of the city's past. They focused on documenting the rebuilding efforts, highlighting stories of community resilience, and giving voice to the marginalized. They engaged in rigorous self-reflection, acknowledging past mistakes and committing to responsible reporting that actively contributed to the city's healing process. Their goal was not to gloss over the city's trauma but to demonstrate that even in the face of immense suffering, the possibility of a just and equitable future remained.

The process of healing extended into the realm of education. The city's schools incorporated trauma-informed pedagogy, creating safe and supportive learning environments where students felt empowered to share their experiences. The curriculum was redesigned to include a comprehensive study of the city's history, both the dark chapters and the struggles toward redemption. This education wasn't merely about transmitting facts but about cultivating critical thinking, fostering empathy, and nurturing the capacity for dialogue and understanding. The goal was to ensure that future generations wouldn't repeat the mistakes of the past.

The city's physical transformation mirrored its internal healing. Ruined buildings were rebuilt not only to restore the city's physical infrastructure but also to symbolize the community's collective commitment to a brighter future. Public spaces were redesigned to foster interaction and community building, creating environments that encouraged dialogue and collaboration. The design of these spaces reflected the city's diverse cultures, creating a sense of belonging and shared identity. The architecture itself became a symbol of reconciliation, a reminder of the city's past and a testament to its resilience.

However, the path towards complete reconciliation was far from smooth. Skepticism lingered. Some residents questioned the motives behind the reforms, harboring deep-seated distrust of those in power. Others remained deeply traumatized, needing long-term support to process their experiences. The challenges were immense, the wounds deep, but the community's unwavering resolve persevered. They understood that reconciliation wasn't a destination but an ongoing process that demanded constant vigilance, empathy, and a commitment to continuous dialogue. It was a journey, not a sprint, and the resilience of the city was continuously tested.

The Festival of Resilience, years later, was a profound reminder of this journey. It was a vibrant spectacle, a testament to the community's remarkable capacity for healing and renewal. But beyond the festive atmosphere, it provided a platform for honest conversations, a space to confront lingering uncertainties and unresolved issues. It served as a powerful symbol of hope, a beacon illuminating the path forward. Alice, watching the joyous throngs, felt the weight of her involvement, the profound impact her work had on this remarkable transformation. The city's rebirth was a triumph, a story of how the human spirit could overcome the darkness of the past and create a future built on the foundations of justice, understanding, and unwavering hope. The city, reborn, stood as a beacon, a reminder that even from the deepest wounds, a community could not only heal but thriving. They organized block parties, potlucks, and children's activities, transforming from instruments of fear into catalysts for connection.

The police department, under new leadership, embarked on a radical transparency initiative. Internal affairs investigations were made public, past misconduct was acknowledged, and officers were held accountable for their actions. A new community policing model was implemented, emphasizing collaboration and partnership rather than control and enforcement. Regular town hall meetings were held, giving residents a platform to voice their concerns and interact directly with officers. This open dialogue, unprecedented in the city's history, fostered a slow but steady thaw in the icy relationship between the police and the community. The sight of officers playing basketball with children in the park or assisting elderly residents with groceries became commonplace, symbolic of a paradigm shift in policing.

One particularly impactful initiative was the establishment of restorative justice programs. These programs brought victims and offenders together in a facilitated setting, allowing for dialogue, understanding, and, in some cases, forgiveness. The process wasn't always easy; many victims harbored deep-seated anger and resentment. But the opportunity to confront their offenders, to hear their apologies, and to participate in shaping the course of their rehabilitation proved transformative for many. The focus shifted from retribution to healing, from punishment to restoration. While not every case was successful, the program's overall impact on the community was undeniable, fostering a sense of shared responsibility and collective accountability.

The city's justice system also underwent significant reforms. Increased funding for public defenders ensured that all defendants, regardless of their economic status, had access to competent legal representation. Sentencing guidelines were revised to prioritize rehabilitation over punishment, particularly for nonviolent offenders. The focus shifted from simply incarcerating individuals to addressing the root causes of crime, such as poverty, addiction, and lack of opportunity. This involved partnerships with community organizations to provide social services, job training, and educational opportunities for those released from prison, reducing recidivism and fostering successful reintegration into society.

The media played a crucial role in rebuilding trust. Journalists, having exposed Martel's corruption, now dedicated themselves to highlighting the positive changes taking place in the city. They showcased the success stories of individuals who had overcome adversity, the initiatives aimed at fostering community healing, and the efforts of local organizations working to rebuild the social fabric. They provided a platform for victims to share their stories, giving voice to their experiences and amplifying their calls for justice and accountability. This positive coverage, coupled with ongoing investigative reporting, helped to dispel the lingering cynicism and foster a sense of optimism for the future.

The role of faith-based organizations in the healing process was profound. Interfaith dialogues and collaborative initiatives involving churches, mosques, synagogues, and temples brought together people of diverse backgrounds, transcending religious differences and strengthening the bonds of unity. These organizations provided essential social services, including food banks, shelters, and counseling services, offering practical support to those in need. They also played a crucial role in fostering forgiveness and reconciliation, helping individuals process their trauma and move forward. Their active participation in the community's healing process redefined their roles, moving beyond mere spiritual guidance to a more active engagement in social justice and community building.

However, the journey towards complete trust was far from linear. There were setbacks, moments of doubt, and instances where old wounds re-opened. Some residents remained deeply distrustful of authority, harboring suspicions that lingered despite the significant reforms. Others struggled to cope with the trauma they had endured, experiencing emotional distress and mental health challenges that required ongoing support. But these obstacles didn't deter the community's resolve. Instead, they served as reminders of the ongoing need for vigilance, compassion, and collective action. The resilience of the community was tested, but it never faltered. Through these challenges, they learned that trust is not a destination but a journey, a continuous process of building relationships, fostering understanding, and committing to a shared future.

The city's commitment to accountability extended beyond the police force and the justice system. Public officials were held to high ethical standards, financial transparency was enforced, and citizen oversight boards were established to ensure accountability and prevent future corruption. This commitment to transparency and ethical governance rebuilt public faith in their government, fostering a renewed sense of civic engagement. Citizen participation in local government increased, enhancing the democratic process and promoting a sense of shared ownership in the city's future. The city became a model for ethical governance, demonstrating how accountability and transparency could rebuild public trust and strengthen the social contract.

Years later, the city stood as a testament to the remarkable capacity of a community to heal and rebuild. The scars remained, but they were interwoven with the vibrant tapestry of resilience, a symbol of the community's collective journey towards a more just and equitable future. The city's transformation wasn't just about bricks and mortar; it was about rebuilding the social fabric, the bonds of trust, and the shared belief in a better tomorrow. It was a testament to the indomitable spirit of the human heart, its capacity for healing, and its unwavering belief in the possibility of a brighter future forged from the ashes of a broken past. The annual Festival of Resilience became more than a celebration; it became a pilgrimage, a gathering of people from all walks of life, drawn to witness the city's triumph over adversity, a beacon of hope reminding them that even from the darkest depths, the human spirit can rise and rebuild. Alice, watching the festivities, felt a deep sense of satisfaction, knowing that her part, however small, had contributed to this remarkable resurgence. The city, reborn, stood as a testament to her unwavering belief in the power of healing and the enduring strength of the human spirit.

Arthur L. Taylor

Reconciliation and Understanding

The air, still carrying the faint scent of smoke and ash from the fires of the rebellion, now mingled with the aroma of grilling meats and freshly baked bread. The annual Festival of Resilience, a testament to the city's rebirth, pulsed with life. Children chased colorful balloons across the Cobblestone streets, their laughter echoing off the newly renovated buildings. Music spilled from makeshift stages, a vibrant tapestry of rhythms and melodies weaving together the city's diverse cultures. This wasn't just a celebration; it was a defiant assertion of life's tenacity against the weight of destruction.

Yet, beneath the festive veneer, the scars of the past remained. The physical wounds were slowly healing, but the emotional ones ran deeper, etched into the souls of those who had witnessed the brutal reign of Martel. For many, reconciliation was not a matter of forgetting but of acknowledging, understanding, and learning to live with the lingering pain.

One such individual was Elias Vance, a former police officer who had been implicated in Martel's corruption but had later played a crucial role in exposing the regime's misdeeds. Elias, haunted by his past actions, dedicated himself to restorative justice initiatives, working tirelessly to bridge the gap between victims and offenders. He found himself in a constant dialogue with the ghosts of his past, wrestling with guilt and striving to earn back the trust he had so carelessly squandered. He organized workshops, facilitated difficult conversations, and became a symbol of redemption for a city grappling with its fractured identity.

His most challenging encounter was with Fatima Khan, a woman whose family had suffered immensely under Martel's regime. Her husband had been wrongfully imprisoned, her business destroyed, and her life upended. Initially, she refused to participate in any restorative justice program, consumed by her bitterness and rage. Elias, with his quiet persistence and genuine remorse, managed to reach her. He didn't offer excuses; he didn't minimize the suffering she had endured. He simply listened, allowing her to express her pain without judgment. He validated her anger, her grief, and her sense of betrayal.

Their conversations were not easy. Fatima's words were sharp, laced with pain and disappointment. She confronted Elias with his past, forcing him to confront the darkness he had once embraced. But through these arduous dialogues, something unexpected began to bloom: a fragile understanding. Fatima realized that Elias was not merely seeking absolution but genuine redemption. She saw his commitment to the restorative justice program and his unwavering dedication to helping others heal. He wasn't just atoning for his past; he was actively building a better future. This recognition wasn't forgiveness, not yet, but a grudging acknowledgment that the process of healing could perhaps begin.

The journey toward reconciliation extended beyond individual interactions. The city's leadership established truth and reconciliation commissions, offering platforms for victims to share their stories and for perpetrators to acknowledge their roles in the city's suffering. These weren't trials but opportunities for catharsis, for public acknowledgment of the wrongs committed, and for the community to collectively grapple with its history. These sessions, often emotionally charged and raw, revealed a spectrum of experiences – accounts of torture, imprisonment, and the silencing of dissent, but also narratives of resilience, resistance, and the enduring strength of the human spirit.

The role of the media in this process was both critical and complex. While journalists had played a vital role in exposing Martel's regime, now they faced the challenge of crafting a narrative of hope and healing without diminishing the gravity of the city's past. They focused on documenting the rebuilding efforts, highlighting stories of community resilience, and giving voice to the marginalized. They engaged in rigorous self-reflection, acknowledging past mistakes and committing to responsible reporting that actively contributed to the city's healing process. Their goal was not to gloss over the city's trauma but to demonstrate that even in the face of immense suffering, the possibility of a just and equitable future remained.

The process of healing extended into the realm of education. The city's schools incorporated trauma-informed pedagogy, creating safe and supportive learning environments where students felt empowered to share their experiences. The curriculum was redesigned to include a comprehensive study of the city's history, both the dark chapters and the struggles toward redemption. This education wasn't merely about transmitting facts but about cultivating critical thinking, fostering empathy, and nurturing the capacity for dialogue and understanding. The goal was to ensure that future generations wouldn't repeat the mistakes of the past.

The city's physical transformation mirrored its internal healing. Ruined buildings were rebuilt not only to restore the city's physical infrastructure but also to symbolize the community's collective commitment to a brighter future. Public spaces were redesigned to foster interaction and community building, creating environments that encouraged dialogue and collaboration. The design of these spaces reflected the city's diverse cultures, creating a sense of belonging and shared identity. The architecture itself became a symbol of reconciliation, a reminder of the city's past and a testament to its resilience.

However, the path towards complete reconciliation was far from smooth. Skepticism lingered. Some residents questioned the motives behind the reforms, harboring deep-seated distrust of those in power. Others remained deeply traumatized, needing long-term support to process their experiences. The challenges were immense, the wounds deep, but the community's unwavering resolve persevered. They understood that reconciliation wasn't a destination but an ongoing process that demanded constant vigilance, empathy, and a commitment to continuous dialogue. It was a journey, not a sprint, and the resilience of the city was continuously tested.

The Festival of Resilience, years later, was a profound reminder of this journey. It was a vibrant spectacle, a testament to the community's remarkable capacity for healing and renewal. But beyond the festive atmosphere, it provided a platform for honest conversations, a space to confront lingering uncertainties and unresolved issues. It served as a powerful symbol of hope, a beacon illuminating the path forward. Alice, watching the joyous throngs, felt the weight of her involvement, the profound impact her work had on this remarkable transformation. The city's rebirth was a triumph, a story of how the human spirit could overcome the darkness of the past and create a future built on the foundations of justice, understanding, and unwavering hope. The city, reborn, stood as a beacon, a reminder that even from the deepest wounds, a community could not only heal but thrive.

New Leadership

The election of Anya Sharma as the city's new mayor marked a significant turning point. Anya, a respected human rights lawyer with a reputation for integrity, ran on a platform of transparency and accountability. Unlike her predecessors, who had often operated in the shadows, Anya promised an open and accessible government committed to actively engaging with the citizens. Her campaign resonated deeply with a population weary of corruption and deceit. Her victory wasn't just a political win; it was a symbolic triumph, a testament to the city's yearning for a fresh start.

Anya's first act was to establish an independent oversight committee comprised of citizens representing diverse backgrounds and experiences. This committee was tasked with overseeing all government operations, ensuring transparency and accountability at every level. They had the power to investigate allegations of misconduct, review government contracts, and recommend policy changes to promote ethical governance. This move signaled a departure from the previous regime's culture of secrecy and self-preservation. The committee's establishment marked a significant shift in power dynamics, granting citizens a direct voice in shaping their city's future. Their meetings were open to the public, and their reports were readily available online, creating a level of transparency previously unimaginable.

The impact of the oversight committee quickly became clear. Several instances of corruption and mismanagement, previously shrouded in secrecy, were swiftly investigated and brought to light. Several high-ranking officials implicated in the previous regime's misdeeds were held accountable. This decisive action, coupled with Anya's unwavering commitment to justice, helped to rebuild public trust in the government. It showed that the era of impunity was over and that accountability extended to everyone, regardless of their position or power. The city's once-cynical populace, cautiously optimistic, witnessed firsthand the tangible benefits of transparency and accountability.

Beyond the oversight committee, Anya focused on rebuilding the city's infrastructure of justice. The police force, heavily implicated in Martel's reign of terror, underwent a radical restructuring. A thorough vetting process eliminated corrupt officers, while training programs focused on community policing and ethical conduct were introduced. The new recruits, carefully selected for their integrity and commitment to public service, were taught to view themselves as guardians of the community rather than instruments of control. A significant investment was made in advanced technology and investigative training, equipping the force to address the evolving nature of crime in the 21st century. The police department, once a symbol of fear and oppression, slowly began to regain the trust of the citizens.

The judiciary also underwent a significant transformation. Judges were appointed based on merit and experience rather than political connections. Court proceedings were streamlined, ensuring that cases were processed efficiently and fairly. Access to justice was significantly improved, with legal aid clinics proved throughout the city to assist those who could not afford legal representation. Furthermore, new laws were enacted to protect whistleblowers and ensure that witnesses felt safe coming forward with information. The judiciary, no longer viewed with suspicion, gained credibility as a fair and impartial arbiter of justice.

Anya's commitment to transparency extended beyond government institutions. She actively encouraged public participation in decision-making. Citizen forums were held regularly, providing platforms for residents to express their concerns and share their ideas. These forums were not mere token gestures; Anya listened attentively to the concerns of the people, actively incorporating their feedback into policy decisions. This inclusive approach fostered a sense of shared ownership and responsibility, strengthening the bond between the government and the community. The citizens, empowered by their participation in the governing process, felt genuinely involved in the rebuilding of their city.

The media, too, played a vital role in supporting transparency. Journalists embraced their role as watchdogs, scrutinizing government actions and reporting on issues of public importance. They collaborated with the oversight committee, sharing information and contributing to the investigation of corruption.

While keeping their critical perspective, they also played an active role in promoting positive narratives, highlighting the city's resilience and the progress being made. This collaborative effort helped to inform the public and keep the government accountable.

The process wasn't without its challenges. Anya faced opposition from entrenched interests who resisted the changes she was implementing. Some individuals, deeply invested in the old ways, tried to undermine her reforms. However, Anya's unwavering resolve, coupled with the overwhelming support of the citizens, allowed her to overcome these hurdles. She consistently reiterated her commitment to transparency and accountability, and her message resonated deeply with the community. The citizens, having tasted the bitter fruit of corruption, stood firmly behind her, demanding a clean and accountable government.

The transformation of the city extended beyond its political and institutional structures. It permeated the fabric of everyday life. A renewed sense of community spirit appeared as citizens worked together to rebuild their neighborhoods, support one another, and foster a sense of belonging.

The Festival of Resilience became an annual tradition, a symbol of the city's collective commitment to overcoming adversity and building a brighter future. The physical and emotional scars remained, but they were now interwoven with the vibrant tapestry of a community slowly, painstakingly, but surely healing. The city wasn't just rebuilt; it was reborn – a phoenix rising from the ashes, its spirit stronger and more resolute than ever before.

The leadership of Anya Sharma proved to be the catalyst that spurred the city's complete and irreversible transformation, a testament to the power of transparency and the unwavering resilience of the human spirit. The city, finally free from the shadows of its past, stepped into a future brimming with the promise of a truly just and equitable society.

Hope for the Future

The air in Wilder City felt different now. Lighter. The pervasive sense of dread that had clung to the city like a shroud for so long had finally begun to dissipate, replaced by a tentative, fragile optimism. The vibrant hues of freshly painted buildings, the laughter of children playing in revitalized parks, the bustling energy of newly opened businesses – these were the visible signs of a city healing, a city reborn. But the true transformation lay deeper in the hearts and minds of its citizens.

Anya Sharma, the city's new mayor, understood this. She knew that rebuilding Wilder City wasn't just about restoring infrastructure; it was about restoring faith – faith in government, faith in the justice system, and faith in one another. Her administration continued to work tirelessly, not just on the grand gestures of city-wide improvements but also on the smaller, more intimate acts of rebuilding trust.

Community centers, once dilapidated and neglected, were refurbished into vibrant hubs of activity, offering educational programs, job training initiatives, and recreational opportunities for all ages. These weren't simply bricks and mortar; they were investments in the city's human capital, a commitment to empowering its citizens.

The police force, under the leadership of Chief Inspector Ava Ramirez, underwent a significant cultural shift. The focus moved from reactive policing to proactive community engagement. Officers were encouraged to build relationships with the people they served, to become part of the fabric of the community rather than simply an external force. Regular town hall meetings were held, providing platforms for residents to voice their concerns and build trust with the police. The emphasis was on de-escalation techniques and conflict resolution, aiming to prevent crime rather than simply punishing it. Critically, transparent internal affairs investigations were launched, highlighting a zero-tolerance approach to misconduct. The fruits of this intensive effort were clear in a dramatic reduction in reported police brutality and an increase in community support for law enforcement.

The revitalization extended beyond the immediate physical environment. The city's arts and culture scene, once stifled by Martel's regime, experienced a remarkable renaissance. Grants were made available to artists and performers, supporting the creation of new works that reflected the city's unique history and its resilient spirit. Public art projects adorned the streets and buildings, transforming the urban landscape into a canvas of creativity and hope. The annual Festival of Resilience, now a city-wide celebration, became a powerful symbol of Wilder City's collective journey of healing and transformation. It was a testament to the enduring strength of the human spirit, a reminder that even in the face of immense adversity, hope could blossom.

The work wasn't merely cosmetic. Anya's administration understood that lasting change required addressing the root causes of inequality and injustice. Significant investments were made in education, creating opportunities for children from disadvantaged backgrounds to access quality education and break the cycle of poverty. Affordable housing initiatives were launched, providing safe and decent housing for families who had previously been forced to live in substandard conditions. Job creation programs were implemented, focusing on skills training and entrepreneurial support, empowering residents to become self-sufficient. These initiatives, though demanding considerable resources, were seen as essential investments in the long-term health and wellbeing of the city.

The process was far from easy. Anya and her team faced resistance from various factions. Some individuals, deeply entrenched in the old system, actively worked to undermine her efforts. There were accusations of political maneuvering, whispers of sabotage, and even veiled threats. But Anya remained steadfast in her commitment to transparency and accountability. She refused to be intimidated or deterred. Her unwavering determination, combined with the unwavering support of the citizens, allowed her to overcome these obstacles. She frequently addressed the public, sharing both successes and challenges, which reinforced trust in her leadership.

The success of Anya's administration was not merely a testament to her strength but to the collective determination of Wilder City's citizens. They had endured years of oppression, corruption, and uncertainty. They had witnessed firsthand the destructive power of greed and deceit. But they had also discovered, in the darkest hours, the profound strength of their community spirit. They had learned the importance of collective action, the power of solidarity, and the transformative potential of hope.

The media played a crucial role in this transformation. Journalists, having learned valuable lessons from the past, maintained their critical role as watchdogs, but they also embraced their responsibility to report on the positive changes happening within the city. Their stories focused not only on the challenges that remained but also on the extraordinary resilience and progress of the people of Wilder City. They highlighted inspiring stories of community collaboration, economic revitalization, and personal growth – narratives that provided a counterpoint to the darker aspects of the city's past. They helped to weave a narrative of hope, perseverance, and collective triumph.

The transformation of Wilder City was a slow, painstaking process. The scars of the past remained, both physically and emotionally. But those scars were now interwoven with the vibrant tapestry of a community slowly, surely, and triumphantly healing. The city was not simply rebuilt; it was remade and transformed from a place of despair and fear into a symbol of hope and resilience. The future of Wilder City was still uncertain, but the foundations were solid, built on transparency, accountability, and the unwavering belief in the power of a united community.

It was a future brimming with the promise of a truly just and equitable society, a promise that, for the first time in many years, felt genuinely within reach. The journey was long, but Wilder City, under Anya Sharma's capable leadership and with the unwavering support of its citizens, was finally on its way to a brighter tomorrow. The city, once shattered, was not just mended; it had been reborn. The spirit of Wilder City, once broken, was. now stronger, more resilient, and more hopeful than ever before.

Alice's New Chapter

The scent of freshly baked bread drifted from a nearby bakery, a comforting aroma that seemed to encapsulate the newfound peace in Wilder City. Alice sat on a park bench, watching children chase pigeons across the newly paved square. The vibrant mural depicting the city's phoenix-like resurgence painted a vivid picture of the transformation she had witnessed. It had been months since the dismantling of Martel's regime, months since the arrest of his accomplices, months since she had last seen the chilling glint in his eyes. The legal proceedings were long and complex, but justice, albeit slow, was being served. Martel's empire of fear and corruption was crumbling, brick by agonizing brick.

Anya Sharma, the city's newly elected mayor, had become a symbol of hope. Her unwavering commitment to transparency and accountability not only restored faith in the government but also inspired a sense of collective responsibility among the citizens. Alice, initially skeptical of Anya's idealistic vision, now saw the tangible results of her efforts. The city was breathing again. The once-desolate streets were now alive with activity, a vibrant tapestry woven from the threads of renewed hope and collaborative spirit.

Alice's own life had undergone a profound transformation. The trauma of her past, the years spent living under Martel's shadow, had left deep scars. Yet, the healing process, though arduous, began. The weight of guilt, the self-blame, and the crippling fear that had suffocated her for so long began to slowly recede, replaced by a fragile but growing sense of self-worth. She had found solace in the simple act of helping others. She volunteered at a local community center, assisting in educational programs designed to uplift the city's youth, those who, like her, had been victims of Martel's regime. The children's bright smiles were a balm to her wounds, a testament to the city's remarkable resilience.

Her work at the community center had brought her into contact with individuals from all walks of life – the mothers struggling to make ends meet, the teenagers grappling with identity crises, and the elderly clinging to fading memories. Their stories, each unique yet interwoven, painted a poignant picture of Wilder City's collective struggle and its ultimate triumph. In their eyes, she saw reflections of her journey, her battles against adversity. It was in sharing their stories, listening to their pain, and celebrating their triumphs that Alice found a sense of purpose, a renewed sense of her worth.

Therapy had played a vital role in her healing. She had initially hesitated, hesitant to confront the demons of her past, but with the encouragement of Ava Ramirez, she eventually sought professional help. The sessions were difficult, dredging up memories she would rather have buried, but the process was cathartic. The therapist helped her to understand the complexities of trauma, the subtle ways in which it manifests, and the path toward healing and recovery. Alice learned that self-blame was not a necessary component of survival and that it was possible to forgive herself and acknowledge her past without being defined by it.

She had also found unexpected solace in the company of Ava Ramirez. The Chief Inspector, hardened by years on the force, showed a surprising vulnerability towards Alice, acknowledging the shared experiences that bind them together. Their conversations were fewer formal interrogations and more compassionate exchanges of stories, confessions, and the quiet understanding that only shared trauma could elicit. Ava had become more than just a mentor; she had become a true friend. The bond between them, forged in the crucible of their shared experiences, provided Alice with the strength, and support she needed to navigate her new chapter.

Her relationship with her family had also shifted. The years of strained communication, the unspoken resentments, began to melt away. The shared experience of surviving Martel's reign of terror had brought them closer. Her father, once a distant figure, now seemed to understand her struggles, offering a quiet understanding and the support that she had long craved. Her mother, always her strongest advocate, provided unwavering love and encouragement; her embrace was a tangible manifestation of unconditional support.

The media, once a source of anxiety and fear, had also undergone a significant transformation. Journalists, humbled by their past failures, were now more committed to ethical reporting, focusing on the rebuilding efforts and the resilience of the city's citizens. Alice found herself frequently interviewed, not as a victim, but as a symbol of Wilder City's resurgence. She shared her story not to seek sympathy but to inspire hope, to demonstrate that even the darkest of times can give way to healing and renewal.

Her story became a powerful testament to the human spirit's capacity for resilience. It offered a beacon of hope to those who had suffered similar traumas, demonstrating that healing was possible, that it was okay to ask for help, and that there was a future beyond the darkness. She became an advocate for victims of abuse and corruption, using her voice to empower others and to fight for meaningful change in the justice system.

Alice realized that her trauma was not a defining characteristic but a powerful catalyst for transformation. It had propelled her into action, motivated her to rebuild her life and, in the process, to help rebuild her city. She found fulfillment in her new roles – volunteering, advocating, and sharing her story. It wasn't about erasing the past but about integrating it into the narrative of her life, transforming it from a source of shame and fear into a source of strength and purpose. The scars remained, a visible reminder of what she had endured, but they were now interwoven with a vibrant tapestry of resilience, hope, and unwavering determination.

The future wasn't without its challenges. The city's recovery was a long-term commitment, requiring sustained effort and unwavering support. Yet, the air was filled with a palpable optimism, a shared belief in the city's potential for a brighter future. Alice, like many others in Wilder City, looked towards the horizon, not with apprehension but with cautious hope, embracing the uncertainty of tomorrow with a newfound sense of courage and determination. She knew that the journey was far from over, but she also knew that she had found her place in this new Wilder City, a city reborn from the ashes of corruption and despair. Her new chapter was not merely a new beginning; it was a testament to the enduring power of the human spirit, a story of healing, resilience, and triumphant rebirth. A story that resonated not just within the walls of Wilder City but far beyond its boundaries, a beacon of hope in a world that often seemed steeped in darkness.

Arthur L. Taylor

Wilder City's Transformation

The revitalized streets of Wilder City hummed with newfound energy. Gone were the shadowy alleyways and dilapidated buildings that had once characterized its underbelly. In their place stood vibrant murals depicting scenes of hope and resilience, painted by local artists who had emerged from the shadows, their talents finally unleashed. The air, once thick with the stench of corruption and fear, was now infused with the aroma of freshly brewed coffee from independent cafes that had sprung up like wildflowers after spring rain. The once desolate parks were now filled with children's laughter, their carefree joy, a stark contrast to the oppressive silence that had once reigned supreme. Even the city's skyline seemed to have changed, reflecting the city's metamorphosis. New buildings, modern yet respectful of Wilder City's history, dotted the landscape, testaments to the city's remarkable rebirth.

The transformation wasn't just cosmetic; it ran much deeper. Anya Sharma's administration had initiated a series of ambitious projects focused on community development, education, and job creation. Abandoned factories had been repurposed into community centers, offering educational programs, vocational training, and recreational facilities. Public transportation has been modernized, connecting previously isolated neighborhoods and fostering a sense of unity and accessibility. The city's police force, once riddled with corruption, was undergoing a significant overhaul, focusing on community policing and building trust with the citizens they were sworn to protect. Ava Ramirez, now a revered figure in Wilder City, had become a driving force in this transformation, spearheading the implementation of community-based initiatives and overseeing the retraining of officers.

Alice found herself often reflecting on the stark contrast between the Wilder City she had known and the one she now inhabited. The city's transformation was a mirror reflecting her own personal journey of healing and resilience. The newly paved streets, once a symbol of Martel's oppressive regime, now represented pathways to a brighter future. The vibrant murals, painted with stories of hope and defiance, were a testament to the city's enduring spirit.

The community center where Alice volunteered had become a hub of activity, a place where people from all social classes came together to share their stories, support each other, and rebuild their lives. She collaborated with a team of resolute volunteers, many of them survivors of Martel's regime, their shared experiences forging a bond of resilience and mutual understanding. They organized educational workshops for children, offering tutoring, art classes, and recreational activities designed to help them overcome the trauma they had endured. They also offered support groups for adults, providing a safe space for them to process their experiences, share their feelings, and connect with others who understood their struggles.

One afternoon, while helping a group of teenagers with an art project, Alice noticed a young girl sitting quietly in the corner, her eyes downcast. The girl, whose name was Maya, had been particularly withdrawn since the arrest of her father, a minor player in Martel's organization.

Alice approached her cautiously, offering her a gentle smile and a quiet word of encouragement.

Maya initially resisted, but Alice's persistent kindness eventually broke through her defenses. They spent the afternoon talking, sharing stories, and creating art. Alice listened patiently as Maya recounted her experiences, her voice filled with a mixture of fear and resentment. Alice shared her own story, not as a way to seek sympathy but to show Maya that she was not alone and that healing was possible.

The transformation of Wilder City wasn't merely a physical one; it was a societal one. The city's legal system, once a tool of oppression, was being reformed, making it more just and equitable. The media, once complicit in Martel's reign of terror, now played a crucial role in holding those in power accountable and in celebrating the city's resilience. The citizens of Wilder City, once divided by fear and suspicion, now stood united, their collective strength a powerful force for positive change.

Alice's own family was thriving, their bonds strengthened by their shared experience of adversity. Her father, having witnessed the devastation Martel's regime had wrought, had become more open and emotionally available. He volunteered at the community garden, a testament to his newfound sense of purpose and community engagement. Her mother, ever the steadfast pillar of support, continued to be her anchor, providing unwavering love and encouragement. Even her younger brother, initially hesitant to engage with her post-trauma, had found a new respect for her resilience and actively supported her endeavors. Their family dinners, once strained and tense, now buzzed with lively conversations and shared laughter.

Ava Ramirez stayed a constant source of support and friendship for Alice. They often met for coffee, sharing updates on their lives and reflecting on the journey they had both undertaken. Ava, hardened by years of policing, showed a surprising vulnerability in her conversations with Alice, revealing a softer side that had been hidden behind her professional persona. Their friendship, forged in the crucible of their shared experiences, transcended their professional relationship, becoming a deep personal connection.

The media continued to portray Alice's story, focusing not on the trauma she had endured but on her remarkable strength, resilience, and unwavering commitment to helping others. She became a spokesperson for victims of abuse and corruption, using her platform to raise awareness, advocate for policy changes, and offer hope to those struggling to overcome similar experiences. Her interviews were not mere recitations of facts; they were powerful narratives that resonated with audiences around the world.

Alice's story became an emblem of Wilder City's transformation – a city that had risen from the ashes of corruption and despair, a city where hope had replaced fear and where resilience had triumphed over adversity. The city's phoenix-like resurgence mirrored Alice's own personal journey, a journey of healing, forgiveness, and the discovery of a profound sense of purpose.

One evening, Alice stood on the newly constructed observation deck overlooking the city, a gentle breeze carrying the sounds of the city's revitalization. The lights of Wilder City twinkled below, a breathtaking panorama of hope and renewal. She reflected on the long road she had traveled, the immense challenges she had overcome, and the remarkable transformation she had witnessed both within herself and her city. The scars remained etched onto her soul, but they were no longer symbols of shame and pain. They were badges of honor, a testament to her strength, resilience, and the unwavering human spirit that had enabled her and Wilder City to rise from the ashes. The future held uncertainty, but Alice faced them with newfound confidence, knowing that she had found her place in this new Wilder City, a place of healing, hope, and a powerful reminder of the transformative power of resilience. The city and Alice were finally free.

Lingering Questions

The city's transformation was complete, or so it seemed. The physical changes were undeniable – the vibrant murals, the renovated parks, the bustling cafes – but the deeper, more subtle shifts in the city's psyche remained less clear. While the overt signs of Martel's reign were gone, the lingering shadows of his influence cast a long reach. The unspoken questions, the unresolved tensions, hung in the air like a persistent fog, refusing to dissipate completely.

One such question concerned the fate of Martel's remaining associates. While many had been apprehended, some had vanished, disappearing into the anonymity of the city's sprawling underbelly. Whispers circulated about potential sleeper cells, individuals waiting for the opportune moment to reassert Martel's twisted vision. The police, under Ava's watchful eye, remained vigilant, but the threat of resurgence, however faint, continued to loom. The very success of the city's transformation raised a paradoxical concern: had the swiftness and completeness of the changes inadvertently lulled some into a false sense of security? Had the celebration of victory obscured the potential for a quiet, insidious return of the old order?

Another lingering question pertained to the nature of justice itself. While Martel and his key lieutenants received their due punishment, many smaller players, those who had participated in his regime through complicity or coercion, seemed to have slipped through the cracks. The legal system, while reformed, was still burdened by its past, and the pursuit of justice for every victim, for every act of cruelty, proved to be an impossible task. The weight of these unresolved cases rested heavily on the shoulders of the city's newly reformed justice system, a reminder of the vast and ongoing effort needed to truly dismantle the legacy of Martel's tyranny. The pursuit of justice was a marathon, not a sprint, and the finish line remained a distant, uncertain point on the horizon.

The psychological scars of the city's trauma also cast a long shadow. The visible signs of healing – the laughter of children in the parks, the community gatherings in the renovated community centers – were counterpointed by the unseen wounds, the deep-seated anxieties and fears that lingered within many citizens. The transformation was a monumental achievement, yet the process of collective healing was far from complete. The city's recovery was not merely a matter of rebuilding buildings; it was a complex and arduous process of rebuilding trust, repairing relationships, and confronting the psychological consequences of years of oppression. Therapy sessions were overflowing, and even with the best efforts of the city's newly established mental health support system, the sheer volume of trauma necessitated a longer-term approach, acknowledging the profound and lasting impact of Martel's regime.

Even Alice's own healing journey, while seemingly complete, left room for unanswered questions. While she had found peace and purpose in helping others, the specter of her ordeal still haunted her in subtle ways. Nightmares continued to plague her sleep, and the constant vigilance and the ever-present sense of danger remained ingrained in her being. The freedom she had achieved wasn't an eradication of fear but a learned resilience, a conscious decision to live despite the lingering shadows. She knew that true healing was not a destination but a continuous process, an ongoing dialogue with her past.

The question of forgiveness, both for herself and for those who had wronged her, stayed a complex and challenging one. Alice had found a measure of forgiveness, not as a simple act of letting go, but as a conscious choice to move forward, to focus on the future rather than remain trapped in the confines of her past. However, the ability to forgive didn't erase the memories and didn't negate the pain. It simply meant accepting the reality of the past, learning from it, and choosing to create a future free from its suffocating grip. Forgiving herself for the moments of weakness, for the times when she doubted her strength, was proving to be an equally challenging, albeit rewarding task.

The transformation of Wilder City was a testament to human resilience, a profound demonstration of the capacity for healing and renewal. Yet, the lingering questions and the unanswered uncertainties served as a powerful reminder that the journey toward true recovery was ongoing, a continuous process requiring vigilance, patience, and an unwavering commitment to confronting the past while embracing the future. The city's transformation was a story of hope, but it was also a story of ongoing evolution, a testament to the enduring complexity of human nature and the persistent need for vigilance against the potential for darkness to reemerge.

The economic resurgence, while impressive, also raised concerns about the equitable distribution of wealth. While new businesses thrived and unemployment rates plummeted, questions arose about the accessibility of these opportunities to all citizens. The risk of widening social and economic disparities, a byproduct of uneven development, continued to be a cause of worry. Ava and Alice, working in tandem, recognized the crucial need for ongoing monitoring and intervention to ensure that the benefits of the city's rebirth extended to all its residents, preventing the creation of new forms of inequality and marginalization.

Furthermore, the political landscape of Wilder City remained volatile. While Anya Sharma's administration had brought about meaningful change, the scars of the past political corruption were still evident. The new political order had to constantly guard against the temptation to revert to old, corrupt practices. Maintaining transparency, accountability, and integrity within the government was an ongoing challenge that would require constant vigilance and commitment to uphold the values that had propelled Wilder City's transformation.

Finally, the case of Maya, the young girl whose father had been a minor player in Martel's organization, represented a microcosm of the larger challenges faced by Wilder City. Maya's healing represented a crucial part of the city's overall healing. Alice's work with Maya and countless other young people affected by Martel's reign served as a reminder of the generational impact of trauma and the importance of providing long-term support and rehabilitation for the city's youngest residents, helping to prevent the repetition of past cycles of violence and corruption. The future of Wilder City lay not just in the physical infrastructure but in the psychological well-being and prospects of its youth, ensuring they would not inherit the shadow of the past. The transformation, both personal and societal, was far from over, a constant evolution requiring vigilance, resilience, and a steadfast commitment to building a better future for all. The seeds of hope had been planted; the harvest remained a work in progress.

Themes Revisited

The quiet hum of Wilder City's resurgence masked a deeper, more unsettling resonance. The celebratory fireworks that had lit up the night sky weeks ago had faded, leaving behind the faint scent of gunpowder and the lingering echo of cheers. Yet, beneath the veneer of progress, a subtle tension persisted, a quiet anxiety that whispered in the spaces between the city's renewed heartbeat. The victory, while hard-won, felt incomplete, a symphony with missing notes, a painting with unblended colors.

Ava, standing on her balcony overlooking the revitalized city square, felt the weight of this unspoken tension. The dossiers on Martel's associates, meticulously compiled and analyzed, still sat on her desk, a stark reminder of the unfinished business. While the high-profile arrests had sent a clear message, the whispers of remaining cells, the phantom threats, continued to haunt the city's newfound peace. The success of Operation Nightingale had been a stunning triumph, a testament to meticulous planning and courageous action, but its success also brought a new set of challenges. The very effectiveness of the operation had potentially lulled some into a false sense of security, a dangerous complacency that could prove fatal.

The reformed police force, still bearing the scars of its compromised past, was now tasked with maintaining vigilance against the ghosts of Martel's regime. Ava's team, hardened by years of fighting against corruption and violence, understood the delicate balance between celebrating victory and maintaining a heightened sense of awareness. They knew that the fight for Wilder City's future was far from over; it was a marathon, not a sprint.

Economic recovery, while significant, also exposed the fragile nature of progress. The gleaming new skyscrapers and the bustling commercial districts were a testament to the city's resilience, but they also masked the widening gap between the affluent and the marginalized. The influx of investment had spurred growth, but the benefits of this growth had not been evenly distributed. Ava saw the statistics, the stark numbers that revealed the increasing disparity, and felt the familiar sting of frustration. The fight for economic justice was now as crucial as the fight against criminal organizations.

Anya Sharma's administration, lauded for its reformative measures, faced the uphill battle of dismantling the vestiges of corruption that permeated the political system. The struggle against entrenched interests and the insidious nature of political manipulation was a constant reminder that the transformation of Wilder City was not limited to infrastructure; it extended to the very soul of its governance. Ava and Anya, working in close collaboration, implemented rigorous checks and balances, established transparent procedures, and fostered a culture of accountability. Yet, the lingering threat of backsliding, the ever-present risk of reverting to the old ways, demanded unceasing vigilance.

Alice, immersed in her work at the newly established trauma center, witnessed the profound and lasting impact of Martel's regime on Wilder City's youth. The children, the silent victims, carried the weight of their experiences, their vulnerabilities laid bare in their hesitant smiles and their withdrawn gazes. Alice's days were filled with the delicate task of fostering healing and helping these young people navigate their trauma and find a path toward a brighter future. She worked tirelessly, her hands calloused from years of struggle, her heart heavy with the weight of their collective pain. Yet, in their resilience, in their capacity to find hope amidst the darkness, she found her own strength renewed.

The city's transformation was not merely physical; it was a deep, emotional, and psychological journey. The visible signs of renewal – the laughter of children, the vibrant street art, the burgeoning community gardens – were testaments to the city's extraordinary resilience, but they also underscored the lingering pain and the unfinished work. The process of collective healing, Alice realized, was as intricate and time-consuming as the process of rebuilding the city's physical infrastructure. It required patience, compassion, and a long-term commitment to addressing the wounds of the past.

The concept of forgiveness, both on a personal and collective level, loomed large in the city's recovery. Alice, having wrestled with her own demons, understood the complexity of extending forgiveness to those who had caused her unimaginable suffering. It wasn't a simple act of letting go; it was a conscious decision to redefine her narrative, to break free from the chains of resentment. It was about reclaiming her own agency, her own power, and charting a future unburdened by the weight of the past. The process, however, remained an ongoing struggle, a continuous negotiation with her own internal landscape.

The economic disparities, the lingering political corruption, and the profound psychological trauma were intertwined threads in the tapestry of Wilder City's transformation. Addressing them effectively required a holistic approach, a coordinated effort that encompassed various levels of society. Ava and Alice, representing the practical and the empathetic approaches, recognized this inextricable connection. Their collaboration became the bridge that connected the tangible realities of governance and economic policy with the intangible needs of healing and psychological recovery. They knew that the city's true recession depended on their combined efforts, on a commitment to address every facet of its transformation.

Maya, the young girl who had lost her father to the regime, represented the future of Wilder City. Her journey toward healing was not merely a personal one; it was a symbol of the larger collective journey, a microcosm of the city's struggles and its potential for redemption. Her story, along with countless others, became a reminder of the generational impact of trauma, the importance of sustained support for victims, and the need to prevent the repetition of past mistakes. The city's future, Ava and Alice realized, depended on creating a society where Maya's story would not be repeated, where the seeds of hope planted during the era of Martel's tyranny would flourish into a future free from violence and corruption.

The transformation of Wilder City was, ultimately, a testament to the enduring power of human resilience, a profound acknowledgment of the capacity for healing and renewal, but also a sobering reminder that the journey towards a truly just and equitable society was far from over. The echoes of Martel's regime continued to reverberate, a faint tremor beneath the city's newfound calm. It was a constant reminder of the importance of ongoing vigilance, the need for continuous effort, and the unwavering commitment to building a future that would be worthy of the sacrifices made and the battles won. The seeds of hope had been sown, but the harvest required careful tending, consistent nurturing, and an ongoing commitment to a future where the darkness would never again overshadow the light. The work was far from finished; it was, in fact, only just beginning.

Final Thoughts

The air hung heavy with the scent of rain, a cleansing storm brewing on the horizon, mirroring the tempestuous emotions that still swirled within Ava. The victory over Martel felt less like a triumphant crescendo and more like a hesitant sigh of relief, a pause before the next inevitable challenge. The dossiers, neatly stacked on her desk, weren't just records of arrests; they were a chronicle of a city's suffering, a testament to the enduring scars of corruption. Each name represented a broken life, a shattered trust, a future stolen. The legal battles, the painstaking investigations, the relentless pursuit of justice – it all left an indelible mark, a deep weariness that settled in the marrow of her bones.

Yet, amidst the exhaustion, there was quiet satisfaction, a hard-won peace. She had faced darkness and emerged battered but unbroken. The reformed police force, now operating under a new code of ethics, was a symbol of that transformation, a phoenix rising from the ashes of deceit. Their meticulous work, their unwavering commitment to truth and justice, was a beacon of hope, a promise of a safer future for Wilder City's citizens. They had cracked the intricate puzzle of Martel's organization, but dismantling the deeply entrenched culture of corruption would be a far longer, more complex endeavor.

Anya Sharma, the newly elected mayor, had initiated a series of audacious reforms, attacking the systemic rot at the heart of Wilder City's governance. Sh faced fierce opposition, the ghosts of the old guard whispering insidious doubts in the ears of the hesitant, clinging to power like barnacles on a ship's hull. Yet, Anya, with her unwavering determination, pressed forward, building alliances, forging coalitions, and slowly chipping away at the foundations of the old system. The fight for true transparency, for accountability at every level of government, was a protracted battle, but Ava saw in Anya a fierce determination that mirrored her own.

The economic recovery was a fragile thing, a delicate balance between growth and equitable distribution. The gleaming skyscrapers stood in stark contrast to the struggling neighborhoods, a visual representation of the widening chasm between the haves and the have-nots. The influx of investment had brought prosperity, but that prosperity hadn't reached all corners of the city. Ava knew this disparity was a time bomb, a simmering resentment that, if left unaddressed, could ignite another crisis.

Addressing the economic imbalances and ensuring fair access to opportunities would require a long-term strategy and careful orchestration of economic policies that prioritize inclusivity and social justice.

Alice, at the trauma center, continued her tireless work, tending to the wounds – both visible and invisible – of Wilder City's youth. She saw the resilience of the children, their quiet courage in the face of unimaginable pain. Their laughter, though sometimes hesitant, and their art, though often infused with darkness, were a testament to the enduring human spirit, a beacon of hope in the shadows. Alice's dedication and her compassionate touch were a vital part of the city's healing process, a testament to the power of empathy and understanding. The healing wasn't solely about repairing physical wounds; It was about restoring trust, rebuilding shattered psyches, and fostering a sense of community.

The concept of forgiveness, so often discussed but rarely understood, hovered over Wilder City like a persistent mist. It wasn't a simple act of wiping the slate clean; it was a complex, ongoing process, a negotiation with one's own soul. For Alice, it was a journey fraught with pain and struggle, a constant grappling with memories that threatened to engulf her. For Ava, it was a quiet understanding that true justice wasn't solely about retribution but about the possibility of healing, of moving forward without being shackled by the past. They both knew that forgiveness wasn't about condoning the atrocities committed but about reclaiming their own power, their own narrative, from the grasp of the past.

Maya, the young girl who had lost her father, embodied the city's future. Her healing was not just a personal journey but a reflection of Wilder City's collective struggle, a microcosm of its pain and its potential for redemption. Her strength, her quiet resilience, was an inspiration to Ava and Alice, a reminder that even in the darkest of times, hope could flourish. The future of Wilder City rested on Maya's shoulders, on the shoulders of countless others who had survived the darkness and were committed to building a society where such pain would never be inflicted again.

The novel closes, not with a neatly tied bow, but with a lingering sense of anticipation, a quiet acknowledgment that the fight for justice, for truth, for a better future, was far from over. The echoes of Martel's regime, like whispers in the wind, served as a constant reminder of the vigilance required, the continuous work needed to ensure that the hard-won peace wouldn't be shattered. The city's transformation was a testament to the human spirit's capacity for resilience, healing, and renewal. But it also highlighted the fragility of progress, the ongoing battle against the insidious nature of corruption, and the relentless pursuit of a truly equitable society. The seeds of hope had been sown, but nurturing them, tending to them, and ensuring their growth was a commitment that extended far beyond the final page of this story.

The true narrative of Wilder City's redemption was far from complete; it was a story still being written, one word, one action, one act of compassion at a time. The future remained uncertain yet hopeful; the fight continued, a testament to the enduring strength of the human spirit and the unwavering pursuit of justice. The city, scarred yet resolute, stood poised on the precipice of a new dawn, its future yet unwritten but filled with the potential for a brighter tomorrow, a tomorrow shaped by the enduring power of hope, resilience, and the unwavering pursuit of justice. The echoes of the past still lingered, a gentle reminder that vigilance remained paramount, but the sun was rising on a new Wilder City, a city slowly emerging from the shadows, its citizens united in their determination to build a future worthy of the sacrifices made and the battles won.

The work was far from finished; it was, indeed, just beginning.

For every crime committed, there's always a "VICTIM."